NICOLAS FREELING

The Pretty How Town

A Henri Castang mystery

WARNER FUTURA

A *Warner Futura* Book

First published in Great Britain in 1992
by Little, Brown and Company
This edition published by Warner Futura in 1994

Copyright © 1992 by Nicolas Freeling

The moral right of the author has been asserted.

The quotations at various chapter heads are from
'anyone lived in a pretty how town' by E. E. Cummings
from *50 Poems* by E. E. Cummings
copyright © 1940 by E. E. Cummings; 1968 by
Marion Morehouse Cummings

A CIP catalogue record for this book
is available from the British Library.

ISBN 0 7515 0161 1

Printed in England by Clays Ltd, St Ives plc

Warner Futura
A Division of
Little, Brown and Company (UK) Limited
Brettenham House
Lancaster Place
London WC2 7EN

Born and educated in England, Nicolas Freeling now regards himself, with accuracy, as a European. For fifteen years he worked as a hotel and restaurant cook throughout Europe, he speaks fluent French, Dutch and German, and he now lives in the Vosges with his Dutch wife while his sons have married German, French and Italian women.

His first novel (which featured the Dutch detective Van der Valk) was published in 1962. Henri Castang first made an appearance in 1974; *The Pretty How Town* is the tenth in the Castang series. With Van der Valk and Henri Castang, Freeling has built up an international reputation and he is the recipient of the Edgar Allen Poe Award in New York, the Grand Prix Roman Policier in Paris and the Gold Dagger in London.

For all my Europeans, and especially for
Geneviève, Ursula, Sylvie

For Thucydides, as for any serious Greek thinker, moral issues and conflicts were an integral element in politics, and also what we should call social psychology.

The word for inquire in Greek is historein. A sustained inquiry, a historia.

from the Introduction to
The Peloponnesian War
by Dr M.I. Finley,
Professor of Ancient History,
Cambridge University

PROLOGUE

Henri Castang

Before leaving Paris I was sent for.

I had been given to understand, and very clearly, thanks, that I was both promoted and sacked, simultaneously.

Promoted, that's simple enough: my "step" up, and rather overdue, to the higher rank of Commissaire which is Divisional. An English reader will understand if I say Chief Superintendent; that's the rough equivalent. But "sacked" needs explaining and so — especially — does "clearly".

Because a senior Police Judiciaire officer isn't sacked: he's like a professor with tenure, irremovable without criminal misbehaviour and a resultant monstrous scandal. He is shifted sideways to what in French is called the garage ramp. He is unstuck. The official jargon says "detached upon special mission". Which is why I have to emphasise the word "clearly". Nothing is ever clear about official jargon, because they might want to contradict themselves later; telling the Press that the pronouncement has been misinterpreted.

But he keeps his rank and pay. The pay anyhow. I wouldn't be using the rank; the Belgians might wonder why the Republic should feel the need to maintain a Divisional Commissaire of the PJ inside their kingdom. Officially I'm just an adviser to a committee working on the standardisation of judicial procedure within the Community. Police officer; pragmatic experience of criminal procedure. Okay: I can also speak some English, some German, even a little Flemish after a few years in the north-eastern corner of France. It's felt to be an advantage. I also have a Czech wife. That's a disadvantage, but once safely outside France, less of one.

While still in Paris I am on the establishment, and if a superior officer expresses a wish to see me – polish your shoes and get over there.

Not the PJ. This was RG. But don't bother with acronyms, let alone their official titles. Even after reading so many spy books, how many English people know the difference between MI5 and 6? I'll tell you: one's home and the other's abroad and each expends a lot of effort in placing banana skins for the other. Secret services, parallel police forces; they're the same everywhere.

This was a vexatious experience. He was in plain clothes but in rank he's a General, the sort that has never seen a shot fired in anger, and feels the need for a military manner as well as a skinhead haircut and an orderly to saddlesoap his boots. With me he was peremptory.

"Now Castang, they're sending you to Bruxelles." Pronouncing the x; like all the French he can't be bothered to learn pronunciation of anything Foreign. But with a cunning intonation.

"We're sending you to Bruxelles." Oh. Or oho. But silent.

"You're a patriot, Castang?" Yes, I'm exactly as patriotic as the President's labrador dog, but there's no reward for saying so.

"Germany!" Doing the hiss and the clenched teeth. "West or East" – for these were the days when there was still an East – "riddled through by the Stasi. I didn't say you could smoke. Now Belgium – right here on our doorstep – that's like their private garden." This in French is called intoxication. As likely as not he was a Stasi man himself. Falsehood; it's in their haemoglobin and their leucocytes, the way you and I have cholesterol. Speaking to the general rule, the most patriotic are on CIA retainers, are told to infiltrate the KGB, are manipulated by true-enough Stasi, and get some money to help with the patriotism. They start carrying handkerchiefs then in their sleeves, to show they've read the spy novels.

"You will use your eyes and your ears; your trained faculties. I want you permeating that nest of crypto-Marxists like the saffron in the rice."

You should always be able to detect French spies; fussy about the food. There was no talk about money, patriotism being its own reward. The Stasi is known for meanness, but French parsimony will always go one better: if you have a meeting in the park, don't imagine we'll pay for the deckchairs.

I decided to say nothing about this and especially not to Vera. Czech Stapo has been sensible enough to see her as a poor prospect, but I've had occasional nightmares in which the French thought she should start being patriotic.

Ay de mí. I get out of the PJ, where I never thought about my country but did hope I was of some use to society, and now there's a new crowd to make me shit. You find this scene ludicrous? I thought it so myself.

Later on, I was to find it less funny.

CHAPTER ONE

Henri Castang

> anyone lived in a pretty how town
> (with up so floating many bells down)
> spring summer autumn winter
> he sang his didn't he danced his did.

I don't know why there should be no capital letters. I think it's an American poet, and he even spelt his name this way: e e cummings. Harold taught me the poem. He is literary, as jurists go. And I have been told, a good many times, that I'm too literary for an ex-policeman.

But this, he says is plainly the pretty how town. And we, the Functionaries of the European Community, are anyone. You notice the capital letters. As he remarks there are far too many around here, in far too many languages, and Mr cummings did well to abolish them. The town itself has too many names. Bruxelles, in French. The x is a very Belgian letter. Pronounced as a double-ess, which is pretty close (but not close enough for some) to the Flemish Brussel. And of course the English call it Brussels, pronounced like sprouts. We mostly call it Bruce. We – I mean my family, myself – have been living here for a few months now, and are just beginning to find our way about.

Harold, officially Mr Claverhouse and my chief, heads one of the Juridical Services in one of the numerous departments of the over-many European Institutions. You see? No, I'm not going to try to explain. It is too complicated, and it is far too dotty. We can't even talk

1

about our part of the town. It does not belong to us, we pay very high rents for it, officially we're only here on sufferance and some would claim that we aren't even here at all: that the whole thing's an illusion. It explains the surrealist cast of the poem.

> Women and men (both little and small)
> cared for anyone not at all
> they saved their isn't they reaped their same
> sun moon stars rain

You are, I hope, beginning to get the picture. No punctuation but "If you are going to understand," said Harold ... because Community prose, in whatever language, is just like this. A skill is called for in the reading; and in the interpretation.

He had invited us (colleague and colleague's wife) to a Christmassy party at his home. Vague, fairly cynical; notoriously Harold is clearing off people to whom he owns hospitality, but I can remember this particular Christmas and so will you. It was the moment when Ceausescu, Genius of the Carpathians, got his come-uppance in Roumania. And when the Brandenburger Tor was thrown open between East and West Berlin: hooligans, mostly British, climbed on top and damaged the Quadriga: police and firemen from both Berlins spent the next day clearing up the beer bottles: HistoryBeingMade.

Lots of the funcs huddle together in a classy ghetto called Off-Louise. So-called because the Porte Louise is the city's grandest gateway and the Avenue (full of banks and posh shops) leads away southward towards the forest country, now all autoroute-exchange and flossy suburb: there are a few trees left. We do not live Off-Louise. The rents are too high and Vera dislikes the quarter; too many funcholes. Nor does Harold. We live eastwardly (most func offices are on the southeast side) and Harold lives further south, in quite a large and decidedly grand villa, with a garden. Around Christmas it was not garden weather and in the house was a monstrous scrum of funcs

2

and wives, drinking hard. Iris floated about hostessing, in an expensive black frock, looking very fine.

We have not been here before. One couldn't tell much from looking since at this kind of party you clear away anything that's pretty or valuable, if you've any sense. A nice house. He must pay a hell of a rent. But Harold is a senior func, and very well paid himself, besides the generous allowances for 'abroad', which to most of them is a frightful fate, demanding heavy compensations. We mingled, as is expected of us: plenty of house champagne to help it along. Some dottiness is observable. Soap in the downstairs lav was Roger & Gallet. Upstairs, reported Vera, was kitchen-Marseille. So I sank a barb, next day. Which is what Harold likes; does it himself continually: it's his style, to promote outrage.

"Yes. Thinking about it. Important point. Marseille's soapier. Olive oil in it? Or maybe Jews?" Now this is downright offensive, since Harold is not Jewish, but I know better than to react. Part of his "abrasive" side, and makes him a lot of enemies, which he enjoys. It was displayed on my very first day, when he invited me to lunch: there were out-of-season green beans.

"Where do these come from? Senegal, is it? Thought so. Smell of nigger sweat." He rubs your nose in it. The best defence is attack. Like his big Cuban cigars; he'll blow the smoke in your face. Or his braces, all outrageous and much displayed. His fearful rudeness to secretaries; they laugh, and some thrive on it, and others perhaps don't. "Who have they given you? Brigitte? Is that the one with the cocksucking mouth?" Oh, says his own secretary, Miss Hunted-Down, it's just Harold being Evelyn Waugh again. I have a lot to learn, and all this literature, too.

That ghastly party! Vera, who is Czech, was in a stew about her abandoned, unforgotten Heimatland, not showing it — she is shy at parties; determined not to let me down. Conversation, in the usual mix of Bruce-French and slightly Germanic English, with some ringing British voices ruling the hubbub; everybody was telling everyone else what the Czechs ought to be doing. And the question that comes up new at every party: where on earth do they get those clothes?

Harold has a smile and a witty phrase for all. His electricity is such that you look up expecting him beside you, when he's at the other end of the room. No cigar, for he is more disciplined than he likes to appear. His suit is extravagant in both cut and material – and he is a big man, a robust presence – but it is his face which dominates, massive and Roman. A portrait bust off a triumphal arch, and even his hair is in keeping. Thick and it waves. No need of a laurel wreath to hide a bald spot, and it's fair, neither dusty nor sandy. It can't be a piece because it grows, and can't be dyed because there are silver threads, if few for a man in his middle fifties. The cop which I still am (there are habits one does not shake off) notices the big flat ears and heavy lobes, the wide mobile mouth, even more than the nose which waves at one, menacingly, or the tiny glinty eyes. Perhaps when young he'd been a baby elephant, but is so no longer: too mobile, and too damn quick on his feet. No doubt he'd be florid if exposed to the sun. The colouring is very northerly. Harold Fairhair, but the secretaries call him 'Beaumains' for his beautifully shaped hands. Surely he would have made a formidable counsel, and any moment now an alarming judge? No doubt. Chose not to, it would seem.

Oh dear. Funcs cover every imaginable political opinion, but I have been trapped among the right-wingers, and the wives are worse. Seized by the Pudding Bore (who is forever telling one new recipes) and the Social Bore (armed with the very latest statistics about alcoholism and the criminal tolerance of the French government towards smoking). I couldn't care less about the French government. Where the hell is Vera? Oh, these Englishwomen who rule everything by divine right – for the memsahib is still quite convinced that her Empire is here and now. Why can one not ship them to Sicily? I am myself contemplating permanent exile in Pantelleria (the Pudding Bore's husband is a decent man, alarmingly knowledgeable about restaurants but quite sound on

4

pesticides) . . . There is Vera, miles away, and very thick with Iris.

I have not met Iris before, though Harold talks about her a lot and in an oddly public way. "Iris would be appalled." As though she were present – "mustn't say things like that, you'll shock Iris," as well as commands to secretaries; "Ring my wife, would you, and make sure she hasn't forgotten the cheese." One had somehow expected her to be not quite presentable; hideous or gross. Quite the contrary is the case. Her electricity is like that of French country districts at the end of a line which fades suddenly: why is this toaster taking such a time to pop up? Here she greeted me with warmth, and then wasn't there any more, until one noticed her standing there beside one, but neither uttering nor, I am sure, listening, though her manners are perfect in an old-fashioned 'ladylike' style.

Things the men notice: she is tall and appears taller because very slim. Nicely dressed. Vera when we were in Paris used to get couturier frocks secondhand, and showed skill in making them fit her own rather meagre figure; this looks like the real thing. Iris' figure can be seen, and is finely proportioned. Hard to say whether she's really pretty. Huge magnificent eyes set wide apart. Harold's, when you can see them at all, are a bright hard china blue: these are deep, deep sapphires. And an immense full-lipped mouth, but inbetween the nose looks insignificant and shapeless. She makes the most of these good features, for the frock is cut high and she has dark shaggy hair cut 'urchin', close to the head framing a delicate oval face, and with a ragged fringe deep all around the forehead, to show up those amazing eyes. In a black rollneck pullover and diamond earrings she'd be as sexy as all hell. Which doesn't mean much, as any man knows. But if the hair were that real Spanish blue-black instead of this ordinary brown-black . . .

Vera would laugh at me. Or be sarcastic. But really it's so as not to listen to the Social Bore who is still being vehement about the extreme wickedness of what she calls my President. The frock fits tight but Iris holds herself

5

straight. No midriff bulge, no 'riding-breeches' around hip or upper thigh; impeccable bottom (and the frock is lined; unlike all these other women, no unseemly display of knickers). At worst a softness of the flesh under the jaw, though she must be fifty and from scraps of information let fall by Harold there are two or three children already grown up; in England somewhere. Enviable, indeed.

Even if laughable – oh, Vera will say, how Susceptible – remember that I was trained this way. "Mark you, when a boy starves in the street" – all right, that is Robert Browning, one of Vera's pet poets, and if over-dramatic, that is the way the painter trains himself to observe and to register, and I was the antique kind of cop. In my day we had lots of street duty, less sitting-on-the-bench, and getting a law degree took much midnight-oil. I did not exactly starve on Paris streets, but I came to understand – later, much later – this Filippo Lippi act.

Indeed, a year or two more with Carlotta, in the Fine Arts section of the Fraud Squad, and I might have learned something about Florentine painters. I wasn't there long enough, and frankly, I wasn't good enough: as Carlotta said truly, I should have begun twenty years before. But I did get taught as a young cop to use my eyes. Other senses, and "the touch", I've largely lost: like a pianist one needs daily practice. The streetwise cop is younger, and a long sight sharper.

People are following me about. Streetwise I am no longer, but a PJ cop, however ex, doesn't miss this. We are like lobsters, we whizz out of rocky holes and pounce. We've had to grow an armoured carapace because there are plenty of predators who think we taste good, so that we scuttle back quick, and glare about, and have also these long sensitive antennae which we wave around. I haven't lost this equipment, which took a long time to evolve.

Who are these people? I don't think they are French. Those would sidle up to my crack in the rock with a coy murmur, " 'nother lobster; pay no attention".

But could they be Czech? Chaps who'd be discreet in

France, or at least offering professional rates to fellow members of the parallel police . . . They'd be less inhibited with me here.

For the word out of Prague is that at the first breath of revolution they all disappeared into their cracks like Jack Robinson. Havel put a good friend into the Ministry of the Interior, but he's pretty worried. Where have they all got to, then? Equally to the point, where's all the money then? They were well supplied. Here's this great big castle and it's full of empty cupboards. Where are all the files? All the gold coins? And all the weapons . . . There could be plenty of all three handily stashed right here.

Vera, who like every woman has fallen madly in love with Havel, is talking loudly and bravely about going home at last. I do not wish to discourage her. Nor do I want to let on that this idea frightens me, a little.

There is nothing useful I can do but to wait, and to see. The German government discovers perfect stacks of Stasi, hidden in every damn crack of the rocks around Bonn.

I was sent here French-style, which is like throwing the child in at the deep end for its first swimming lesson, and can be like the hangman's trapdoor opening beneath you. Nobody in Paris had any help or information to offer. There is an admission that Bruxelles exists, and is probably to be found in Belgium. But this country only exists in a variety of French wit, which holds that Belgians are unbearably dense and primitive; a game run on Little Audrey rules.

> Why do Belgian lakes run downhill?
> To make water-skiing easier.

Harmless enough and the Germans have exactly the same jokes about Ost-Friesland; but the French problem is that they start believing their own myths. Thus Belgium is known as 'Outre-Quiévrain' and can be reached from the Gare du Nord, and that's the sum of French knowledge. I have worked for some years in the North, have had occasional dealings with Bruxellois cops, magistrates,

7

lawyers, and still know little of the place beyond the big axis between the North and Midi Stations. Of the eastern area beyond the Ville Haute, where the European Community sits, or rather squats, I knew nowt. This part of Bruce, enslaved to the automobile, is horrible, as everyone there is at pains to make known. I fell upon a hardish, dryish French stick in the purlieus of the secretariat, determined to be unhelpful.

"I don't know, I'm sure."

"Is there no plan?"

"There's no plan for anything around here. Except promoters – they plan; to destroy and then build, to buy and then sell. Chiefly sell, as you will shortly become aware." French rhetoric; I'm used to that. Naturally, the concierge was more help, and produced a little map. Well, you see, (coughing) these are the Community offices.

Yes. The secretariat had been easy enough and everyone knows the big Berlaymont 'star' . . . but this: there are thirty-five of them. Four are called Archimède and four more Loi. There is a long, straight, exceedingly dreary street called Loi; I could see I'd have my work cut out, abiding by all that Law. One or two had happy names like Joyeuse Entrée or Marie de Bourgogne. It wouldn't, I imagined, be my luck to fall on those. Much more likely Triangle, or Astronomia.

"Heavens, does the Communauté own all this?"

There was an indulgent chuckle at my naïveté. "Man, the Community owns nothing at all. Pays enormous rents for whatever it can get. Has paid enough for Berlaymont to buy it ten times over."

"What do they use for money?"

"Yours and mine," the chuckle now sinister. But with his help I was easily directed towards Mr Claverhouse. For my new Chef de Service was English.

I am familiar with bureaucracy. Supposing I had been still a police officer, cross-posted to some French city of this size . . . I now hold rank of divisionnaire: a chief superintendent, quite important. In police terms I could be a departmental director. Under me, first, my adjunct (a

8

job I have held), Principal Commissaire charged with Security. There would be two more Principals in charge of Sureté Urbaine (the criminal brigade), and the district police stations; a flock of underdog commissaires below them: I would have lorded it over quite an empire.

Not here. There are many thousand international functionaries in Bruce and I was small fry, like a dogsbody commanding the tinpot of Means. "Well, why is car-seven said to be unserviceable? One of those clowns hit a tram with it, again? I hold you Personally Responsible."

I may be senior, but my status here is lowish. As indeed the Director of the Police Judiciaire in Paris told me, together with the fact that he sent me here to get rid of me. Even buried in the Fine Arts detail of the Fraud Squad I was an embarrassment to him, and to two or three Ministers. Here Mr Claverhouse is the Divisionnaire, and I am nobody. He is a mighty man, but there are too many mighty men in Bruce for him to be noticeable, except that he is noticeable by himself: he sees to that.

The new concierge was fussy about security. Men with guns hung about the lobby: it's in case anyone upstairs were writing satanic verses, and an ayatollah on the street were overcome by indignation. Harold bellowed down the phone. Bullshit ceased. Miss Huntingdon, a calm and pretty Englishwoman of mature age and respectable appearance, met me at the lift. She is there indeed to create an aura of respectability and efficiency: Harold is the second but not the first, or not all the time. She is generally known as Miss Hunted-Down, is serene about it.

Harold got up, came to the door to greet me, politely. It is quite true that he can be terribly, appallingly rude: he can also be the soul of courtesy, punctual, gentle, considerate. He wore one of his notorious striped shirts, the still-more notorious braces (on one side, pictures of can-can girls, on the other, western gunslingers). And of course the cigar. If I say "wore" the cigar it is almost literal; like the way some cops wear guns. In the centre of his mouth it points at people; in the corner it expresses derision for those slower, dimmer than he is – almost everybody. In his hand it intimidates. Always it bullies, is very macho. Left in the ashtray it drives people away, despite the air-conditioning. Relit, it puffs in your face. It is of course Cuban, of excellent quality. Harold does not spit in your face when talking, but it's all but. One can see how the legend took root.

Although a large and greedy eater and a powerful boozer he has less belly and that harder than given general credit for. Fast around a tennis court, and stays well: Ausdauer, as the Germans say. But his best gift is his voice, that of the trained advocate, at times deep and soothing, at times a resonant tenor, quite often an unseemly screech and always with a musicianly pitch and timing. The accent has no ridiculous affectations at all. It shows his skill because Harold's father was – or so he says – a Nottinghamshire coal-heaver. Sometimes, wanting Huntingdon to make tea, he'll ask, "Have you mashed then, love?"

"Now we're going to lunch. We'll talk about business over – on second thoughts no, it'll spoil the lunch. Let me introduce you to your colleagues. Here," throwing open a door, "is Columcille McCorquodale. Pretends to be Irish but a Scotsman obviously: beware. A Black Ulster Protestant." A grin from a quiet, loose-jointed man. It is self-evident nonsense. I don't know whether there are Irish features, but there's definitely an Irish face (and his name is Eamonn Hickey). Great legal expert; the Irish love law. A nice colleague. Doesn't utter much, but when warmed by a few jars will be voluble on the subject of De Valera.

"Our international code – trickiest of all or is it totally meaningless? Herein lurks the civil code, our Mr Suarez, aka Unamuno. The Grand Inquisitor as you can readily see." For Mr Suarez has a little black pointed beard, but the diabolical look changes suddenly with beautiful white teeth and a flashing Spanish smile. "The commercial gentleman, this bald French genius is Mr Lesniak, but we won't disturb him because he has no sense of humour whatsoever." True as it happens. "Social legislation, oh,

10

that's very theological, Frau Heinemann worries about the Immaculate Conception, as indeed do all Germans, and Herr Vrielynck, just to fox indiscreet enquiries, is not Dutch at all but Danish and his particular crown of thorns is Sovereignty, meaning all those people who prop up the bar in the National Assembly, frigthened of losing their free writing-paper.

"Now," said Harold banging himself into an armchair behind an untidy desk, "let's get you sorted out. We've a number of people working on criminal law, including the betwitching Nadia who's away at present because she has an Aged Parent in Bologna who causes her concern, and who is very brilliant indeed." (I was to learn later that Harold's private opinion was that Nadia "can never see the papers on her desk because her fringe keeps getting in her eyes.")

"I do a bit myself on these lines, but I'm forever drowned in admin and fending off busybodies. Our work has been over-theoretical and I asked for somebody with pragmatic experience of the field. Now for example this quasi-metaphysical debate between the inquisitory system *à la française*, and the accusatory procedure *à l'anglaise* . . . that's right, the work done by the Delmas-Marty committee about the reform of Instruction, you see I do know a tiny bit about the subject."

Flashing gestures; a lot of cuff and cufflink.

"I want specifics from you. Just as the Brits are begging for a judge of instruction, the French are doing their best to get rid of him. I want some crime fiction from you. Graham Greene was undoubtedly right to say that the best example he knew was *The Tale of Mr Tod* by Beatrix Potter – we can do better than that."

(B. Potter, well-known crime fiction writer? I must ask Vera.)

"The Rights of Man convention – no, Nadia has that on her plate. But the police official's trade – I want a memorandum from you on deontology. The defence of the child; there's another, I'll have a schedule drawn up. And frontiers – the 'European space' – there'll be one after

11

your own heart. Who has a right of pursuit on other peoples' national territory; when, and how. These are only guidelines. Let's go to lunch and you will tell me about yourself. We've got to get you settled in, too – oh, those terrible flats, in Woluwe Saint-Pierre." Harold's mind covers a lot, but it was nice of him to think about housing.

I remember thinking that I had a lot to learn about rhythms and procedures. Like all cops I'm accustomed to working from a given point, being told to produce a result inside twenty-four hours. This is not like being a scriptwriter in Hollywood, asked to come up with an idea in six weeks, and being very well paid. But would I continually be told "the script's no good"?

One mustn't take Vera too seriously when she talks about the hell-hole in Woluwe Saint-Pierre: it didn't last all that long, though I do admit the hatefulness of speculators' flats which make a brazen pretence of luxury while lacking all comfort, because badly planned within their meanly allotted space, they claim to be spacious and succeed only in being cramped.

"This may be nice for Abner Brown but not so nice for us – O." Vera looking round with the eye of experience.

"And so we plan to let him drown without unpleasant fuss – O." Rum-Chops' song, from the *Box of Delights* which I have been reading aloud for Emma, to improve my own English as much as hers. Lydia is a little too old for Masefield's Kay books, though in revulsion against a French school – Paris children are in general too old for their age – she was going through an infantile stage, and probably reading nothing but Enid Blyton. Now of course they have to go to the international school, where subjects are taught in their own language, and at least they learn that there's a world outside France.

We have moved too often, and only once have we had a place of our own. I think we are all "disturbed" by now. The children show it plainly; even the normally placid Emma behaving mean and snippy. Vera bottles her emotions; bad, bad. Nasty little sharp lines of strain on that face, which has never been pretty but has quite often been

12

beautiful. A man who has a job to challenge him and to concentrate upon feels the strain less.

Vera is a country girl in origin; she uses the word "peasant" in its original sense of gente del pais, people of the country. A strong feeling for land, soil, trees, animals, and she had always wanted a house in the countryside.

> Where the breadfruit bun toasts in the sun,
> And comes to lunch on trays – O.
> While the gang will still be in Pentonville
> In cells for all their days – O.

Those "model" prisons, designed in England around 1860, all still in use and over-populated: they were built in a star shape, like many modern apartment blocks, or the Berlaymont building.

"Yes indeed," said Mr Hickey. "I had an IRA friend who'd done time in Strangeways."

"You did?" I suppose my eyes opened rather too wide.

"Certainly. Why not? Don't think that I approve. But one must try to understand, even when it's impossible." A kind man, and who brought a lawyerly mind to my problem, as well as much warmth and generosity. "It's only inside Ireland that the Irish are really impossible to live with." And he is already quite an old Bruce hand.

Meeting him in the metro and remarking, more to make conversation than anything else, that one would like to live in the Saint Catherine quarter he said quite casually, "You ought to look at Schaerbeek."

"Full of Turks, too, no?"

"Not all of it. And some lovely houses. Want me to look? I may conceivably hear of something."

I must make this story short, but it belongs in the larger tale, and it had so much importance for us, that . . .

I was frightened. Prices go galloping up, one hears hair-raising tales about wicked Swedish profiteers, the Ville-Basse is full of revolutionary posters bravely declaring "Bruce is not for Sale", but Vera went to look at those lovely houses, which most people call ugly, and fell in love with them.

13

"Marvellous, and no question about it. I can't see it, though. We'd need an enormous mortgage." She has a horror of debt, hates banks. Mediaeval reaction towards usurers.

"It can't do any harm to try," I said.

And kind Mr Hickey has been as good as his word.

Bankers have been all beaming smiles. And having taken a good legal look at the title, Eamonn Hickey came to look at the house and strengthen my spine.

"Unless there's dry rot or something that's a very good buy."

It was at this moment that I stopped being a cop. Irony? I am a functionary, a householder, a bourgeois. A police officer even quite senior remains rootless. He hasn't faith in anything, much. So that I think yes – it was from this point that a new self-assurance stemmed. And a new sort of self-respect.

Vera was enchanted, and peacocked about the demesne – even if the usurers still own a lot of it. We stand quite high; one looks down upon "the Turkish quarter" (and Schaerbeek railway station, whose architecture she has fallen in love with). The air is fresh, the avenue wide, and there are trees on the pavements. The school bus picks the children up at the corner – and the children are gleeful. A sober func, I catch a tram to the Gare du Nord, and the metro from there. The car 'when I can't help it'. Everybody agrees that the automobile has ruined Bruce. I should like to bicycle, but car exhausts at bicycle level have taken the pleasure from this.

Perhaps, and it is for the first time, I do not feel a failure.

14

CHAPTER TWO

Henri Castang

I was no more than a competent cop. True, there are few
good ones. As with doctors; the job calls for contradictory
qualities. To be sharp, as well as blunt, and most of us
settle for being merely dulled. Like an old razor-blade,
kept for shaving pencils.

I don't think I'd be much of a spy, either. I'm not
meticulous. Can't one divide people into the noticers, who
quantify and analyse, and the unnoticers who don't know
where they parked the car, but who might have an instinct
for the significant?

I'd be too sloppy. The matchstick in the door, the papers
in a neat pattern; I'd either forget or leave them crooked. I
notice a few things though, because I was trained to.
Somebody is taking a close interest in my doings. Poking
into my microdots, wondering if there are messages in the
filtertips of a forgotten packet of cigarettes: thus someone
in the office. That's about two hundred people counting
security types and cleaning women. Likewise my car; and
not to support a drug habit by stealing radios, or the small
change for parking meters. Am I going to look out of the
window some day soon, and see a Third Man, when all the
witnesses will swear there were only two?

Paranoiac, am I? As bureaucrats go, I'm very small fry.
But a police officer always has grounds for suspicion. The
juniors look to grab credit, often by sticking a colleague
with the discredit. Further up, the manoeuvres become
political; the place was always riddled with cliques and

15

pressure groups. Towards the top when I hadn't even climbed the stairs, I now found myself sliding down the oubliette. There won't be very many real spies, like Gunther Guillaume, though if I'm to believe what I hear, there are a great deal more than were first thought of. The majority will be people exactly like me.

Wherever a bridge in East Germany crossed the main road, the former government put up big banners to edify the populace: "Are You Hardworking? Orderly? Disciplined? We are!"

Right, that's me.

The populace of what we still think of vaguely as East Berlin got restive during that indeterminate time before the formal takeover. Kicked the door in of the former Stasi Headquarters, broke a few windows, burned a few tons of paper. Just a gesture. Despite alarmist stories about the missing agent-files, none of this makes much difference. Half the Volk were Stasi agents without realising it, and generally acting through high and honourable ideals. Not just policemen. Municipal functionaries, the mayor's secretary, the schoolteacher, the dentist. People like me. I was a Stasi man myself and didn't know it; the sort of idiot who believes in tolerance and social justice and trying not to be racist.

But take a big stick to the ants' nest, stir up the political institutions of a country, and you have a lot of smelly sediment muddying the waters. A lot of people out of jobs, looking for ways to feather their nest and not too scrupulous how they do it. Bruce is full of them, too.

But real life is like this, full of things seemingly inconsequential and piecemeal patchwork. The history of a crime is full of people's lives. Criminal trials are in general very boring because the story has been worked and kneaded interminably beforehand, through a hundred police reports, a score or more of witnesses taken through what they thought they saw or knew a score of times, a lot of experts (the thing to know, and to remember about experts is that hardly ever do they get anything right), and above all twenty lawyers arguing about what is

16

or isn't legally admissible. I tell you, it takes an unusually good judge to get some yeast back into this heavy dough and make it rise . . . Why, do you think, does 'the accused' sit there nine times out of ten so dulled and apathetic, so total a stranger to the goings-on? All this has nothing to do with him! His real story will never be told. The exception is the professional criminal, exhibitionist as they all are, delighted at having a captive audience, chatterboxing to his heart's content, being funny, scoring off the prosecutor, getting into the papers. They keep their press clippings, and love showing them . . .

It was just after Christmas. Long before we got into the new house. Back in the hell-hole flat. The rest of us were stretched, coming to terms as soon and as fast as we could – or Lydia would – to our new existence. But Vera sat there in that stinking flat with nothing to do.

These apartment blocks have cable television and saucers on the roof: one of the toys the promoter feels he can offer in return for robbing you blind. Vera spent hours zapping at the thirty-six channels, or is it a hundred and six? Who cares? She did, because – just recall the times: revolutions in Roumania; everyone storming up and down the street in Leipzig; secret police (you couldn't even give them away in the supermarket, not even this year's luxury model with four-wheel drive and central electronic locking); and the "velvet" turnaround in Prague. Pretty good television; lots of flowers and nightlights burning, thousands of little bells – you remember the bunches of keys, ching-jing and Marta Kubisova singing from the balcony and "Havel – to the Castle!": everywhere that face. The whole of Europe fair swept off its feet and small blame to them. And who knows what Vera went through, hour by hour, looking at all this? She's been paralytic with guilt these last twenty years because of running away from bloody Czechoslovakia.

As a young girl, substitute on the gymnastics team, she was in France for a competition and she dodged out still in her practice costume. I was a young cop on crowd control; she fell into my arms. And then a few months later, demonstrating a jump for schoolchildren, she slipped off the bar, came a hell of a bang on her arse. Oh yes, there were cracked vertebrae, she was paraplegic for a few years and she still limps a bit. But the extremely good surgeon who handled her said it wasn't enough to account for that period of paralysis – traumatic yes, but physiologically some unexplained . . . quite! He didn't tell her, what good would it have done? What are the mechanisms which will paralyse you psychologically, and which are just the same as falling off your horse? Do you say that she fell off her horse on purpose? Because of feeling guilty about your country and your parents and your whole life up to a moment of childish romantic impulse?

She did some crying there all alone in front of that fucking television set, and was red-eyed when I got home, and didn't want to say that she wanted to go home herself. That she had to put it right before she could go on living.

I had to work this out, and I was abominably slow and clumsy doing so. We aren't very good at that sort of thing, in the police. You clonk Jack with the poker. Bury Jack, wipe the poker, arrange to have been in Kansas City on business while all this was happening. We'll do all right with the physics of that, but don't ever enquire into the metaphysics. This was also a complicated affair. Plainly she had to go, and quickly, and alone, but I couldn't just bundle her on a plane. I had to arrange things, and then the children . . . Luckily I have her own words. She wrote it all down, alone in hotel rooms, in cafés, on park benches. Listen to her account.

CHAPTER THREE

Vera Castang

Once Henri had it fixed firmly in his head that this was serious, he was good about it. He has a strong sense of justice. Rather a fuss was made, but men are like that. I mean that nobody asks them to put themselves out and then they do put themselves out, much further than they need, and rub it in to show how self-sacrificing they are in reality. He could perfectly well have stayed here with the children who wouldn't have minded a bit. Having decided that it was right and reasonable for me to want to go home, nothing would suit him but to come with me as far as Berlin, under the pretext that it was too far to drive by myself. He kept maintaining that the plane fare was too dear. Which it is, but it was useless to point out that he'd spend more money this way. He'd have said yes, but this way one gets more for one's money. He hates planes and I don't mind them. The truth is that he wanted a pretext to go to Berlin. Giving himself away fatally by saying it would be such a good experience for the children. As though it would mean anything to them at their age! Pure sentimentalism. Their idea of fun is riding up and down the moving staircase in the Ka-de-We department store, and eating gigantic Mövenpick ice-creams on the Ku'damm.

I know, I'm getting my story back to front, but I'm going to be catty and female, because he had rather a fiasco, poor Henri. Monsieur le Commissaire, late of the PJ in Paris, who is forever lecturing me about prudence, and

19

telling me off for leaving the car keys in the ignition, had his pocket picked! That put a stop to the ice-cream racket!

Not of much money, at least I hope not! I can't be sure he told the truth, but to believe him it was only the day's spending money and the essential was in his belt. His identity card was lifted though, and his driving licence, so that Big Chief had to go and eat humble pie at the police station, and I just bet they laughed. Before I got back, Henri had time to polish this story and work it up into a neatly turned joke against himself, told with a properly rueful face.

"You remember Fabrice at Waterloo? Setting off with high hopes that at last he's going to fight a battle, and then of course he never sees anything at all; his horse bucks and he finds himself sitting on his arse in a pool of water, and if it wasn't for all the kind motherly women he'd have left his skin behind, too. Such a splendid deflation of romantic bullshit. I know now just how he felt. Quiet elderly gentleman, had his hat knocked over his eyes – cunningly jostled by smart Berliner hooligans."

I would have liked to spend a few days in Berlin myself; instead the family got whipped off home with great speed, told we couldn't afford to hang around any longer. But the children had a marvellous time riding around on the S'Bahn. The oohs and ahs lasted all the way back to Bruce. Emma naturally refused to utter, far too self-conscious. Lydia however clattering away in German as though born to it. It did her good, anyhow.

I set off with my own heart beating. The very first thing was going through Checkpoint Charlie. As you'd expect, the most squalid point in both West and East. The Berliners can walk across anywhere they please and quite right too, but I was an Outlander. One can cross at the Friedrichstrasse station, but not in a car, naturally.

I didn't see anything of Berlin, West or East. Once we found a little pension-hotel I was very kindly allowed to rest for the night, and got taken out to eat in the pub on the corner. It was nice, too. I can't remember what I ate. Being a little bit French, Henri attaches enormous importance to meals. A bad one will throw him into despair for the whole day. He had liver with apples and onions, that's Berlinerisch enough, and drank a lot of beer. The children had steak, I suppose. They're never very adventurous. I longed to go to bed, but of course we had to have the classic stroll up and down the Kurfurtsendamm "to stretch our legs". Schrippe in the morning. I packed some, to eat in the car, and got shovelled off with a perfect volley of warnings and injunctions. I can't say I listened. I was very keyed up and nervous. Five marks for the visa, at Charlie, and then they just waved me on.

Well, it's a drive, of course. One sits through those pine woods, and bumbles along. Autoroute, though the surface isn't up to much. Henri had made a to-do about not going over a hundred or the Volks Polizei would pounce. I didn't, much. All the Westies whizzed past me. Henri would have done a hundred and thirty, saying, "They can't pounce on all of us." A longish day, though. Easties used to go this way in flocks, when Czechoslovakia was the only country who allowed them in without an immense poohah. There were still plenty of little Trabis scuttling along – they stink less when once up to trundle speed – but not what we'd call heavy traffic. It was climbing the hills, past Dresden, up to the frontier in the middle of that sad desert, that my heart came in my mouth. The Erzgebirge is terrifying, but I was too frightened to think about it. At the pass the Germans waved me through after taking the visa paper, but then there was the barrier. The uniforms. And the flag flying.

So foolish. I'd made my mind up I'd just push my nice handsome passport saying "Communauté Européenne", keep my mouth shut, speak German if I had to utter at all. But I had to get out of course, and park the car, and fill in stupid forms. Sit in the photomat for pictures of my sweet clock, looking unbearably criminal as they always do, and then to hear a fuss about obligatory money-changing. I was feeling a bit peppery by then. Yes, I am conscious of my disloyalty. To my poor father. That was worse because my father was proud of his job and proud of doing it well, but here in charge of tourist visas at an important frontier post they had put an old fool with three words of German to mumble between his unbrushed teeth. He went through the papers word by word, looked at me, short and nasty.

"But you were born here. You're Czech." He was a thick, sour captain, one of the real old Stalinists.

And Meddlesome Matilda (which is one of Henri's names for me) replied, "No, I'm not. I'm Slovak." Equally short, and equally stupid.

He glared, and he wanted to say You are a stinking traitor, which I am, but I think he was afraid to. He stamped the papers as though he were stamping on me, with his big cheap boots.

Three hundred metres up the road was the barrier. Several cars had passed me, and were being checked by two army girls, slim and smart in uniform trousers. The lieutenant in charge saw me waiting and came across. He saluted. He actually smiled. Young. Needing a shave. The face framed in the car window had humour along with the five-o'clock-shadow. He took the visa papers.

"*Geldwechselschein*," and waited patiently while I fumbled like a fool. I'd stuffed the exchange-control slip in a purse along with the Czech money.

"Sorry. But you've time. And pretty girls." He smiled with his steel-mended teeth. But they were clean.

"Lots of pretty girls," in English, eyes gleaming, "Thank you. Have a good trip," stamping my passport, without looking where I was born.

This is my country. The good and the bad and myself in the middle. Around me the mysterious, artificial-looking peaks of the Erzgebirge. Aztec-like, utterly befouled by the pollution, yet clean-seeming and peaceful in the still, sunny, smoke-hazy light. Ahead of me the road. My heart was beating, strongly, I could feel it, but steadily, now. I concentrated on the driving. Those old, old trucks, and every one enveloped in a black belch of filthy fumes. I was alternately exhilarated and cast down. Physically it is so beautiful, and it is so shabby, so dirty.

22

A garrison town, full of tanks and soldiers. Concrete bunkers and the smooth masonry, star-pointed bastions behind grassy moats of an old Vaubanesque citadel. I was through it before I realised it was Theresienstadt. We did not need Germans to teach us bestiality. We were always apt learners, skilful practitioners. Neat flowerbeds and smart paint, the camp orchestra striking up a jolly piece of Schubert, sadism towards women, all that is also very Czech.

And then it was Prague and my heart started bumping again. You see it long before you get there because of the same old trams. I had the window down and there on my left, keeping pace, clank-clank. Suddenly the car was flooded with the smell. An illusion, of course. Familiar? No. I had never been away. I'm sorry to say it but my eyes filled with tears, so that the red traffic light in front of me hazed and splintered and danced in front of the windscreen. I snuffled and jerked at the tight packet of paper hankies, and a smart new Skoda – black market no doubt – swerved angrily past me and tooted, cross and patronising at the stupid Westy who can't shift her arse when the light goes green.

I drove on into the old town and parked. The Starometske Square chock-full of gaping tourists. I am one too. No question of going on tonight. I am very tired.

These grimy, over-ornate, once-grand hotels. When I was a girl I looked at them awestruck. I should never have dared go in. I thought they were full of people eating caviare, in evening dress, under the elaborate wrought-iron chandeliers. The lobby now has been 'modernised' with sheets of cheap plastic and plasterboard, tatty and peeling. Formica tables broken at the corners, showing the strawboard below greasy with spilled coffee and dirty dishcloths.

Two or three reception girls, all looking the same, peroxided and much painted, smelling of synthetic perfume. They did not even look up, said, 'Full up, sorry,' and I trailed out humiliated. I went back to the car, sat and smoked a cigarette, pulled myself together. I am Czech, no? Those lobbies were all full of unshaved-looking Turks hanging about, waiting to sidle up behind Westies mumbling about money and girls. Qué, Turks? They're Czech. Czechs have turned into Turks from forty years of being treated that way; of dirt and sliminess and slummy behaviour. I went back to the grandest hotel within reach and when the tinny voice said, 'Full up, sorry,' I slapped my palm down with a hundred-crown note under it and said, 'How about special circumstances?' It went straight into her bra, and the voice said, 'Bath or shower?' and I was looking into nice grey eyes, she was a pretty girl. Turks are nice people, too. They are poor, and we are stinking rich Westies and we bribe them and treat them with contempt and this is what they turn into. My lovely Czechs are all thieving beggars. When I went to get my overnight bag a hooligan had unscrewed the chrome VW symbol off the front of the car. The French used to do that with the Mercédès stars. When I had jolted upstairs in the pre-war lift longing for a shower, I discovered she'd given me a huge rusty old bathtub. She didn't care. I was too tired to make a fuss. I stripped and fell into it. The water was rusty and stank of chlorine, but I didn't care either. It was hot, at least. This expensive hotel, far too dear for Czechs, is ludicrously cheap to my juicy-Brucey D-marks.

When I went out into the passage a naked boy had just come out of the room next door. I don't know whether I looked startled or amused. He scruttled off to what I assumed to be his own. What did it matter who he was sleeping with? But I felt dirtied, and not just by the dusty carpet, the greasy woodwork. Henri finds me a fearful priss. He would have guffawed, thinking it funny.

I idled round the familiar streets. On the square newspaper boys were bawling. I didn't buy a paper, I have no interest in politics, I'm complicated enough already. I looked up the avenue to where the king sits on his horse. I didn't go up there. I was depressed again, and felt ashamed. I mooched off along the Narodni. There on the left is an alcove in the arcade. A boy had been shot there, or perhaps been beaten to death. There were faded flowers against the wall, trails of guttered candlegrease, and one pathetic night-light burning. I'm not sure that I know what I believe in. But I'll be honest. I stood and said a prayer. Who – or what – for? For wholeness perhaps, Us-ness, Me-ness. For who we are, and why. If I'd had a candle then I'd have lit it, set it. I remember as a girl, an old man pissing in that same corner, caught and given a ticket by the police, laughing at his disgusted face. One sees no police at all, now. I think Havel may have said he didn't want to see them on the street for a while.

Down at the end, where one hits the river, is Café Slavia. When I was a student we thought it the centre of civilisation. So I went in, for old sake's sake and a glass of white wine. Then, I could afford a coffee once a week. They've still got the "absinthe" picture on the end wall. The bearded artist, 1900-style, sitting at a round marble table – in Paris we supposed – chin on hand, gazing at the ghostly vision of a naked woman posing, on the chair opposite. Typically bad anecdotal sentimentalism and, supposedly, we were learning to understand why. And it's still the old art déco setting, and there was still a guru at the end table, smoking a cigar, his hair needing washing. Five hours on one cup of coffee. How unreal it all seemed.

And the lobby is still a Treffpunkt for the youngsters who haven't a penny to go in, crouching on the plinth under the statue. I've done that.

I was so downcast I wanted to get drunk. Too many ghosts here. But outside on the Narodni a tall, very pretty girl was roller-skating. She wore professional cyclists' tight black knee-length shorts, but that is "mode". She flexed, surfed on the tramlines, slaloming in and out of parked cars, hop on to the pavement and down. She was agile and fast, certain and beautiful.

My pavements are not dead. The tiny squares I loved so, of dark red porphyry and bluish granite, so well made. They used to take trouble over such things. Then – not now? Oh yes and yes, and yes, they still can. So I turned into the Kavarna next door to the baroque church, where the tree grows out on to the pavement. It was still early but they were full and didn't want to give me a table, so I bribed them. Then they started the nonsense about the International menu or the Russian one. I spoke German, because the Czech Vera would never have dared going in here. I had a vodka-orange, and good dry Böhmisch red wine, and real cognac in a glass the size of my head. Utterly ridiculous. Henri would have had a fit.

What was so pathetic, here, was the waiters wearing evening dress, terribly old and shiny – greasy. But mine had a clean shirt. A lovely boy, too. My word I must have been drunk. The especially nice thing was he was a really good waiter, properly trained and beautifully deft, like the skating girl. I was drunk, look at all those adverbs. In the West the men are too grand to be waiters and are merely pretentious. But here it's worse because they're ashamed and so do nothing properly at all. This boy still had pride in his job. Every movement had a lovely professional neatness. He set the shashlik on fire and made the sauce over the lamp, and do you know, the pudding was pure crêpes Suzette, nobody in Paris knows how, now. They can't be bothered – except when you pay the millionaire's price at Lasserre for the duck – rubbing the sugar on the lemon peel. Curaçao and Grand Marnier. Yes, once, a birthday treat from Henri.

No fancy gestures, no flourishes, no smirking. I gave him a ten mark tip. I know, outrageous.

Out on the street I was accosted by two American tourists, old dears, who stood gassing in that friendly way they have. Did I know the way to the "Ostriches"? Yes, of course, (though I've never set foot there, it's Posh). "Oh, it's just so romantic," said the nice kind woman. Over the Charles Bridge. That's the one with the statues? Wonderful! Isn't it a lovely night!

Sure. If a man had come along and said, "D'you want to fuck," I'd have said yes. At least I think I would. Cognac-bravery, more like. I'd better tell the truth since Henri will read this. I said no such thing to anyone. I walked straight back to that horrible hotel, I took off my clothes and stretched out on the bed. By myself.

They just don't bloody care! Sitting on the throne next morning. You'd call that a relatively safe vantage point. Cleanish, yes, but spills and stains everywhere from paint and plaster slopped about. Everything slovenly and stupidly botched. I reached out for the paper, and the whole throne tilted sideways. Triumph of communist plumbing.

Breakfast was okay. The rolls were made of the white tasteless dough that is soft and at once goes dry and crumbly. The waiter was scandalised because I yelled at him in Czech. Is there no real bread? I paid my bill, and I drove away as quickly as I could.

Slovakia, and now every kilometre makes me younger. The bony woman, with the lurch in the walk, though it's ever so slight and doesn't show in the car, dissolves: 1930s movie. In her place there appears a little girl who sings, whose party-piece was to climb walls and dance along them. Good equilibrium. Natural that they should accept me for gym school. I could do front and back flips on the balance beam. The promising child promoted to Bratislava at cadet level. As a junior to Prague. I don't think the Beaux-Arts scholarship would have come my way without that. Athletes in Eastern countries were much privileged. If you can call it that. Sixteen-hour days and harshly disciplined. Aged eleven, twelve, I recall being hit with a switch. It used to catch us just above the back of the knees. And being called a lazy dirty little Slovak.

We were dance-trained, too. Not like the Russian children, but to this day I like hard, upright chairs. To sprawl was the worst of crimes. This is how they get their results. Early selection and intensive training, and the parents are told that there may come a day when they will be very proud of their daughter.

So from the age of eight I went home only on holidays.

> In an old house in Paris all covered with vines
> Lived twelve little girls in two straight lines.

That's Madeline and me. It was important that the line be Straight.

I've told the story often, how I was deprived of privileges for slacking. Because by then drawing interested me more. Sulking on the substitutes bench, and a harsh word from Miss Clavel. She was gentle with us as a rule. A dry old stick but a trusted Party-member. Funny musty smell she had. My crime must have got painted very blackly, back in the village. Oh yes, my father could be proud of me, all right. There was a fuss made. "Applying for political asylum" is a French tradition, but I was a child, and irresponsible, and I think they'd have handed me over but for a stiff Czech bureaucrat putting their backs up. They granted me a temporary permit "pending enquiry" and would likely have gone back on that but for Henri, who knew their ways, marrying me. But it is so awful, being grateful.

More important is to try to understand my father. He's a Communist from way back, the old-fashioned radical, very puritan. I, too, have my puritanical side. At least, that's what Henri calls it. So I understand, you see.

I'm still saying "he's". He died a year ago while we were still in Paris. That's all I know.

In the early years I wrote, often, big emotional screeds. The "crime" was only a childish misdemeanour. I couldn't imagine being unforgiven. I imagined my letters were censored, that perhaps they never arrived. But I was sure that in the end I would find an envelope addressed with that small, very clear, pointed handwriting. I never did. He was a railwayman, he had those big rough and gentle banana hands, I sat on his lap when I was tiny and played with them. He was good at administration, and helped out in the commune (they were a pack of peasants) with paperwork, and later when an incompetent idiot retired (or got rusticated for being on the fiddle) he became a sort of unofficial secretary, not just a Party pillar but something much much rarer, the man liked and trusted by everyone because he was never on the fiddle. He was Straight. And that was the trouble. He was straight with me too, according to his lights. Nothing must go wrong with the trains, even if he had to sit up all night. He was chief signalman on the section. But now that I've read the book,

I can see that he was Weir of Hermiston.

So after a time I learned to write more briefly, and less often, trying to be factual and to keep the line open. Birthdays, occasions like that. A photo of the children, a word about Henri's work, and mine, hoping that in the end, they'd understand. And very occasionally, perhaps once every two years, there would appear "a word" from my mother. Big round handwriting, rather straggly, on a couple of small sheets, and not very informative.

Do not misunderstand. She is not illiterate. On the contrary, she was well educated, her grammar and spelling are impeccable and she speaks a vivid, flowery, racy language. But she does not belong to a people who "wrote" or exchanged letters. They went to see one another, be it every day, or week, or once a year, and their joys and griefs, the events and the gossip, were expressed orally. They didn't know how to put things down on paper, and the result was stilted phrasing. *Dear Vera.* She didn't mean "dear" but it was the way one started a letter. *How is it with you? With us all is much the same. I have some trouble with rheumatism. The chrysanthemums did well this year. I hope the children work hard at school. Your ever-loving Mother.* Never a word about my father.

I did not show these to anybody. Henri has much delicacy behind the crude manner. He has a tactful respect for secret areas. I am a secretive woman.

And then one of those awful death notices cut out of a local paper, in the special language more stilted than anyone's writing, full of stuff about the lifetime of service and devotion, much regretted and sorely missed. And a heartbroken note.

He was out digging the garden and he fell over still holding the spade. The doctor said it was a rupture of aneurism, it happens suddenly and you don't suffer. It was a lovely sunny day. As always he was doing a job, one he was good at. That's better than an illness. Hána came from Bratislava and stayed with me two weeks.

Hána is her sister, a silly woman but a good one, who talks without punctuation in a powerful local accent. Works herself to the bone for others and then complains that they're exploiting her. Shrill, hot-tempered, full to the brim with love. Who wants brains? Who needs common sense?

There was a police car parked by the side of the road. All my old irrational fears returned in a rush. *One feels that the most unexpected and the most inhuman will arrive at any instant, that danger is behind every phrase pronounced, every street corner, every car slowing in front of any building, every sound of boots in a stairwell.* William Shirer's well-known description of the Third Reich, and a classic comment on all the Stalinist régimes. You see, I've never been back and if I'd tried Henri would have stopped me. "They" let it be known that they were much vexed and I'd certainly be arrested. I'd caused a public loss of face. I was frightened.

"They'd hold you as a hostage," said Henri bleakly. "Sell you back for money. Make some absurd claim – a hundred thousand dollars invested in your education. It's been done before. The West Germans have been paying that sort of blackmail for years. All right, now you say you've got to go. If something happens we'll tell Havel. But not the children . . ."

I stopped for coffee and a pee in Brno. Do you know what my compatriots had done? Bought a new lavy, didn't even bother to unstick the brown paper tape round the edge. Shoved on a plastic lid the wrong colour, and walked away. We'll tell Havel? Oh, Havel knows. A whole generation, mine, is lost. But not the country, I won't believe that. Not the children, the tall boys with their pale skin and pale blue eyes, the sharp-featured pointy-nosed girls, and now I'm here in the south you start to see the darker, podgier Slav looks.

Funny – I have the pale Czech colouring, but Slav around the eyes. I'd never really noticed before. Lydia takes after her father. But Emma has something of her grandmother's look.

It was, I'm afraid, a disaster. I had come with all sorts of ideas, that I could persuade her to come back with me to see the children, that sort of thing. One look, I knew she'd never budge. The distance between us is now too great. We were formal with one another. "Fille," she called me. "Mère," I said. Like two nuns, one the younger.

When my father was alive, the moment he got home and took his overalls off he took everything off, washed from head to toe and put on a collar and tie. If he had any business to take him outside then he put on his suit, and his big silver watch with its chain in the waistcoat pocket. If business took him to the pub – and it had to be business – then one beer, never more. At home with his dinner he had one glass of our own country wine. She was the same. She would never even go outside the house with her apron on, like the peasants. Always a dress, and clean shoes. He polished all the shoes, every night, his workboots as highly shined as her court shoes. She was wearing a shawl now, a little old woman with sunken features, and sabots stood on the step outside the door.

She made pathetic efforts at welcoming me. She went and "got a duck" from the neighbours. I had to eat that most Czech of meals, a roast duck with dumplings. ("Those awful dunlops," as Henri calls them. I used to make them at home, Semmelknödel as they're called in South Germany, when I was young, until he said, "I never want to see one of those things again." Do you notice, I say "Home", and it means him?) I tried to tell her about Brussels, and the job we have now. I don't think she understood anything. "Yes . . . yes. I'll pick some flowers shall I? Too early for gladioli." My father was proud of his gladioli, the bed beautifully dug with decayed straw and old horseshit, each stem carefully staked. Henri hates them so I never buy them. But as it was the end of April, she found some daffodils left where they've always grown, in the cherry orchard. Never once did she say, "I knew you'd be back." Only "I didn't expect you", while making a fuss about laying the table with-a-tablecloth, and putting the poor daffs in a vase, and finding a bottle of wine. I'm sorry to say I drank it all. I needed it.

"You'll have to go and see your Aunt Hána. She'll be thrilled." Herself so plainly disappointed. I showed photos of the children. She stared dully. "They do grow up, don't they." They're your grandchildren. "Your girls," she said. But they're yours – this is Europe. And it's ours. It isn't Outer Mongolia here.

31

I'm afraid I lied, abjectly, concerning poor Hána. I said they'd made a fuss at the frontier, and they'd only allowed me a visa for one day. It was the sort of thing she seemed to expect. Took it as "normal".

Another pathetic effort while eating, to recall what would be sure to interest me, what had happened to girls I had been at school with, childhood friends. Zdana . . . Ivana . . . All resilience was gone, the old inventiveness, the quick, funny spontaneity, the irreverence. But it used to be there. I haven't sentimentalised it out of nowhere.

"Havel – he's a Czech!" Not "he's a playwright," or what I could understand, "he's a bourgeois, an intellectual!", but "he's a Czech". Such a miserable, provincial, Slovak thing to say.

"Dubcek's too old though, really, too tired."

"He's one of us. Havel – sucking up to the Germans, the French."

"Is that what they're saying, in the village?" My voice was far too sarcastic.

I bought some flowers for the grave. I kneeled down to ask for his forgiveness. They'd put him in the churchyard, too. A man who'd died in his old-Communist principles, and I respected him for it. I went into the pub as well, knowing that tongues would be wagging in the village. I endured some reminiscences of little Vera, and more of my father, and both as sententious as they were tinsel. Forgiving him for having been a just and honest man. Oh, we are very Catholic hereabouts, and all the Communists now call themselves Christian Democrats. It won't be long now before they're all busy canonising Monsignor Tiso again, their great guru during the Hitler time and a famous denouncer of the Jews and the Freemasons. There are five million of us Slovaks, a good solid right-wing bloc. The Clerico-fascists. I can hear Father's cutting voice. No. I won't come back. Those sentiments I can hear, loud and ringing, in any Western country. What is Success? What's Failure? I keep hearing these two words. What do they mean?

". . .And my regards to Zdana when you see her. And Vlasta of course. And my best love to Aunt Hána." I drove away sorrowful. But very, very proud of my Father.

I travelled a lot faster on the way out. I didn't stop in Prague. I went straight on, and on a sunny April evening I was in Dresden.

I've seen, since then, the Memorial Church in Berlin. It's a bit of a self-conscious fraud, stuck up there so righteously at the top of the Ku'damm and surrounded by glitter. No wonder the Berliners snigger rather and call it the hollow tooth. This is the real thing. This colossal empty space bitter with draughts. This blackened shell is the Zwinger, the finest baroque ensemble ever known. Black from the fire, black from forty-five years of solid Marxist shit, black of my shame. A few hundred brave boys, poor wretches, did this, aimed and directed by criminal imbeciles: they are the same everywhere. Are the English just more inescapably pleased with themselves? I don't think any of us has much to be smug about, do you? I stopped being Slovak here once and for all, and were I English, would it be different? Here is my why, for being a European and wanting to be an artist and daring to be alive forty-five years after the others died.

I wonder whether any English poet has stood here, moved as I am now. And if not, why not?

If Henri were here he'd be making a joke, the way he does when very much moved, and it's more English than French – the Aquitanian Bastard. "You know, under a microscope, my lungs must look exactly like this." "Yes, mate, but not such good art." On one blackened dart of masonry I caught a glint of gold still; the "AR" monogram. Augustus Rex. In Berlin Henri just had time to whip me across to see the Opera. They've restored that, thank God, and beloved Erich Kleiber made them put back the gold inscription "Fredericus Rex Apollonis et Musis". Appalling people these kings, but ours, and they belong. The bastards in Dresden have done nothing. Sort of tidied it up a bit, and there's a tablet on a wall to say that Ulbricht or some such saint had Here Combated Fascists. There won't be anything sillier than that in England.

CHAPTER FOUR

Henri Castang

someones married their everyones
laughed their cryings and did their dance

Vera got back in a stew about her mother and her homeland, but controlled about it: I am trying to do as much. Truth is that I felt shaky about the entire enterprise, watched her through Charlie with stones in the chest and jelly in the gut. To her the important thing is that she went at all; to me that she came back. This secret service crap is like finding grit in the spinach when it hasn't been properly washed – you're eating comfortably and pliff, ptoey, you're spitting with your teeth on edge.

Goddam cheek – in my notebook. Every cop carries one, and mine is sacred; known to the children as The Book and Lydia, when small, was whacked for drawing faces in it. Now, pinned in with a staple, is a shitty piece of printout paper with a laconic message: *Tuesday 18th 19:20 Gare du Nord southbound tram platform.*

There's a celebrated passage in Gide, describing Verlaine up for trial. The judge enquired whether he were a sodomist. "One says sodomite, monsieur," replied Verlaine.

I said both.

Because this is the when-did-you-stop-beating-your-wife trick. Go, and you'll likely make a fool of yourself. Don't go, and you'll always wonder whether you haven't made a greater fool of yourself.

I tore out the whole sheet, crossly. Flung it in the waste-basket. Got it out, uncrumpled it. Of course there isn't any bloody "clue": standard paper, standard fussy electronic clusters supposed to be lettering. The whole thing as turned out by any airline booking desk from here to Chicago.

I won't pay attention to this sort of tripe. But I am paying attention whether I want to or not. That's the trick.

It would be easy to pick my pocket, say in the southbound tram which I habitually take, and put the notebook back a minute later. There's a message in the style of delivery: we are clever, we can do this whenever we like. Or done here in the office – there's a stapler on my desk. I had looked at the book last night, so who was here this morning? Oh yes, am I now to get paranoid about Eamonn Hickey?

I won't react. It is an obvious come-on to see if I am malleable – one always is, calling it curiosity but in truth it is fear.

The Gare du Nord is a ghastly place. Modernised – meaning the architect made a balls of it. A stranger can't tell his arse from his elbow: the corridors are interminable, the levels confusing – main line, suburban line, metro, tram (which goes underground here). Head for the Gents and you'll come out in the car park. A triumph of technicity over common sense.

The other day I was watching an old Woody Allen movie on the TV. A classic nightmare passage: he's on a train surrounded by morose faces bleakly staring – dream effect of silence and the tick of a clock. Through the window he sees another train full of laughing people; a girl blows him a kiss. He blunders about trying to get off; can't. It was just like this. Life's like that, too. This was the joker's message as well as the movie's.

I saw nothing, of course. I was being told that I could be manipulated. The joker will declare himself when he judges me sufficiently softened up.

I see a good deal of Harold; because of my own

35

inexperience he is my guide in the byways of bureaucracy. And of law – I was brought up in the French tradition, that a judgement based on equity is worthless without law behind it, and Harold is an admirable jurist. The most opaque piece of prose becomes lucid, lively, instantly apprehensible. One mustn't give the impression that I'm forever popping in, but he conducts things in the most open manner; wants me to appear saying there's a point on which I would like him to take an opinion. Partly kindness; he's a kind man. Partly getting-on-with-it; he'll listen to a paragraph of snarled syntax and answer in three monosyllables. And partly the flamboyance that comes naturally to him: the Persian rugs in the office, the insistence on having "a pretty car". "It's very difficult to get a pretty car." Harold will stop in the middle of law to discuss this. He appears and disappears, both fast and noisily, in a competition Lancia, Italian racing red. Suarez, who used to work in Geneva as a legal adviser, says that he's often reminded of Henry Kissinger.

There's a lot of everything in this complex personality: energy and brilliance, childishness and petulance. It can be trying, but it's stimulating, and mostly it's funny.

Trying because he introduces personalities, which makes one think he must be vulnerable in his own relations.

Complaints about Iris, for example. Punctuality is a thing with him (it would be worth asking why) and he can't bear meals not to be on time, "won't go to houses which keep Spanish hours," and so forth.

"Iris has to be three quarters of an hour late with everything." (Why? Probably a sort of armour adopted in self-protection.)

Since meeting her he is much fascinated by Vera. "Wonderful woman. Beautiful too." I had mentioned that since coming back from Prague she'd said that there was no difference between success and failure.

"Ha!" Harold delighted! He's brought this up two or three times.

Then there are crude, childish provocations.

"I rather fancy Vera." Stupidly, I was provoked.

"Wouldn't, if I were you, mate. Bullet up the arse from me is nothing to what she'd do to you." This was very indiscreet, as Harold had of course designed. The cunning cross-examiner. I was senselessly infuriated. "Killed a man for trying to rape her."

"Really?" In his "high voice". "Doesn't brood about that?"

"No." I had to make the best of it, now. "Artist. Detached from the present. Broods about the past and the future, but in between, highly sobersides – "What are we going to have for supper?"

"Ha!" The information had been tucked away, and would be used some time.

He's just back from England; charged in bellowing for a paper. He comes himself, likes one to come to him, hates things brought by secretaries. "What are you doing, skulking in that office?" Cf. the tiger-spring across the room – to consult a law book? Feet apart, glasses pushed high, looking up a word in one of his numerous dictionaries.

"And how was London?" I asked.

"I was walking in the park, met a small pathetic procession; a dozen gardeners dressed up as Yee-oh-men, trundling a very small brass cannon, greatly battered, beautifully polished, plainly much beloved. Officered by elderly party with mutton-chop whiskers, on a horse.

"This appealed. Bag-Men, Mace-Men, so like being Recorder of the City, or perhaps Master of the Rolls. I followed.

"When they reached Marble Arch a young police-woman, very pretty, extremely elegant, looked with that cool smiling calm, cantered her immense horse a few effortless paces, held up a sexy majestic hand with the air of 'negligent woodcraft'. The entire traffic of the Bayswater Road, Oxford Street and Park Lane came to a solemn two minute silence and this preposterous group with total dignity vanished up the Edgware Road.

"What, I asked myself, could they conceivably do there? Could this have been the Queen's Birthday? Bicentenary

37

of the Capture of Seringapatam? I'll never forget her. Not a man alive could have dragged her off that horse and raped her. Though it was certainly in my mind to try.

"God knows, what the future of England may be. This vision, of the present so kindly guiding the faltering footsteps of the Victorian Age, exalted me. I should so have wished to go straight off to Whites, and tell Evelyn all about it."

It had gone on just long enough. The secretary stood there open-mouthed.

"I'm not quite clear about the negligent woodcraft."

"Oh, that's the *Sword in the Stone*. Robin Hood. 'And you, Robin, stop leaning on your bow with that air of ' – is that my paper?" But in no hurry to go.

"Are you loyal to the Throne, Harold?"

"Oh, I don't know about that, dear boy. Royalty is now exceedingly squalid. Just imagine asking the Duke of Cambridge whether he were a pederast." Slipping easily into the Duke addressing the Sandhurst cadets. " 'You boys have been putting your dicks where I wouldn't put my umbrella!' Venereal disease was the great obsession of all nineteenth-century British Commanders. Get dick caught in the computer, now," whisking the paper out of the girl's hands. "One hazard we must try to avoid."

Leaving me bemused – the sword in the what? – but I learn a lot of English from Harold. He has a fine antique vocabulary. Whipper-snappers. Jacks-in-office. Kitchen-maids'-followers. Pettifogging-attorneys. Plumber's-mates. Rat week, for a negligent secretary.

An hour later I was standing dreaming in the men's lavatory and found Harold next door to me. Hissing conspiratorially over his shoulder.

"And how's your loyalty to the Republic?"

"Singularly shaky," suiting the action to the word.

"Good, good. But one must be loyal to something. Not the Commission, I hope."

I had to pass my hands several times under the magic tap before it would run. "One wants a piece of soil, and I haven't one."

"We are the dispossessed," wrenching at the roller-towel. "I have a little magic patch, on the Welsh border. Seekings House," mysteriously. It took a moment before any penny dropped.

"Not the Midnight Folk?" Emma, bewitched, can talk of nothing but Abner Brown and Mrs Pouncer.

He did his act of the eyes widening. "Oho. You know. I must keep an eye on you." He marched off leaving me flabbergasted (one of his words).

There are odd bonds between us.

He called that evening at the flat, unannounced – a thing which annoys me; what were phones invented for? – but so polite, in the most formal sense, that the most old-fashioned and punctilious of men could not have taken exception. It was quite late; indeed the children were in bed and we were reading. He did not outstay his welcome and can't have been here above an hour, the time for a drink and a refill, enquiring of Vera whether she found occasion to complain of his cigar. He concentrated upon her throughout.

"What was all that about?" she asked bemused, after he'd gone. She was getting ready for bed.

"Penitence. I'm rather impressed."

"What on earth for?" I had not mentioned Harold's coarse remark concerning herself, having taken it as no more than the usual vulgarity: nor that I'd grown rather warm about it. Vera can be very prim, and unexpectedly she broke out laughing, "struck an attitude" in her underclothes, and took it as a compliment.

"Those very ministerial manners! – and enquiring in such detail about the children and the house – I couldn't make it out," struggling into her nightdress. "In fact, if you hadn't been there I'd have wondered whether it wasn't a pass."

"That wouldn't have surprised me, but for being so pointedly in front of me. D'you still want to read a bit?"

"No," said Vera. Decidedly . . .

*

39

I can't help wondering about Harold himself. This coming to see me, apparently pointlessly, is that a hint? That (irrelevant?) conversation about loyalty; is that another? One never knows with the English, but why ask about my patriotic sentiments?

I'm fed up with games. I left a piece of scribbling paper in the typewriter, late at night, as though to be a reminder to myself of some piece of research.

"To come on out of the woodwork and I'll see what can be done." Meaningless to a cleaning woman. And there was an answer next morning. I've been careful with the notebook – neither over-careful, nor ostentatiously careless. It said simply, "You've a lunch date."

Another tiresome trick; the last-moment phone call so that one cannot play cop, and stake out a meeting place. Worth it though, if I'm ever to learn anything. Everyone had left and I was catching up on chores when it rang. Man's voice with a strong local accent.

"Nip along then – taxi waiting."

"That's nice, but skip all the bullshit, just say who, how, where."

Coarse cackle of laughter. "Don't be frightened, you're not getting kidnapped. Not Beirut, is it?"

Genuine taxi; a number, a meter, even the authentic smell. "Jump in then, chief, not a lot of time. Only Les Sablons. Restaurant, innit? Birthday surprise, what?" laughing. "Big bottle of champagne." Plainly he knew nothing. "That's all right chief, all paid for," braking to a stop. "Here," handing me another of these infernal bits of paper.

Les Grands Sablons is a sort of square. The paper said "Entrance next the picture frames. Table to the left, opposite the antique shop." A passage full of arty expensive shops – the whole quarter is like this – with a precinct in the middle. I was sniffing at it when a familiar, flustered voice said, "Sorry, am I late? Difficult to park." Vera. I have walked into a trap.

I caught hold of her wrist.

"No! Go straight home. I'll explain when I see you.

Somebody's idea of a joke. But go – go now!" She was looking at me with enormous eyes, but conquered that fatal need to argue. And she has experience of being married to a police officer. It didn't take above a minute. I was angry, though.

I'll give these clowns a piece of my mind!

Inside is a nice little patio. Tables with awnings, greenery. People drinking.

"Have you reserved, sir?"

"No – yes – meeting someone. Don't know what name he gave. Castang, was it?"

The head-waiter thought I was having him on. "Without a reservation I can't do anything for you at all, I'm afraid."

But at that moment everything began to happen quickly. Two characters came sidling in; nondescript, but with the clothes cops wear to conceal the fact that they're also wearing guns.

"Mr Castang? We'll make no fuss in a public place. Raymond, narcotics detail," flashing some sort of warrant card. "We'll just move along a step." The businessmen, being hearty over apéritifs, hadn't even looked up.

We took a discreet pace along the passage; one stood to mask while the other patted me down. Professionally done. There could be no real embarrassment; I have lots of identity papers. They were polite.

"Apologies for troubling you. Some error in transcription."

They were gone, slipping quickly into a grey Opel parked on the back street. There's no point in kicking up a shindy, any more than there'd be in taking a note of the number.

I strolled back along the passage. The table was occupied by the sort of man who wears a fluorescent bow tie, chatting up three women whose merry laughter made a great show of their teeth. I stopped to read the menu. I'd been done out of the soufflé de Saint-Jacques and the mille-feuille of wild salmon. Perhaps even some Corton Charlemagne, for Czechs may be poor but the Stasi isn't. I went back out to Les Sablons and had a hamburger and a

41

beer on the pavement; walked back to the office reflectively, getting the dried-up bits of frites out of my teeth.

I rang Vera, making noises of reassurance to us both. Some woman had phoned her, saying my secretary was off that day. She'd thought I must have something to celebrate. Yes, I said, like getting a recorder to tap incoming phone calls. Don't react unless it's me: that's the way the house gets burgled.

I rang the Kripo and asked to be put through to the narcotics detail.

"Somebody called Raymond, Rémond. Plain clothes, don't know his rank."

"No one like that here; what's it about then?"

"Somebody with a phony card and a grey Opel." They wanted to know more: I didn't know any more.

Trudging in next morning I noticed that the door to Harold's office was shut, which is unusual. Miss Huntingdon gave me a corner of her sunny smile.

"Deity is in rather a black frame of mind."

"Oh dear; leave these with you then, shall I?"

"No, no, it isn't Captain Bligh." Flogging moods are mostly contrived for effect, as she well knows. "More sort of wrapped in cloud and communing solitary upon the mountain top. Go in, if I were you; might be salutary."

Harold was sitting sideways on a corner of the desk, one foot dangling, holding two ballpoint pens, with which he was trying out a drummer's rhythm on the edge of a metal tray holding more. He paid no attention to me.

"You said you wanted this stuff." The bright good mornings were out of key. I dumped the paperwork, made to leave.

"Don't go. Siddown," in a growly voice.

"I've a lot to do."

"Listen to this," paying no attention. "Came to me suddenly from – must be fifty years ago." The drum beat a melancholy pattern of flat, sullen rimshots. Harold sang, softly; he has an agreeable baritone voice.

42

" 'My mama done tol' me—
When I was in knee pants' – you know that? –
'She give you the glad eye—
But when that sweet voice is done'," going into the high register,
" 'A woman's a two-face—
A troublesome thing what leave you to sing—
The Blues, in the Night.' "

He began to whistle, in complicated clarinet fioriture, good like all his imitations and I recognised that . . .

"Artie Shaw." Way before my time, but I can recall the Duke Ellington records too, from my student days.

"Good, good." Apparently I'd got an A. Change, from my usual B-minus. He dropped the drumsticks and swung round.

"I distinctly recall telling you to sit down. Now you're a star in our firmament. Our krimi-expert. A real cop, no less."

"Yes," frivolously. "Like Schimanski." The outrageous commissaire on German television is my favourite fictional cop. He gobbles junk food and yells at everyone. This is true to life. Even Schimmy's innumerable ways of falling in the shit are familiar to me, though no cop I know is that tough or that talented; least of all me.

"I'm serious." Glaring. "This isn't 'Tatort' – this is an office where we do delicate and valuable work."

"Well, it was you who started being Artie Shaw."

"Shut up. Now as a working cop, you've investigated a lot of crimes, including homicides."

"From time to time. They aren't all that frequent. The camera can be very clever but it leaves out the smells. Unwashed feet and unaired rooms, a lot of dirty laundry both real and metaphorical. Physically and morally, they're grimy and they stink. There are specialised teams for the gangsters and narcotic dealers. Ordinary Kripo like me got the smelly socks and the broken marriages."

"You make quite a fetish of your marriage, don't you."

It's a bore, having to explain this. "Almost all cops are

43

divorced. The wives don't like the lousy hours and the lousy work. Cops live in squalid apartments where nobody does the washing-up or changes the sheets, and the casual girlfriends are as squalid as themselves. They don't see their children. They nearly all drink and they nearly all take pills. It takes a woman of strong character to survive this. I had to make my mind up that she came first, no matter what. Price one pays. Your fictional detective may look raffish and bohemian, but the real one's more apt to be stilted and suburban."

And, I could have said, I'm bloody glad to be out of it. At the cost of being sent here. This is regarded by most people as a sort of Siberian exile. It is fashionable, even, to pretend that it is a fearful punishment, for which a high salary and easy conditions can barely begin to compensate. And if the men don't feel that way, the wives do: the place fair seethes with discontent.

Harold pretended to have lost interest.

"Ho," picking up his drumsticks. "I've just recalled another line . . . 'Clicketyclack, they're echoing back, the Blues – in the Night!' "

There's no doing anything with him when he's like this, as Miss Hunted-Down had sagely concluded.

One hears tales, which lose nothing in the telling, so that they come at a heavy discount. One reads of some engineer, Parisien to be sure, offered a job at eight hundred thousand – good God that's sixty thousand a month – and who turned it down because it meant living in Metz: for some obscure reason they're frightened of the East, and of course Bruce is the north-east. Naturally, we're all devoured by jealousy at the thought of vast salaries offered to technical or marketing people in the private sector.

One tends – or I do – to believe that only one's own compatriots are like this: they and the English, notoriously as xenophobic as the French and complaining about sausages and the climate (they're all paid far more than they'd be getting at home). My own German colleagues are mild souls, but Vera who trots around among the wives, conscientiously, reports that they all moan.

"A perpetual snivel about the quality of their life not being as good. Really? I asked, you'd rather be in Stuttgart? Oh yes, every time. The Dutch all think that nobody else takes their pet grievances seriously – Oh you know, wearing fur coats, smoking in the canteen or buying South African fruit or Belgians are sloppy, even if the place is clean, it's never Dutch-clean and so on."

And the Belgians, themselves? They still have the immensely strong assumption, carried to outrageous lengths, that in Flanders they're all sub-human. A tale is going around of some executive here, I mean native Bruxellois, threatened with a posting to Antwerpen. "Vancouver if you like, Buenos Aires if need be, but never, never will I take Anvers."

Vera and I, who like it here, who think ourselves damned lucky, look at each other and wonder. What's wrong with us, then?

A reader might think that I am being unduly devious. Is this a crime story? Then come to the point. As in the adventures of Schimanski where you see him perpetually in action, rushing about, eating and drinking and changing his clothes (he is forever falling into the extremely polluted waters of Duisburg harbour). But this is the physics. They leave out the metaphysics because that would bore the television audience.

This is about us – the Europeans. We do not find it easy, to abandon several hundred years of nationalist propaganda; of having it drummed into us at school that we are French, or English, or Czech: Vera's struggles with her Czechness are altogether apposite.

I found it easier: some accident of birth, some hereditary genes, some atavistic instincts (and, perhaps above all, the detachment of cop-training); these produced a very unFrench character. And my own theory is that the French make such a closeknit Thing of being so precisely because they are so disparate in origins, in blood.

This story is about Harold – who is extremely English. About Iris who is Anglo-Irish, and that is something very peculiar, but between Vera and Eamonn Hickey, who is

Irish, I begin to get a glimpse. One will not understand Harold without some effort to understand Vera, or myself, or Eamonn.

And as for the pretty how town, it is a very suitable home for us. Belgium (politically a recent and artificial invention) has been quarrelling – with be it said immense enjoyment – for forty years about the status of Bruce. A French-speaking city in an enclave of Flanders. In the end – tired out – they have given it a status peculiar to itself. The city has become the Third region of Belgium. We – the Europeans – live in it.

The house that I have bought is in Schaerbeek, a commune on the north-eastern fringe of Bruce and, as the name implies, "in Flanders". But is it Flemish? – is it hell! Like Bruce it has a High Town and a Low Town. Up at the top of the hill we're all bourgeois, you could call it a French ghetto and you wouldn't be wrong. Down at the bottom it's all Turks, long dresses and cowled headscarves.

It occurs to me, I've still got some formalities to see to, which will mean a lot of excessively meaningless paperwork at the Schaerbeek Town Hall.

I am looking forward to verifying what truth there may be in some hair-raising tales: that, for example, the Burgomaster has installed a special Apartheid desk, for registering the births-deaths-and-marriages. People say that this is labelled "Only for Flamands".

Harold conducts his cross-examination in his own devious way. Without alluding to previous conversation he will fire a sudden shot. A day or so later—

"What was your parentage?" apropos of nothing at all.

"Really, I don't know a great deal about it. They died, or ran away. All rather obscure. I was brought up by an Auntie." He can see, I presume, that I'm not over-anxious to talk about it.

"But you're French?"

"I suppose so. Vaguely. France is full of people called Schimanski and who knows where they come from? I don't always have a French mentality. Vera claims I'm part

46

English – "the Aquitanian Bastard" – you know how the English are; think half of France belongs to them, really."

"Yes, I do see. And Vera taught you English?"

"I don't know. Taught one another, I think. I was always quite good with languages. She's much better than me, but she reads a great deal more. Literary. Will suddenly find an outlet in Alfred Lord Tennyson."

Harold suddenly concentrated on the centre of his desk, which was full of messy papers, and the voice went deep bass.

" 'My great agony, my bliss – my anxiety,
My lovely paradise;
I love her bitterly too, and hate her affectionately always.' "

"What's that then? Some sort of *haiku*?"

"You're not all that far out. Translation by Jan Morris of a traditional Welsh verse form."

"Means a lot to you then, Wales?" I was recalling the little plot.

"Not especially. To Iris it does." And changed the subject.

What can – should – one take seriously? The jurist; that for certain: an acknowledged expert like Suarez speaks of him with respect. It was not favour or nepotism that got him into this job. A good administrator: his powers of synthesis as well as analysis are striking and Mr Hickey agrees. The advocate; I have mentioned his ability to make ponderous complexity into lucid, simple phrases. Persuasive; the various boards and committees with which government is thickly sown, in Bruce as everywhere else, are said to view him as formidable. Even funding, first of all departmental requirements, seems to be no problem. We are squashed for space (as everyone is here), but those who have been here longer tell me that what Mr Claverhouse wants, he gets.

And the actor. This gets explained to me in terms of "Englishness" – that the law courts are theatrical, and that the Garrick Club has traditionally been as full of judges as of strolling-players. I suppose so. Some people find the excessive drollery distasteful. But the animation is vivifying (Harold would look up "anima" in the dictionary and declare this phrase a tautology). He is away for days on end: the office is silent, studious, and, it has to be said, rather boring. You know it when he's back: Aha, la Joie de Vivre, says Miss Huntingdon.

We've just had one of these week-long absences. I was sailing down the passage past the office shared by three or four of the secretaries, and overheard scraps of song, not just Harold's though his is as usual the most powerful, intermixed with giggling. I put my head in. We have acquired a new girl, tall with straight fair hair; shy, but it had been discovered she has a pretty contralto voice. Harold had pounced.

"Now with me – both together—
'Maybe I'm only supposed to stay in your arms awhile'
— and then you look over your shoulder, sexy, reproachful at old Bogart, and in Singspiel,
'As others have done',"
in the deepest bass voice. The poor girl was embarrassed but encouraged by the others, unmaliciously.
"Now you alone from the beginning—
'Maybe it happens this way . . .' Oh, that's good."
And himself with a flourish, up into his tenor register.
" 'I hope in my heart that it's so
In spite of how little we know!' "

"Captain Macheath," Huntingdon was saying joyfully, "but will turn into Lotte Lenya any second now." The girl was smiling despite threats to be tearful, self-conscious at the teasing.

He is addicted to these sentimental lyrics of the forties, when they have any real music to them – that one was surely Hoagy Carmichael. Why these strange survivals from adolescence? What's the meaning? What significance has the haiku? But I'm sounding like a cop; the last thing I want to be.

And "Nonsense," said Vera. "He enjoys singing. Sings well, by your account. Harmless display of vanity, and does the girls no harm."

Just "English". They have an amateur dramatic society. You'd never catch the French doing that. The Germans have a chorale, and among the Dutch there's said to be a string quartet. Why the hell not?

CHAPTER FIVE

Vera Castang

I've become friends — and there I stop at once. "Friends" is too strong a word? I've never been one for friendships with women. And that sounds as though I've had a lot of friendships with men, which of course I haven't. Writing words, and getting them right, is just as hard as drawing lines. Still, since being "home" I'm more "at home" in my skin, inside myself. Does that make any sense? Can I say that Iris and I get on well together? I doubt if she'd talk, either, about "becoming friends".

I've a terrific amount to do with the house. It's filthy, and I scrub and scrub, and wonderful things appear. Marble in the entrée, in a lovely smooth inlay. Some good wood in the staircase. On doors too, and windows, under a thick slab of beastly old paint. There's fine plasterwork on those cornices, the lovely high ceilings. I've got Henri up there on the step-ladder whitewashing, before a huge paint and paper programme. One begins to be able to see out of windows. Rather splendid. Yes, I like Schaerbeek very much!

Blowed if I'm going to be house slave, though. I seem to have spent my entire married life cleaning house. Aha, says Henri, when taxed with this fact, but this time it's Your house.

So what? The "cottage" was my house, too. Anybody who has lived in an old country-built French house ought to know what it's like. Stone flags on a kitchen floor and uneven pine planking. Everything crooked. It rambles, steps up and down. The children were tiny, played in and out, brought in mud. Roof space full of dust and cobwebs. Old houses may be very romantic. Wait till you live in one, too poor to afford a femme-de-ménage. I'll make damn sure of the Portuguese Putzfrau here!

The other grievance from way back – why did I never get properly trained for a job? Being a cripple, that's why. At first I was actually in a wheelchair, and even today try going to university lectures, or just getting up the steps of the post office. I limped afterwards, awkwardly. People, even kind people, look dubious. Your back, is it? Yes, or my leg or my bottom or something. They get the idea you're probably mental, as well. Fit you in as a switchboard girl or something – think you could manage that? I wanted real, professional training, and what at? There were the babies then.

Now there's nothing I'm sufficiently good at.

Virtually all these women here in Bruce have at least part-time jobs, filling in. Library, Registry, Kindergarten, hospital. The grander ones are Les Dames Patronesses, organising what Henri calls the little-white-beds (neglected, abandoned children). There's the usual social usefulness, warm clothes for Roumanian babies. Worthy, and amateur. None of these conscience-saving biddies ever realise that one trained pro, nurse or teacher or technician, is worth lorry-loads of junk and pious sentiments. And a professional is just what I'm not. I went to good art schools in Bratislava and in Prague. I draw well, I can paint a bit. I'm still a sodding amateur. Iris understands this.

I remember my prison-visiting days. When young, I was idealistic about Henri's police work. He put them in jug; I had to do something about that. The most valuable thing I brought them was toffees. The tea-and-sympathy isn't bad, it's valid even. I did some good, I believe, before the Director took a dislike, decided I was subversive. All he wanted was that they should stay QUIET. Lots and lots of Valium. Anyhow, what those boys need most is sex. I wasn't professional enough for that. Even were it possible, which it isn't.

The flat, in Woluwe St Pierre – yes, I agree it was nasty. I agree this house is marvellous, even if it is early nineteenth century and I do hanker still for something modern. I thought I'd learn Spanish. Henri talks a bit, fluent and bad. It doesn't really work because, honestly, I go much faster than the class and that's a bore. The dance group is fun, we dress up and click our heels, swing our skirts and show our knickers. It does us lots of good pretending we're Andalusian and it's also perfectly RIDICULOUS. I'm getting worked up, as Henri calls it. That likewise is ridiculous.

Iris also had decided she'd learn Spanish. She says she knows nothing, which is untrue, she is highly educated. She's older than me, a good fifty-five. Beautifully dressed, and beautiful. I am fascinated watching her. Please do not misunderstand. It is fashionable to go les, but sorry, that is not for me. There are heaps of women round here comforting one another. I can understand this because most women live comfortless lives. Do Iris and I comfort each other? I believe so, but we don't take our clothes off.

Her face is one of great beauty. Full of feature, framed by that short shaggy hair, painterly. Immense eyes, great big mouth. I'm having shots at painting this, not very well so far. She despairs about the big lumpy nose. Isn't it better than having none at all, like so many American women, looking like Pekinese dogs? At home, at school, it was drummed steadily into her that she was very plain indeed. The English, the Irish, do not admire big strong features. Which is she? It's rather hard to make out. "Anglo-Irish" – what's that?

She has explained, at length, because Irish history is complicated. Roughly, the English invaded and colonised from early time: Normans, and she's Norman, one of these old families. Not Hauteville – I know about Robert Guiscard! – but like that, tough bandits who left Normandy looking for land, and found it in Sicily or in Ireland, became landowners, castle-builders. Her brother – she had one brother, twelve years older, and then a heap of sisters – was the last Baron, but by then they didn't have a penny. The boys all had names like Tancred and

Humphrey. The girls got flower names, or virtues. She nearly got called Prudence (a joke probably because she was the youngest).

Isn't this remarkable? No, she says, nothing extraordinary about Normans, you'd still find them, if few enough now with titles and money.

This was all right, in the days when everyone was Catholic. When the English Crown changed religion, then the trouble started. And her family was not only Catholic but Yorkist (I am vague about that), and got into very bad odour. Dwindled, from then on, because successive English governments penalised and confiscated — all right, I know about religious wars. They're invariably the worst. We've had them at home, up to the neck. Cromwell sounds like the Butcher of Magdeburg. Caths or Prots, interchangeable when it comes to barbarism and bestiality. There was a moment when the family went Prot, to save their skin, though if I'm following aright it wasn't their skin as much as the land.

Odd couple we make. Little Mrs Castang, decidedly plebeian, installed in a wooden armchair, the one with the straightest back, knees together and eyes cast down because of the pad on her lap. She is making a pencil sketch of Iris who likes to curl up sideways on a sofa, head in hand and many carefully arranged cushions. Classic pose, with the two big counterbalancing curves, the arm and wrist against the hip and thigh. Mrs Claverhouse now definitely Lady C. Rich drawly patrician voice.

This turning of the coat is the great family shame. It was put a stop to by some great-grandfather; frankly I don't have enough of the historic background. People two centuries ago are vivid to Iris, she can engage in conversation with them. It is important to remember that being Catholic is to make you more Irish, and culminates in being very anti-English. We have reached the crux of all this.

I sat there and got told. I would not break Iris' confidence. It is all right now. Her secret was safe with me, poor woman.

One elder brother, and a flock of girls. Patrician families cherish the boy, when he's the only one. The descent, the tradition, the title. A great burden for the boy, too.

It went on cooking in his head, the Catholicness and the hatred of England. You can see it all to this day in the IRA. We see it through the optic of the English. No better at whitewashing their own crimes, but I'm convinced that Iris is right when she says they genuinely don't understand. They don't see it as a crime. They were the just, kind, tolerant masters. The Irish are mad thieves and assassins, with no truth, no honour.

I have read up enough, barely, of the modern history. Ulster, the northern province, filled up with Scottish Presbyterians taking over the confiscated land. A famous military caste, supplying the Empire with soldiers and administrators, and when the other three provinces at last got their independence Ulster would not follow. Black Scotch Protestants – I know something of that Calvinist mentality – saw the Irish as riff-raff. A Norman family that has been on their land for over seven hundred years does not see itself as scum. Nor mad. From their viewpoint the boy did nothing mad.

He was twelve years older than Iris: in 1941 he was eighteen. A tall, strapping, fair-haired lad, to whom sitting a horse and carrying a sword came as naturally as breathing. Went and joined the SS. I know of plenty more. What about Léon Degrelle, right here in Belgium? The being Catholic, all the poor wretches (Iris was too young) brought up pro-Franco! It wasn't only our own Dear Tizo who preached red-hot Fascist enthusiasms. Lots of mad monsignori led crusades against the Bolsheviki. Degrelle had a famous one called Lupe de Mayol, official chaplain to a whole SS division, and you should have seen Himmler's face when told he had to swallow that. Holy Church keeps very quiet about all such episodes now. Iris, enormous eyes stretched to the maximum, has fantastic tales (very probably they are not fantasy) about the Irish clergy.

The boy got a Knight's Cross, too, posthumously. Left

54

his bones in front of Smolensk. General Gottlob Berger, that decent man, saw to it that the decorations went back clandestinely, with his personal citation, through the German Embassy in Dublin. Well, that was the end of that family. The father didn't live another six months, the mother maybe two years. Bled out. These old families are often strangely ineffectual and when a crisis comes they've no resistance. They'd lost all their money and then their house burned down.

That, too, is strange. Iris sees it as the Doom. The house was called Spanish Point. Not a castle (they'd had a castle but that got knocked down three or four hundred years earlier) but it had features – low round towers and curving colonnades joining to a central block. Her description, coloured by every sort of nostalgia, is confusing, and she can't draw. A great many of these houses were burned, especially during the Civil War in 1922. The usual reprisals. Theirs wasn't. Occupied in turn by both sides, and not so much as a piece of furniture got scratched. Only for it all to burn down by accident, around 1947. Iris' childhood burned down with it. I'm no psychiatrist, thank you. The girls had a rotten time. She speaks of it now with humour. One can see a lot that was good about De Valera's Ireland. A lot, too, that wasn't.

This all took several days. I listened, and I drew. Iris went off and made tea – Irish enough to drink tea by the bucket. Once she started talking there was no way of stopping her.

How many of us are there who cannot go home?

I was Slovak and am I now Czech? Iris who does not want to be English and is afraid to be Irish. Eamonn Hickey has become a friend in his withdrawn way and says he can't decide which is worse, the Irish Catholic or the Scottish Calvinist. Or Henri, who doesn't know what he is but it's increasingly unFrench.

Doesn't Harold Claverhouse belong here too? – so English, and so ready to say he hates it. I can't make it out – the dreadful class gulf, the north-south thing, the rich-poor thing.

Everywhere one meets Russians who long to go home and are afraid to. And as for the Germans! They're pushing through the unity as fast as they can go, and say they're delighted. And very frightened. Nobody knows how many Germans there are in the East (and wait till you meet one whose parents were Silesian). They are like the Sorcerer's Apprentice. Huge crowds are coming marching, and they've forgotten the incantation.

We're trying to make a Europe for us all – yes and also for those who sit tight at home and make noises about their sovereignty. One can study it all right here in Belgium, which wasn't a country at all until they'd got rid of the French, and the Dutch, and found themselves left with the Wallons and the Vlamingen (and the Bruxellois), all fighting furiously: they still do. Is that all we are, little squabbling tribes? What are we going to do about the Hungarians in Transylvania?

It has to include Iris and me, and Raisa, too. It's going to be terribly hard work.

CHAPTER SIX

· *Henri Castang*

> when by now and tree by leaf
> she laughed his joy she cried his grief

I'm getting backwash from Vera, who is having a hard time unlearning her Czechness – for never in all these years has she felt remotely French – and becoming European. I should understand, because I am sloughing my own French skin; I've got friendly with a neighbour who comes from "the bit shaved off Germany" after 1918. His name is German, he is German; no, he's not, he's Belgian. One of our more enlivening Community characters.

It is giving me a rough time on the ex-policeman level also. I have made my mind up that I will not act the flunkey to any parallel police. They (whoever They are) have had two shots at softening me up – "playing with my bollocks" is a phrase I learned in Flanders. There won't be a third, I can promise them. But cop-sense as well as ordinary prudence says in my ear "sit tight". Yes and loose, too.

Vera has got very thick with Iris, and won't tell me anything about it; being female. I have my little private battles, and say nothing to her. It gives them too much importance to call them spies, but I do wish I knew who they were. Eeny, meeny, or miney.

I have been drawn back, inexorably, into a police criminal enquiry. Why not? – it's all I've been trained for.

Oh God, I should have seen something coming. Ach,

57

that's the silly thing one always says afterwards. Not "It" – but there were warning signs and they did not lack. What is experience for?

One says that, too, and the answer is "nothing". Every time is the first time.

I've never had one remotely like this. Oh yes, I've had homicides come out of a blue sky: very respectable gents, the last person one would ever dream – et cetera. This, though; it's so very public, and so very private. Headlines in *Bild*, and naturally the entire gutter press ramping, with emphasis on the English. The Belgians are doing their nut, and I – I have to cope. Sorry, just letting off steam: I realise I am making no sense.

Of course, in a bureaucracy one has to go through the hierarchy. And I found myself shot straight upstairs as though in an express lift. As the English say, nobody would touch this with a barge pole. No bad metaphor, that; one finds some nasty things in canals which come floating upward when prodded. I ended outside the door of the Secretary-General, no less.

He doesn't waste his words. Looked at me with the famous invisible eye. The voice does not alter in pitch.

"Everything goes on as before." He never has trouble in sounding bleak. "I lose a valued administrator. Nobody is irreplaceable. I am not. You are not."

Message received.

"This will be treated like any other newspaper item. Nobody has anything to hide, and nothing will be hidden.

"You – you have an adequate professional background." By God, he had his sources on the desk – my dossier. Nothing like being adequately briefed, and it was the very phrase he used.

"There'll be trouble with the English. With the Belgians, I've no doubt. I'll handle them. Your job is to see that I'm adequately briefed. I want reports from you, daily if need be, until this dies down. I'll see that you have facilities. I'll get you all possible co-operation from the police and judicial authority. They'll have their enquiry, and you will make yours.

58

"There might be discrepancies. I should even expect such, and I would want to know the exact situation and in precise detail. You need not be afraid that your comments or conclusions will reach eyes other than mine. You need not fear libel, gossip, or political manoeuvre." He put his hand flat on the folder in front of him, as though to stop it flying open.

"I have here the letter of recommendation from the Director of the PJ, naming you to the post for which he was asked to find a candidate. I know him. I have spoken to him. Beyond the banal formulae of usage and official eulogy you are undeniably able, and as undeniably indiscreet. I should hope that lesson has been learned.

"Take heed of that. I'll back you with the authority you'll need. You'll be given some title to impress commissionaires and secretaries – say Special Advisor. It is not designed," the smile was like the edges of broken glass, "to get you into restaurants without a reservation. I want the facts, the factors, the suppositions. If you find yourself with something you cannot cope with, see my secretary – I'll give an instruction for access and don't abuse it. Very well."

"Sir."

"And Castang."

"Sir?"

"These are human beings. Poor people. Recollect that we are the same."

"Sir."

I saw the secretary. She is, if anything, more frightening than the Secretary. She had a card, like an invitation to a wedding, engraved – the case is foreseen – with a formula about special empowerment and confidential facilities. She filled in my name, signed it, went in and got his signature, too.

"We don't exactly dish these out. You'll return this to me, in due course." And her own card, with the direct phone number.

"When I'm not here, it rings through. He's told me what he wants." I nodded. It was all rather like the Battle of

Britain. When my little green dot appeared upon the radar screen it would be followed for a moment, until a voice in some underground vault said, "Make it friendly." But nowadays it wouldn't be a Waaf uniform with trim blonde hair and a Roedean accent. Japanese robot more like, saying "Palmprint" or whatever gets you into the underground bunker at Fort Meade, Maryland: I can't think of anybody who'd know; or would want to.

The Secretary, at least, was still a human being, even if his secretary did look, and talk, a bit like J. Edgar Hoover.

I went home. I wouldn't be going to the office awhile. I had rung up with some hasty explanations about Absence, received with bottomless calm. Harold very often is absent, and this time it would be rather more prolonged. As for me, who the hell cares? We are both in Limbo, but such is the nature of bureaucracy. It isn't as though I were an authority upon criminal law. It just so happened that they wanted someone with my sort of experience, as an empirical sort of check-and-balance to Harold's genuine expertise. We have been struggling with Roman Law – appalling legalists those Romans – and that very English concept, difficult for anybody trained on the mainland, the Common Law. Harold very strong, as was to be expected, on that impressive tissue of customs and precedents. A good, and a patient mentor. Recently he has been taking me through the labyrinths (full of minotaurs) of United States law, Canadian law, et cetera. "You don't look very like Ariadne," I'd said. "I'm sure she stank of fish," (typical). "All those octopuses on Cretan pots. Or does one say octopi?" (rushing to the dictionary).

We have got more friendly. Is that the word? Matey? Harold has – I just cannot say had – a concept he calls "Jolyon Wagg". This is the brilliant English nomenclature of Seraphin Lampion, the pally insurance salesman in the Tintin books – one must understand Tintin if one is going to try to understand Belgium . . .

Harold is "Jolyon Wagg" with nearly everyone, using his persuasive jollities to get his own way in whatever he's pursuing. It is also a mask, for the sensitive, vulnerable and secretive man within, who does not make friends easily.

We were both exhausted after a tiresome passage among Torts. Who the hell invented torts? Sounds like the Normans, in their tedious fashion as legalistic as Romans: do outrageous things and produce tortuous, you said it, and hideously complicated legal justifications for raping girls or putting people's eyes out. The Plantagenet monarchs were especially good at this. We were having a drink, in the office, rather late.

"Come home with me and I'll show you something."

"All right. I'll just give Vera a buzz that I'll be late."

We climbed into the famous Lancia – sixteen carburettors (or is it valves?) Turbo. Very rally-Rally, turbulent is the right word. Mr Toad, says Eamonn Hickey (it's one of the basic texts for understanding the English, like *Alice* or *Brideshead Revisited*). Who was it went Poop-poop? Along with Blackstone's Commentaries one has to learn about Jabberwocky.

His house has one of these male rooms Americans call their den (but the English don't) where they flee from bossy women; a sensible idea because a man, even if he has no need to be all hearty and masculine among the stuffed tigers, needs somewhere where he can make a piggy mess without that frightful tidying. The women want a place of their own; it's just the same. This was full of books and music; a basement full, say, of toy trains would have surprised me. Not that one ever knows what is behind the façade of a house.

I felt flattered, I think. Being thus invited into a man's private domain is not just a sign of friendship: it shows trust. Men are distrustful creatures. As a cop, I would have been distrustful – oh what complications can ensue – but I was trying to learn not to be a cop. I was moving among people whose public lives are full of responsibilities, subject to lots of political pressure, and whose privacy is organised to compensate. I wouldn't have been aston-ished, I think, to find Harold with a radio transmitter,

61

playing chess with lighthouse keepers. Even the toy trains – I mean why the hell not?

"Like a drink – or something else? Coffee, even?" I was thirsty and took some Perrier. There was no sign or sound of Iris: the house seemed empty. I recall wondering what she did with herself. A solitary movie goer? Did she flit around the town in dark glasses like Greta Garbo? Did she have lovers?

The room was big, with space for a lot of furniture. He had two desks, and two enviable cabinets, intricate Victorian work, lots of little mahogany drawers exquisitely fitted, designed for "collections": butterflies, or minerals, or toy Napoleonic soldiers. It takes money, and it takes leisure. A cop never has either. Cigar labels? – no, that seemed too trivial for someone of Harold's calibre. He saw my covetous looks. I do a bit of elementary woodworking, but not up to cabinet-making standards. Perhaps now that I am "senior" I will hunt for bits of cedar or cherry, and get more ambitious: I like to use my hands.

Harold got his cigar going nicely, swigged at a generous puddle of cognac, reached over and opened one of the little drawers. Bed of plum-coloured velvet inside.

"Bit of luck getting these. Made specially, and I bought the whole thing." What he has is old photos, I'll say daguerrotype because I don't know anything about the subject; there are several technical processes and variations, on glass, on specially prepared paper of ivory or vellumy surface, some silvery, others sepia – beautifully delicate graduations of light and shadow. The sheer craftsmanship of those old boys (women, too) in the last century; I'd no idea: breathtaking. Many mounted in elaborate frames: sprigs and curlicues, gesso work, gilding, carved wood and cut velvet: must have been worth a great deal of money, but that's not the point. The point is that they were all erotic. Harold guffawing heartily.

"The Voyeur, my boy." Capital letter, definitely. One enters into the spirit of the thing; they weren't porno, although some came damned near it. The borderline is impossible to draw in a court of law (like a lot of our

62

concepts, in which framing legalistic definitions is as delicate as any task that could be set a Victorian photographer). Hereabout, one would ask how fastidious was the subjective, personal eye of the collector.

"That's just it," said Harold, delighted. "Some of those old sods were decidedly unfastidious, in fact downright coarse. So one weeds. Porn or pederasty one can sell back to the dealers, which eases the finance because this stuff comes damned dear. I've a few right now, I'll show you." Fishing in another drawer and coming up with twenty or so of the usual; capped and ribboned housemaids and lacy Edwardian ladies having their knickers taken down to be beaten by the equally usual bearded gentleman in clerical or academical regalia: quite good fun and perhaps not so much coarse as . . . "I think so," said Harold, "what one doesn't like is the wish to humiliate, to denigrate or take revenge, mm, no?" Well yes, and these hairy Victorian dicks, poking amazingly bushy Victorian pussy, ripe buttocks enclosing overripe figs amid moist mossy undergrowth, are coarse TOO.

"But these I like." Balthus girls, being mysterious on a shabby armchair in a poorly-furnished French château. A lusty vintage going on outside, probably, and hefty peasant girls being détroussées in the chais by Georges Simenon ("Little Anny went down to the cellar for a jug of wine"; celebrated monologue by Lotte Lehmann, reducing Richard Strauss to helpless laughter). But here in these faded Louis-Philippe rooms, grey-and-gold tarnished and rather moth-eaten, in filtered, muted lighting, the girls taking their clothes off are distant, withdrawn: there's no heavy breathing. Even the lesbian ones, tremendous favourites around 1880, young girls already undressed and being swooningly embraced and caressed by mature ladies themselves in a pleasing négligée of loosened staylace, are seldom vulgar and rarely dirty. A Nabokovian delight in the repeated triple patterns of axillary and pubic decoration, it's very Ada-Lucette, but one would be hard put to bawl dogmatically that it's porn. One is not in the world of Bergman bishops taking too close an interest in

Fanny sitting on the pot, or Alexander's sailor collar.

So that I remember leaving Harold placid with his cigar, comfortably unwound with his broads. "When does this word date from? Up to about 1920 they were broad, weren't they? Skinny girls weren't fashionable." Beaming and chuckling and not a care in the world.

This Harold on the sofa opposite me, sitting anyhow, disjointed and disoriented, his clothes too big for him, is unrecognisable. The big smooth advocate's voice jerks and lurches, the pitch wanders away along with the eyes, the healthy pale brown face is patchy and mottled. He's not all there. Quite certainly he's non compos mentis and even his physical co-ordination is badly astray; how he got here in that overpowerful, quick-footed car, without an accident, passes belief. I crossed to the front window; we were in the first-floor living-room, yes, the Lancia is parked outside and half on the pavement: only a bit crooked. Shock takes odd forms. Outside the big ring boulevards there's not that much traffic this time of night.

Eleven o'clock. Vera has gone to bed and is by now, I hope, asleep. We are both morning people. Just as well; a morning bird marrying a night bird can produce stresses. Twenty minutes ago I was pottering in a dressing-gown, the late-night chores; is the gas shut off, the thermostat turned down, the shutters closed and the door locked and the garbage bins out? She may have heard the bell, wondered vaguely what that could be – as I did – somebody mistaking the house no doubt, and drifted off to sleep: whatever it was I'd cope. Opening the door the width of the chain, seeing it was Harold – of all people – I'd automatically made a gesture of keep-your-voice-down for voices echo off that marble floor and up the stair-well. He was stumbling and I thought he was drunk. Not until I got him up and parked on the sofa did I realise that this was some bigger trouble. Eyes awry, slurred voice, oh lord, here's old Harold totally pissed and that's most unlike him. You understand? – it was a purely social embarrassment.

"You'd better not have any more to drink." What could I give him that wouldn't have him falling down steps? The lavatories here are on the half-landings; that sensible last-century design.

"I've not had much," surprised; the voice clear, the tone no more than taken-aback. I thought of pills, then. But Harold is no drug-taker. Some sudden, shattering virus?

"You want one, then?"

"Yes. Some whisky. Anything you've got." There was half a bottle of red wine standing there left over from supper; that wouldn't hurt. His teeth were chattering and he had trouble with the glass, nearly spilling his drink on his shirt. He got it down, clenched his jaw but the eyes cleared.

"Killed Iris," he said. He didn't say I, or He, or They. But my own sleepy wits focussed. Harold has come here for help. Because I am, or was, a cop. Something bad has happened at that house. A violent break-in? Iris fell down the stairs? She does, I know from Vera, drink a lot; and by herself.

So I started putting cop questions; brief, simple. But the answers weren't making any sense, didn't add up. What became more and more apparent was that I would have to go and see, because whatever it was, he was in no fit state to look after it, or himself. He finished the bottle and steadied up, but his eyes closed. I came to a decision.

"I'll take care of it. Give me your keys." Our car was in the basement garage and his was blocking the pavement. "Take your jacket off, and your shoes. Stretch out on the sofa and get a bit of sleep." He obeyed without fuss. But this was a lull; he could wake up again and then what? I would have to get Vera. She woke easily, and was cross only for a second. As always in any crisis she was cool-headed and reliable. The moment she understood, she was up and climbing into trousers and a shirt. No dressing-gowns for Vera with a stranger in the house. Harold is my friend, not hers.

It was a quiet, fine summer night. Our street was already slumbrous; a few lights here and there, the odd man putting the dog out. The beautiful motor started at once with a bellow and I took my foot off the accelerator in a

65

hurry: this is not the Volkswagen. I was tense and my feet felt stiff, and I moved the gears carefully. Crosstown there was plenty of traffic, but it was relaxed, home-going, fluid, and I needed only to keep the eyes peeled at crossroads and keep the feet light. Having to pay attention, be sensitive to sensitive machinery, helped me to take the drama out of the situation. No matter what has happened a cop does not get excited. I am still cop enough for that. The Lancia's sweet, easy pace and smooth cornering was just what I wanted.

Plainly, Iris is badly hurt and perhaps even dead? Harold came home, found something frightening enough to throw him totally out of balance. He blames himself, feels guilt, it's a common enough transference. That sort of hyper-nervous organism, things come straight up to the surface, shock is traumatic, he doesn't know what to do. He came to me, a good and even touching demonstration that he sees me as a friend. I'm a cop, and he can see this one facet of our relations; that I will know what to do, unemotionally and without drama. Harold is first and foremost a dramatiser: all his reactions are theatrical.

Are my reactions getting over-theatrical? – there was a car behind me; the spacing of the lights and the profile of the outline were getting to look over-familiar. I slowed down while fishing in my side pocket for a cigarette; it didn't overtake. I speeded up a little and it kept pace. As though wanting me to know it was there.

So I tried a simple trick, pretending to be unsure of the route, pausing at a fork as a puzzled driver will, hunting for a direction sign. It sat there, a little way back, like a dog herding a stray sheep: cajolery and intimidation.

I thought of bolting; there are plenty of handy autoroutes and few cars as nimble as the little Lancia. I'd enough on my mind already. I decided I didn't care. Questions – had he come with Harold? Or had he been hanging about in my street? When I arrived, we would see what happened.

Nothing did. I slowed, to turn in to Harold's driveway, and he went straight on past. Stuck between the trees I could see nothing. There was no reflection; he'd turned his lights out. Maybe he stopped; I still didn't care. It could have been muggers looking for a prospect who would frighten, like the types who will follow a woman at night, hoping to get her rattled.

Oh, forget it. Concentrate upon the now, and the here.

The house was dark and quiet. This seemed odd. If something abnormal happens, you don't just turn out all the lights and go away. Or do you? People keep odd fragments of habit intact. Economy with the electricity bill; I get furious with Vera's habit of leaving all the lights on in empty rooms. I could see another, blacker possibility: that Harold, finding something horrible in this house, moved instinctively to block it from sight. Cops are not paid to imagine things and I flicked a lighter to see the front-door lock and find the key. This is not a town house but a country villa, and the living rooms are on the ground floor. I have been here enough times to know my way, but I had to fumble about for the light switches. I found Iris.

I am, I have been, a criminal-brigade officer. I have been to all the police schools; I was trained, and my formation was on the streets of Paris, so that I have seen everything. The sheared, twisted metal of a bad road smash cuts like a scythe. Prick me, I'll bleed. But scythe me, and you'll be covered in it. And as for doors — pass them. No scene supplied by the imagination will be as revolting as the reality, but the cop, like the nurse, has learned to block it off.

And now I am a tidy little pusher of clean paper. Here in the European Community we have plenty of dirty minds, but physical violence belongs — oh, let's say, in Corsica. I'm out-the-habit. I stopped short, and I turned my back. I know where the drinks are kept and I went there stiff-legged. It took me a moment and a jolt of Harold's whisky before I had concentrated, controlled myself, and turned, again. Cop now, and cop only.

That mauvish colour is cyanosis and belongs with asphyxia, but those deeper-coloured marks mean strangling. Exorbited eyes, burst blood-vessels, some bleeding from the ear, one can have no doubt of death or of cause of death, but we'll have to have the médecin-légiste here. What is he called in English? – a, a forensic pathologist. And we'll have to have the local PJ. The CID. What odds can it possibly make, you'll ask, what they're called in English? I'll tell you; it's a gesture of detachment, an automatic distancing effect. One learns this, here in Bruce. Speaking English conveys English thought, and the same in French. Harold speaks both languages indiscriminately, and equally well, but he has taught me, when examining any concept, to stop and ask myself "How will that strike them in Denmark?" Danes, you see, are as important to the Community as the German-French axis. Don't ever think about England unless you're thinking of Ireland too. As Mr Hickey says, vive la différence.

Because worse is to come.

Iris was wearing a housedress, a long thing of green and black stripes buttoning down the front. She had nothing under this, as was all too apparent. There looked to be some vaginal bleeding, too. I went through to the back part of the house, and I found the kitchen door unlocked.

Some sort of scenario was beginning to sketch itself here. I do not know whether she was in the habit of going about naked under this sort of housecoat. Perhaps she liked a shower or a bath before bedtime. Perhaps like me she had undressed and gone to check the locks or the gas. Perhaps she had heard a noise. I wasn't here. It is possible that Harold will be able to tell us: it is possible that a careful perimeter ("cordoning off"?) and meticulous Identité Judiciare work will give us (who's Us?) the reconstruction. I shook all this out of my head for the moment. I am Polizei; this is "Tatort"; I have gone belting over here in my racing-red Lancia like Schimanski. I am Harold's friend, and my first loyalty is to him. My poor Iris. The buttons had burst, the two wings of the coat wrenched brutally back leaving the woman exposed from the throat down. A classic rape-murder. I could not stop the memory flooding back of how Vera – yes, my Vera – had had a nastily narrow margin between herself and – it

68

could have been, the same. She had found a weapon, and cracked her assailant's skull with it. I have other reasons for this being an unpleasant recollection, but they are irrelevant. Iris had not found a poker or a Chinese vase handy. She had struggled, poor wretch.

Don't let your own veins start swelling, or begin yelling like Schimanski. It won't help.

But I can understand now that Harold, rolling in late at night and turning on lights, could be knocked clean off his normally solid trolley.

There was nothing I could do here, and I mustn't mess about or the Bruxellois PJ would have some nasty remarks. I must get out of here, and back to Harold, and do what is needed. I had better bolt that kitchen door, and leave the lights on, and go.

When I was here last? A couple of weeks ago, to look at the collection of erotic photos: damn, the PJ will find those, and have a good loutish snigger at them. What had Harold said then? (Echoing, sarcastically, a former British Attorney-General.)

"Porn is what you mustn't leave lying around for the servants to see. Or your wife," he'd added. And this was porn: Iris left lying here, naked, raped, dead; for the servants to find. It had hit him that much harder.

And porn, too, is the invasion of privacy. (I was back outside, sitting in the Lancia, and I realised that I, too, had my hands over my eyes. Sitting here like a lump of meat; a fine figure I'll cut if a cruising police car should happen to notice and stop and enquire what the hell I think I'm doing here.) Shaken, I drove slowly.

I'm afraid that the Police also make gallows jokes. Please do not think this pure insensitivity; it is much more of a defence mechanism. But that pale colour, something between blue and violet – I've heard it called lavender. It is the colour of the common or garden iris. The dead woman had been well-named.

She is dead and nothing that we do can now dirty or diminish her. We try, though, to give respect to the dead. That is an article of faith with all peoples. The crimes of the Hitler-Stalin time are to us loathsome because they massacred the living, and because they treated the dead with ignominy. The profanation of a cemetery is horrible to us on this account, that we have taken from the dead their dignity.

My poor friend, I could not even cover her. It's a rule, I'm afraid, and I have seen too many police enquiries botched because of well-meaning sentiments. There will be many heavy feet and many peering eyes. Much depends on the type of police officer who gets the job, but they may bring you back there and force you to look at her. It will be in their minds, you see, that you may have killed her.

How am I to explain this to Harold? How am I to say that it is also in my mind, because, you see, it has to be. They will attack your privacy, your dignity, while they disregard the dignity of Iris dead. It is one of the nastier aspects of criminal-brigade work.

Belgian justice has no very good reputation, which is the cue for my saying, no, Shouting, out loud "Whose Has?" When it comes to a homicide, you are going to find a fact you know (we have talked about it) but which you will reject with an instinct you cannot control: like vomiting. You are going to find that the legal mechanisms of a murder enquiry, and the mentalities which execute the same, are insensitive, brutal, and frequently incompetent. Your wife is lying there on the floor, naked, with her legs open? A lot they'll worry, about her privacy. Or, be it said, yours.

And these were just a few of the unpleasant thoughts passing through my mind, as I drove the Lancia rather slowly, very soberly and not very skilfully, back through the summer night towards Schaerbeek.

CHAPTER SEVEN

Vera Castang

What could I do? Harold there, half in a coma, half in that state of over-excited nerves? He might do anything. I couldn't talk. I am not much good at conversation at the best of times. What was there to talk about? I don't even know Harold at all well. I know quite a lot about him, but that's different. He is my husband's colleague, and superior. To some extent, friend. I'm no great judge of that. Men's friendships are formed in ways we women do not enter into. I'm friends – yes, I'll accept this word – with his wife. So through Iris, I know, or I can conclude, guess at, things about him. Not much. Women are much more reserved than men think. Men imagine these hen parties and all the women being girls-together, quacking out their intimacies and secrets. Baring themselves. Not in my experience. I don't, Iris doesn't. What can have happened to Iris? This is worrying.

So I made some music. The clearest, the most steadying thing I could think of. My collection of records, tapes, whatever, is not anything to boast of. I felt I couldn't cope with anything operatic, or even orchestral. What about Beethoven piano sonatas? Harold didn't react much. They certainly did me good. These are the sort of pianists I like. I don't like the emotional ones such as Rubinstein or Horowitz, people made such a fuss about. I don't know much about music. Henri doesn't either, but agrees. Irreplaceable Schnabel: lucidity. Balance, is it? Exact equilibrium between cold detachment and a sentimental

71

involvement. Henri used to say, "How I wish the Policîa could come near that."

He was away a long time, but I didn't look at my watch and I didn't feel sleepy. He came in with such a black look and so heavy-footed that I knew something was gravely wrong.

Harold spoke in a quiet, collected voice. "Vera has very kindly been keeping me company. We've had the Waldstein, and the Appassionata. Marvellous pianist Backhaus was. And then the Hundred-Eleven, fantastic." It was his social voice.

"How are you, Harold?"

"A great deal better, thank you."

"Okay to put it on the purely rational level? This is best handled as a logical progression. Point A to point B and so on across country. All right for sound?"

"Yes. Thanks to you both." A sort of heavy briskness from each of them. It is, I think, their professional manner.

"Very well, then, Camera. I have looked. It is bad. She is dead. There was nothing I could do. Everything points to a criminal assault. I don't think anything has been disturbed or stolen, but the back door was on the latch. We must hypothesise an intruder. We must suppose that Iris was upstairs, perhaps getting ready for bed, that she heard some noise and came down. Is that consistent with her likely behaviour?"

"Yes," said Harold. All the emotion had drained out of his voice. "Whatever else – she had courage."

"We have to face this, then. She came down, tackled him – it was certainly a he – and he was caught. Virtually always they'll run if they hear anyone. It could be a big man with a gun, but in general they don't like risks and complications. They'd rather get away, and write it off. But if pinned in a corner they'll fight. As frightened people will. You understand, I'm extrapolating from generalised experience." Harold nodded, gravely. "There was a struggle. This turned out very badly for Iris. Perhaps she yelled. He took her by the throat.

72

"The likelihood is then that he cut and ran without any thought of what he came for." Harold bowed his head. Acquiescence. So much unsaid, there was a question in my mind. I would not voice it. Henri saw it, felt it, swung round on me with the face of a judge passing a death sentence. "Yes. What you're thinking of is also true." I could not stop putting my hands to my face. The men were controlled.

"I'm a cop, Harold. I've experience of these situations. I'd no choice, you know, but to leave things exactly as they were. I mean that I could touch nothing." Harold nodded, in bleak understanding. "And I've no choice now." Henri pointed to the phone on the side-table. "Bruce cops. PJ. Criminal brigade. Police pathologist. The lot. Procureur du Roi. If I don't it's my skin: the more since they'll find out my professional background. They would not forgive me any deviation from standard practice. I couldn't forgive it myself. Neither, I can say with confidence, would you. But they won't listen much to me. Or not at first. I have to warn you – they'll concentrate upon you. You were there, you found her. Tell them the simple truth with no emotional overtones. Can you stand that?" And again, Harold nodded.

He had one of the quite commonplace names. I think it was Deguelder but I can't be sure for several reasons. His local accent was almost comically strong and he mumbled his words so. I was never sure I'd understood, and said things like "Yes I'm sure", as one does when unsure. I called him "Monsieur l'Inspecteur" in a respectful tone and this went down quite well. Nor did I learn his name later because Henri took a strong dislike at first sight and referred to him as "Dégueu" which is one of Lydia's words, schoolboy slang for "Vomit".

Because he was rude as well as crude, and nasty with it. Afterwards, one finds excuses. It's easy to say that he was probably tired, certainly cross at being called out late at night, hauled all the way to Schaerbeek only to find another long trip to the other side of the town. He wasn't

73

sure of his ground either. Belgians in general have strong reasons for disliking Communauté people. We are suspected, with a good deal of truth, of being underworked and overpaid. To them we are parasitic, occupying the good housing and driving the rents up, responsible for traffic jams and huge, ugly, expensive buildings, paying fancy prices for things the locals can't afford, behaving in general in a superior and supercilious manner.

So that he made a thing of being the Common Man and speaking platt. Not liking Henri's Parisien French or Harold's educated voice. You could see him thinking "Fancypants". At pains not to be dodged about or man-oeuvered. One can't blame them, an awful lot of jobbery goes on and I'm sure he was quite right to suspect cover-ups. He knew that he was only the duty dogsbody, and wouldn't be in charge of things for more than a few hours. But he would be the first on the spot of a long row of legal and Policía (to borrow Henri's word) authorities, and he was going to make his own authority Felt. He was a tall, tough chap, all bone and muscle, good-looking in a conventional sense with straight features and wavy fair hair, facial expressions made deliberately harsh, and an electric blue eye which glared at one. Harold, who was looking terribly tired by now, he treated as a criminal from the start, and Henri as accessory after, and doubtless before, all sorts of enormities designed to conceal and generally to obfuscate the truth.

Naturally, Henri was wrong-footed. Anyone, in common decency, would be supporting, even protecting a man who had just gone through so appalling an experience. And he dislikes the bullying sort of cop. He claims, and I'm sure he's right, that an investigating officer gets much more out of the preliminaries by being patient, polite. He ought to know. He's done hundreds of these. Experience, professionalism. He became irritated at what he thought sloppy procedure.

"And who are You then?" crudely asked Mr Inspector. (Another damn little lawyer, no doubt. What's this cocksure way of speaking?)

"Well, greetings then, colleague." And not just an ex-cop but a divisional commissaire, no less. Which put the local man into a flaming sulk and one can hardly blame him. They were both at fault. If he hadn't felt strained, and unhappily aware how vulnerable Harold must appear, Henri wouldn't have got so irritable. I couldn't help seeing both sides.

A lot of palaver. Police surgeon, photo team, all the apparatus of "Identité Judiciaire" – all of them having to be got-out-of-bed at this hour. Midnight by now and I was getting very tired myself, and told Dégueu rather abruptly to keep his voice down (a grating, metallic voice, like his hair). "There are children asleep, in this house." He felt the hostility.

"You Community people are all the same. One idea, to ensure yourselves preferential treatment. You'll get the same as anybody here, no more and no less." Off they all went at last, Henri laying his hand on my sleeve and saying, unnecessarily, "Try to get a bit of sleep now." By then I was feeling thoroughly harried, and of course I couldn't sleep; lay there worrying.

I had to be up as usual, to see to the girls' breakfast and get them off to school, and naturally, to behave as though nothing were amiss. Henri appeared red-eyed, curt and monosyllabic, being polite with me to practise for a day of people he'd have to be polite to. Children are very sensitive to an atmosphere of strain, and behave badly themselves in consequence, and it seemed an age before I had them bundled off.

"Well?"

"Bad. They took Harold off to the commissariat for the night. Night! – two hours ago. You can imagine how much sleep I got."

"I was at last so heavily asleep myself I didn't hear you come in."

"Roaring at them to let him sleep, trying to persuade them he just wasn't fit to answer questions: he'd say anything at all in the state he was in, and did, too, which of course made matters worse.

75

"Dégueu's convinced he killed Iris himself. Maybe he did, there's no proper evidence either way."

"Oh, Henri."

"Start with a fuckup, it goes on getting more entangled. Then I got into trouble. Said I wasn't going to have a cop standing over him, so he was sitting around while they were palavering in a corner; I could see they were going to pull him in so I told him to go get some clothes and stuff, and the silly ass, before anyone realised, was standing under the shower. Gazed at them blankly, and said he was feeling so crummy he thought a shower would clear his head."

"But why shouldn't he have a shower? Sounds like the most sensible idea he could have."

"Vera, dear. If there is a legitimate ground for supposing a man killed his wife, there is also ground for supposition that he also raped his wife."

"Oh my God."

"Get him back at the commissariat they'd suggest a medical examination. Just a straightforward physical by the police doctor, but they could insist, and if he makes a fuss it looks bad and a note goes on the file. But if there's no observable evidence they can say — and will — that he took a shower to obliterate it."

"And is there — what did you call it? — legitimate ground?"

"Negative grounds. There's no trace of a breaker-in. The IJ people seemed fairly thorough about that. Found the traces of where I'd come in. Trouble about that, too! Took me down and printed me, suggested ever so nicely I submit to a physical as well. Because if there's no housebreaker, and I didn't rape Iris, then Harold did."

I stopped myself in time from saying "Oh Henri" yet again.

"Yes my dear, quite so. Marital rape is an established legal concept." And a little flicker of black humour. "Wait until you've had a few more husbands."

Since I'm trying to be honest, can I say that if I've never been raped by my husband he has come near forcing me at

76

times when I wasn't ready and wasn't willing, and I should think every wife under the sun has known this experience, which she generally manages to disguise at the time. But does she always suppress it afterwards?

"That's only the way it looks," he said briskly, to cheer me up. "Can be a lot of other things. Which is why I have to go down there now to sort them out. But first, a lot of telephone calls. Like to Eamonn Hickey – 'D'you know any good criminal advocates?' "

Secretaries, and the hierarchy: Mr Claverhouse is unavoidably detained, this morning. A shave; the effect is disastrous. A scraped bleached look, and glassy; the eyes are sunk further in the head than ever, above a dark suit and an Honourable-Fishmonger kind of tie, but he had to make a good impression at Headquarters.

I was left to my thoughts, and nasty they are.

My marriage means everything to me. Like a goose, I mate for life. I am more than the housekeeper, just as Henri is more than the breadwinner, and we are both more than the father/mother of our children. That's not a truism, though it ought to be. It became so immensely important to me when I was overcome with guilt at being a failure, the awkward Czech drag who had so damaged my husband's career and prospects. Iris felt something similar, as good as told me so. Hard for her, with so obviously brilliant a man as Harold. I remember telling her that it wasn't until I got back to Czechoslovakia that I felt in any real way whole, that I'd come to terms with my early life and all the wasted years, that I began understanding something of the real meaning of success or failure. If she went back to Ireland, perhaps she'd get it all out of her system. For it's very hard work to be a European. The place where we were born, which made and shaped us, and whose air and soil and water we absorbed in childhood, gets muddled with the flag-waving sentimentalities of nationalist patriotism, and it's especially hard for the Islanders. All this quack about Solidarity – it starts with our individual truth and loyalty to one another, come no matter what.

77

If Harold has really done this dreadful thing to Iris it fragments me.

She has two children, boys. They are in England, students, one already a graduate I think. What will this mean to them? I forgot to mention this to Henri. They have to be told. How, and by who? But Henri has more than enough to worry about. Harold's secretary, Miss Huntingdon, is said to be good as well as competent. She will very likely know. I have no acquaintance with her.

I see it all the time in our "Accès" work. Ninety-five per cent of it is brought about by broken marriages, or better defined, by people who don't work hard enough at their marriages. Too many reasons for that. I'm due there today (we take it in turns) and I can't cancel it. Thinking about this will anyhow help relieve this new calamity from sitting on my back like the black dog. In fact this is a typical Accès situation, though they don't often go as far as killing people. I'll talk about this. It'll straighten my mind.

Quite a few of us in the Community, husbands and wives, thought we should do some social work, and the hell with feeling guilty about being overpaid or overprivileged. And the hell with people who said What, yet Another bureaucratic structure in Bruce. It was a good place to start. We have some ambitious people who say we can make this into an internationally known and respected organisation, like Amnesty or Greenpeace. But Henri and I just slog along at doing what we can. He was a catch, as an ex-senior-police-official, though he said that really was a fundamental disqualification. I'm not much use, but we all muck in, bookkeepers and secretaries, there's work for all of us.

It began from the idea of the "Point Jeunes" in Lille. They started one in Paris and, typically, no one would finance it. But in Lille they got help from the department, and the town, and they've a place opposite the station, strategic because all the children who run away from home, in Valenciennes or wherever, end up at the station.

It's simple enough. Adolescents come in looking for help. Here they can get a meal, sleep, take a shower, wash their clothes. The principle is simpler still. That the children should find their breath, have a moment to think, and take themselves in hand.

They have ten or so people, run a twenty-four hour permanence, give some advice, but try to avoid dictating a line to take, because it's all too easy to impose solutions on bewildered and inexperienced youth. One tries to give them a bit of confidence, the feeling they're not going to be cheated again – "Go home first, and then we can try and work something out" – they get that from everyone, and naturally they feel defrauded. One tries to nudge them, without hurrying, towards a notion of their own responsibility and how to feel able to go about taking it.

Henri was sarcastic and sceptical, at the start.

"What, yet another amateur do-gooding group! Look, France is chock-full of them. All very worthy, all with complicated names they reduce to ridiculous acronyms. There's even one called the Snatem, the *Service National d'accueil téléphonique pour enfance maltraitée* . . .! I could find you a dozen more. They're splinters, they quarrel, none has any proper status, finance or programme, no co-ordination, nobody's ever heard of any of them and nobody could ever take them seriously."

"But, Castang, this isn't France."

"Yes, I do take the point."

Perhaps because a couple of us are senior functionaries, influential in a clubby departmental way, wise in the ways of bureaucracy, we do get some state help (and don't ask me how, some finance). And the city of Bruxelles (or is it the Region?) gives us a house. When Henri managed to overcome his own inbred cop-bureaucracy he was an acquisition.

"No, please, not the Institute for Childhood and the Family. Look, all these names like Open Door are both vague and sentimental; it's a fatal combination. Ac and Seil, a welcome and some counsel, one could say Access." Someone objected that Access is a credit card. "Yes, well. Accès isn't," said Henri being French.

It was Henri, too, who said they needed lawyers.

"Few are real criminals, but the police treat them as though they all are," from long and disillusioned experience.

One gets all sorts. Young girls with glassy expressions and hands clenched round empty tubes of pills; we do learn when to call the emergency service. And young aggressive boys, who say they'll break the place up. They frighten me. I suppose that it's because we no longer have wars, and all the generals in Nato are terrified of finding themselves redundant. Boys need things to bash, and even a stone-throwing Intifada would focalise the violence now going into football clubs. I'd think it normal, even rather a good instinct, to throw stones at government, but jellyfish that it is, it presents too few satisfying targets. Except the police, as Henri says, Laughing Heartily.

I am of no great use. I don't even speak Flamand. However, we do get plenty of German and English children. Doubtless soon there'll be Czech hooligans leaving the train, all set to rip off the wonderful rich Westies. They aren't all children either. Those sad men who are over forty and whose skills nobody now wants. In our world you're supposed to be young. I see women older than me, dressed up and painted like girls of fifteen. And because it's so Fashionable to be homo, one gets girls who turn out to be boys, and plenty of vice-versa. Of course they all take drugs. Their lives are nasty and boring. Stopping drugs is like stopping sex.

CHAPTER EIGHT

Henri Castang

(sleep wake hope and then) they
said their nevers and they slept their dreams

The Central Commissaire's name was Mertens. A
dark-skinned man with fine dark hair and expressive
eyebrows which cocked and frowned and conveyed a lot of
quiet-spoken scepticism; as short as me which is shortish
for a cop, but a lot broader: an intelligent blue stare giving
away nothing of his thoughts, which was what he intended.
Krim Comms come in all shapes and sizes and my
experience of them is wide. In his office he smoked a pipe,
in a fashion giving me to understand that he didn't believe
a word I said. He was polite, friendly, and called me
"Colleague" with an amiable indifference to whatever
position I had held in the past. If you'd been smart, he was
probably thinking, they'd have kept you in Paris instead of
pushing you into this job here, but he went on smiling, in
no hurry to make any judgements.

I was counting on two factors to help me. The Bruce PJ
has been blotting its copybook a good deal of late: so, of
course, has any police force you care to name, but here
some senior officers had incurred the displeasure of their
Minister and got suspended for practices one won't detail,
because I'm well aware I don't know the half of what went
on, and never will. Mertens no doubt was Mr Clean, but
he'd be a bit more amenable to my suggestions that this
was no moment to go hogging press publicity.

The other was that a job of that sort is very largely political. One gets there by being, as I conspicuously wasn't, a good politician. This would make him sensitive to a lot of important things, like the Commission, or the Islanders as Harold calls them; his being English would give all the senior officials pause. Nobody has forgotten the immense scandal of the Heyssel football ground a few years ago. Bestial behaviour (I query that word "bestial"; only mankind behaves quite that badly) by Brit louts brought about the death of many harmless people. Skilful manipulation by the Islanders, who have colossal cheek to put on top of their arrogance, made this appear as entirely the fault of the Belgians, whose faces were covered with egg because of sloppy crowd control, but who hadn't killed anyone. Even the manager of that other well-known football team, the Auschwitz Trusties, never thought of this brilliant and very British argument: Jews would never have got killed in such numbers if they hadn't pushed so inside the shed.

Mr Night-Duty Inspector had been over-anxious to show these Brits where they got off, and the sodding Frogs, too, while we're at it. Technically he was within his rights, but this had been crudely done by a heavy-handed boor who was Mertens' Minion and needed his knuckles rapping smartish.

Mertens smiled, smoked his pipe, and gave no ground.

"Yes. I have his report. Quite so. Written reports, Colleague, as you will know well . . . I wasn't there. I dare say his behaviour did leave a good deal to be desired. You and I are a bit senior for that sort of thing, but we both remember that night shifts are hard on everyone. People have drunk a good deal. Your Mr Claverhouse," mild, shuffling papers till he found the medical report, "seems to check out rather high on blood alcohol level. I make no reproach; he had a shocking experience. But he's the key witness, isn't he? My man had no choice but to bring him in. You'd have done the same."

"The manner . . ."

"Yes. There's no mention here of any bruise or

laceration. I don't think you claim any physical ill-treatment, do you? Not like those people who need to be calmed and somehow fall into the typewriter in the interrogation room. Or that doctor in Paris, a black man I believe, who was left in those very tight handcuffs for so long he got bad circulatory trouble. Hm?" He picked up his telephone, spoke, waited, spoke, put it down. "He's had his breakfast. Gone back to sleep. Nobody's taken his bed away. Rest will do him good. I'll be wanting a word with him, to be sure, but where's the great hurry? I'd rather like to see this house. Drive out together, shall we, take a look at the Tatort? Be a pleasure, to have you with me. Benefit from your experience. As I understand it, you know the way. You were there." Yes.

"Then there'll be the Proc, won't there," still conversational, quiet in the back of a police car, ordinary black low-level Mercédès exactly like a taxi. He'd left his pipe in the office. No need to be Maigret. "Judicial transport; he'll want to have a look, too. Judge of instruction, all familiar to you. How many sets of keys are there by the way? I've got one, you've got one?"

"No, I borrowed those. He was, as you've said, distraught, shocked. In an emotional state. A bit pissed. I'd no means of knowing how much of it was real. If anything. They imagine things. Just as they imagine guilt. I don't need to tell you. I had to go and look. You'll appreciate that as soon as I verified, no time was lost in calling your people."

"All perfectly proper," said Mertens soothingly. "No cleaning woman or anything, who might have keys?"

"I doubt it. The lady had no job, and would have been at home to let people in, I'd imagine. We'll probably find her keys in her handbag or wherever."

"I wouldn't suggest that you, or anybody, had snuffled about."

"Oh yes you would, only that no, I hadn't."

"There is that open door. We've found your hand on that, where you very properly shut it. You could have opened it first and shut it again, to confuse the issue. No, you're too clever for jiggery-pokery."

"Either that or too honest."

He turned his head for a long look. "On what evidence we have, we'll agree to call on the face of it, no one else was in the house. But she was strangled, wasn't she, and raped. Which leaves the two of you. Yourself, that's hardly serious. Your account of matters is good. Seeing that you're a professional, it would be. It's verified by the husband, and I don't think we can suggest collusion between you, can we?"

"I don't think I've given Mr Claverhouse any grounds for jealousy or rage."

"No and your wife doesn't, either. And nor do I. As a matter of pure formality, the Proc wouldn't want to exclude a technical possibility."

"Autopsy."

"Yes, he'll want that, won't he? And so do I. Automatic for a homicide, but it's for him to order. We've a body temperature, not very conclusive, and we'll have the contents of the stomach. But she was on her own as I gather, could have eaten a bit of bread and butter at any time. Time of death could be earlier – or later – than we're supposing, am I right?"

The car stopped and Mertens got out for a slow circular look at the greenery-shrubbery surroundings, the country road and villas set back from it. Lawns and conifers.

"A neighbourhood enquiry isn't going to do us much good, is it?" He produced the keys and we went in. I had to be professional about seeing it again. He went over the house carefully, a good thorough cop.

An IJ team takes careful measurements and will produce detailed drawings. It will take a great many photos from every imaginable angle, with good lenses both close-up and distance, and very clearly lit. It fingerprints things like door-handles and window catches, telephones and light switches and the commands of all the electronic gadgetry; rarely conclusive, but one can always come back for more. It sniffs in kitchens and bathrooms and makes notes of smells, of moisture and temperature levels. Because it can be important to know whether the toaster was used, or the soap still wet. Ours did, anyhow, and I saw no reason to suppose theirs wouldn't: Mr Mertens gave the impression of knowing his job.

They focus on the body if there is one. The detective things; hairs, buttons, tiny scratches or tears; polished, dusty, or greasy surfaces. One gets to know how well the housekeeping has been done. They have little tubes and envelopes for samples, and a great many labels. Their own equipment is not all that sophisticated but it is to be hoped that the lab is thoroughly equipped. Police departments in France are chronically and outrageously short of money, but Germans have plenty. I don't know how well the Belgians are fixed.

A police doctor when he comes wants to turn a body over and fiddle with it; rectal temperature, signs of bruising, lividity and so forth. One wants everything fixed for the record first, and again afterward. One can be greatly hampered by well-meaning folk who have applied their notions of first-aid, or "made things decent". Really the investigating officer, pretty often myself, hasn't to be the great detective but ought to be an exact, scrupulous and fussy archaeologist. Everything verified and countersigned, because people can be sleepy, lazy, negligent, absent-minded, hasty, or have simply had a few drinks. Commissaires come afterwards and pick holes in procedure. They may or they may not cover up for subordinates. That tends to depend on whether they later find a need to cover up for themselves, or one another. Or their friends, and people to whom they owe favours, and influential chaps who know an ear, and whisper into it. Oh well, I'm out of all that now. Or I thought I was.

Mr Inspector Dégueu who had done this work was crude, and even brutal, in his dealings with human beings (I didn't altogether blame him though it wouldn't do to say so; he found us a tiresome crew). But I had no cause to suspect him of mishandling factual, evidential materials. As for Mr Criminal Commissaire Mertens, he walked about with his hands in his pockets, said little, looked a lot, acquainted himself thoroughly with the topography, asked me to reproduce as exactly as might be my moves, observations, thoughts, and reactions, and made no comment. Could be as honest as he was (plainly) competent, and could be a sly-boots: he wasn't giving anything away. About the photo collection, after opening and shutting a few drawers he only said, "Worth a lot of money, no doubt, wouldn't you say?"

Leaving, after locking up carefully, "Think I'd better put a guard on this house. Lot of valuables. Can't have another intruder," – sarcastic emphasis. "Proc may want to put seals on it. Mm, mercy of God, no Press as yet. Won't take long. Neighbours must have noticed some of the doings, last night. Mm, where's Mr Claverhouse got to, then? Drop you back in the town, shall I?"

I had to go and have a word with the Hierarchy. This led, with remarkable speed, to the Secretary-General. And when I got back from that, there was a phone message. Things really were moving: the Proc would like to see me. More exalted company.

For the Procureur du Roi is a big wheel in the administration of justice. There are several sorts, as with Commissaires, ranging from bemedalled Generals to Substitutes thin and pale as stalks of celery, and I got a pretty grand one, judging by some mellow panelling and a fine Empire desk with lots of bronze acanthus leaves for me to trip over. Paul-Albert de Coninck was fiftyish with a handsome deer-hound head, the shape showing several generations of aristo breeding and emphasised by brush-cut grey hair. A long pointed nose, long shaved jaw. Delicate hands fiddled with a Dunhill cigarette despising it even if the adverts do say it is the Best. With a courteous manner and a quiet voice he came straight to his subject.

"The facts as known to me are few but salient. If I recapitulate, will you have the goodness to confirm or clarify? You seem the one person in possession of the material knowledge relevant, up to this moment." Beautiful French.

"Mr Claverhouse." A Frenchman would have said Cleveroose, to rhyme with loose or perhaps noose, but not

86

him; been to Oxford. One could not but recall Harold when "in good voice", kettle-drumming on his tabletop, declaiming, "Up with the banner of Bonnie Dundee." "A key figure in the Communauté. His wife's been killed. He appears as a logical suspect. Mr Mertens tells me that technically you could be the same and recommends that technically," slight ominous smile, "we can disregard that. He'd rather you were there where we need you. Furthermore, the Secretary-General asks me to offer you facilities. *Dont acte*," a laconic French version of "Le Roi le veult". "Because this is not a business one would wish to see handled indiscreetly. One will need *doigté*; our German friends would call it *Fingerspitzgefühl*." Illustrating, a wedding ring on one parchment-coloured hand and a plain gold signet on the other.

"Very well then, Monsieur Castang, as I understand you have held office, judicially, under La République. Try not to exercise your talents in any way embarrassing to myself, since then I should find myself compelled to annul these facilities. I may tell you that I haven't as yet had the pleasure of meeting Mr Claverhouse. Probably I shall do so in the course of this day. It may happen that I recommend his further detention in his own interests as much as those of justice. I shall also hope," courteously, standing, "to further our acquaintance, perhaps in less formal circumstances." Upon the command to Dismiss, as I recall, one executes a right turn, brings the left foot down smartish, before breaking ranks.

Council of war was in progress in Mertens' office. Eamonn Hickey, duly briefed, had come up with legal advisors. Gregor, Advocate, was tall, sandy, massive. Laetitia, Advocate, was statuesque, in a handsome, Jewish way. They were pushing Mertens, sounding quite bloodthirsty.

". . .placed in conditions of some dignity and comfort."

"Naturally we'll press for inculpation, in order to have access to the entirety of the dossier, which will prove as I suspect to be remarkably thin."

". . .*se constituer partie civile*." The Civil Party is a legal fiction by which you disassociate from criminal proceedings but get very vehement about damages. Mertens had the tight wide smile of a fighter watching two opponents both clutching broken beer bottles.

"Ah, Monsieur Castang. A party at issue," pleasantly. "Let me introduce you."

"No conflict of interest?" asked Laetitia, spry. Vera may complain about Pigs, but any man views a woman casually glimpsed in an optic of desirability. The pigs prickle, a wee bit. They'd describe Laetitia as a toothsome morsel. Yes, deplorable, isn't it.

"Well no," spoke up Filthy Castang. "I represent the defence, entirely. The whole procedure is preposterous."

"As neat a piece of self-incrimination—" Mertens laughing in a nasty way.

"Proc have a word with you, has he?" I asked. Jovial nod and a pull on his pipe. "Access to my colleague? And privileged?" It means on the same terms as Greg and Lettice. Lawyers are entitled to a "parlour" with their clients, and no nosy prison officer sitting by, but other visitors as a rule are not.

"You Community people are Very privileged. I'd rather incline to join issue, but Monsieur de Coninck rules and I submit, graciously. You'll have the same standing as the present company."

"In that case we can—" they both said together before begging the other's pardon. A silence, which I broke.

"There are a number of points." Cosy. "Proc inculpates, he can hardly do anything else if Mr Claverhouse so requests – as you will no doubt advise. So I can say first, the house is about as open and draughty as the San Siro stadium, the back door was open and I shut it, I'll go on oath on that. She could well have answered the front door. Nothing we know of marks her as a suspicious or fearful woman, she was both casual and confident. She might have thought her man had mislaid his keys, or someone may have gained her confidence with a plausible tale, it's nowise ruled out. It's dry summer weather, those carpets are just averagely dusty, leather-soled shoes would leave no trace observable to IJ examination."

Mertens smoked his pipe and said nothing.

"We've thus a perfectly respectable hypothesis. Man gains entry, burglarious intent, finds himself faced with a highly attractive woman in a housecoat and naked under it, thinks of a bit of nooky first, she starts to struggle and it goes too far, and he bunks the way he came, shocked out of any interest in the valuables."

Tap tap went the pipe, on a large marble ashtray looking like a Christmas present from loyal underlings: it was polite but tepid applause. "An A-minus, I think, Castang. Not quite first-class."

He knew, I knew. Der-Die-und-Das knew that this was carrying water in a sieve. Any findings sent to the police lab hadn't been processed yet. Nobody had even looked at the photos carefully. But as the English say, six to four on that there was no more clue to an intruder than to where Captain Blood buried his treasure. If they didn't peg Harold, they could always fall back on me.

"You're whistling past the graveyard," went on Mertens. "Supposing I were to tell you that this morning I had a little talk with your friend. He's rested, recollected, all the marbles in place. Simply, he admits the whole thing."

"It would have no evidential value in any court."

"It would be viewed as extorted, by reason of multiplied traumatic conditions."

"As simply, it would be meaningless." The simultaneous quack was hardly harmonious: the three of us smiled, shrugged, and begged each other's pardon.

"That," said Mertens, "is as the eminent professor from Louvain University may determine." A self-imposed next step; the Proc would order a psychiatric expertise as a matter of course.

"One would put," said Gregor a scrap portentously, "that such is the reaction of any sensitive man jarred off his balance by an appalling discovery."

"Mertens," said Laetitia in a surprisingly deep voice, "I've no idea whether you are married and if so whether this has been the case for a number of years."

"What people say to Commissaires of Police is universally unreliable," a remark I could make with deep-felt sincerity.

"Good God man," said Gregor, "he spends the night in jail and doesn't know which nightmare is which."

"I'd like a word with him myself," I said. "You'll make no obstacle, Mertens?" For answer he picked up his telephone, muttered, inserted a pencil in his other ear and twisted it pleasurably against a tickle, rolled his eyes at us.

"He's gone up to the Proc, been inculpated, and transferred to comfortable surroundings at Queen-of-Heaven." Which is a cop joke; Regina Coeli is the notorious central prison in Rome and its nickname has been adopted for all such institutions. "For the necessary permissions, apply to the Judge of Instruction. So you can all quieten down. A few weeks for the sediment to settle. As you're all aware, preliminary hearings are fictions, to allow of this process. When we've some clear wine, we'll taste it." *Dont Acte*, as the Proc says.

The Palais de Justice of Bruce, perched up at the top of the hill crowning the old town, has a splendid view from the terrace and that's about all that can be said for it. So has the Hradcany Palace in Prague, which is also gigantic. And that is very beautiful, which mildly is not the case here: it is in the very worst of neo-classical nineteenth-century taste.

Our own Dear Palais in Paris (I've my hand on my heart, like a United States dignitary before the Flag) is hideous, too, but sanctified by historic associations, like the Conciergerie, and the Sainte-Chapelle, and Marie-Antoinette: an astounding maze of dungeons and secret passages and Salles-des-Pas-Perdus (the Hall of the Lost Footsteps is the most poetically appropriate nomenclature I know of). There are courtyards and long-dead clochards, and even a tiny garden planted with Busy Lizzie by the holy nuns who look after female prisoners. There are lots of ghosts, and a permanent doctor, and I can tell you, he's never short of work; people die and go dotty fresh every day. Most invigorating, except of course for prisoners, judges, or policemen.

This is almost the same size but a lot less funny; a monstrous kremlin, sombre monument to heartbreak and injustice. The ghosts here are of the Belle Epoque, Georges Simenon with his pipe and Maigret with his, and the Juge d'Instruction Coméliau, with pince-nez and umbrella, nagging. So strong are the smells of mothballs, bowler hats and velvet-collared damp overcoats that I was pleasantly surprised to find the judge a young man in jeans, smelling of deodorant but otherwise quite human. "Permissions to visit? – yes of course. And your wife too? And by the way, Castang, there's Press lurking about, just thought I'd warn you, oh yes, I'm being very tight-lipped, the Proc told me any leakages and I'd get hung up and Flayed, whosit, Marsyas, enormous boring picture, Rubens is it, or Titian? We'd have plenty of gallery space here for that, and how appropriate it would look."

The television adverts for deodorant are full of young women who melt, cling, and drop things, shortly to culminate with their knickers, but the clerk (all judges are run by their clerks) was an austere biddy in a black shirt and skirt. Not the melting type, and likely to keep her judge on the straight-and-narrow.

I'm tired, my God, Harold will have to wait until tomorrow. It's an Accès night, too. Vera will have made my excuses. They are of course extremely flexible about one's hours of attendance. I don't think I could face any delinquent teenagers this evening. I have enough work with my own. The girls have a big airy second-floor bed- and workroom full of pop posters and strange instruments of music. I said I'd cook them supper. They didn't look very grateful, but one does what one can.

CHAPTER NINE

Vera Castang

"I brought you some clothes and stuff." They'd searched my bundle and patted me down for guns and beer bottles the way they do now outside a football stadium. But it was casual and they left me alone with him. Undoubtedly this is privileged. I could have had files or screwdrivers taped to my inside leg. They make you sit on the other side of the table, and there's a man to survey your good behaviour. Nowadays they have sinister little love parlours for the wives. I haven't been in this situation. I should think they'd call a woman to search the wife before letting her in. Drugs for instance don't take up much space. They can object to all sorts of things. They could have pointed to the eau de cologne saying "glass is forbidden".

"I hope these trousers are all right. Men have always such quantities of clothes they never wear or can't even get into, and refuse to throw away." I was talking too much because I was embarrassed. Harold had been in jail for three days and I don't know him at all well, yet here we are having to make conversation under unpromising conditions.

"Oh, now I'll be very comfortable. I've even got a clothes-hanger. I've a room to myself, it's absolute luxury. Personal wash-basin and lavy, shower twice a week."

"Do you have any contact at all with the others?"

"They found it rather difficult to know who'd make suitable company. I share the yard at recreation with two elderly gents. They're both very nice. One's a mail-order fraud and the other a crooked bookkeeper. I was prepared to be bored, but they're full of fascinating tales."

"Television?"

"No, thank God. They did very kindly ask, but I said no thanks. One is quite infantilised enough as it is. They come around at bedtime asking if one wants a sleeping pill. But I've library books. This is absorbing; they bring the catalogue, one marks one's wishes. They've unheard-of wonders. You expect Agatha Christie, but they've super stuff like Peter Cheyney and Daphne du Maurier. Treasure-house of 1930s masterpieces. I've become the greatest living expert on the Saint. Did you know that one could tell the time by him because he smoked exactly four cigarettes an hour? And after a hard day's work coshing Jews he could still run a hundred yards in under ten seconds? Of course you didn't. I only need bound volumes of the Hotspur to be the world's happiest man."

"Food all right?"

"Marvellous, so unconstipating. One ethical point I do find difficult. Which is to be preferred, clean stainless steel or dirty silver? Iris was such a snob, always claimed that Inox tastes greasy however much you wash it. But the silver was always filthy because she hated cleaning it, and of course the *femme-de-ménage* won't touch it." I didn't want him talking about Iris, or not in that tone of voice anyhow.

"So there are no petty persecutions you find too trying? Not that I could stop them, but there might be ways and means to alleviate."

"Well some people apparently get very uptight at being locked in, and want to bang and scream, but I find it rather restful. I mean when someone does come clattering at the door he's invariably kind, polite, and often interesting. There's a weird language one has to learn. Like being a number instead of a name. So when you turned up just now, the chap comes clonking with his keys and says things like, 'Come on Immatriculation, you're about to be Extracted.' And then of course late at night they peek in at one through the Judas. I hope they won't

93

be vexed at my talking like this, do you think they're listening and taking it all down on tape."

"I don't care at all whether they do or not." I was feeling a little irritable, but I had to recognise his need to be jaunty.

"And one misses women. I suppose that gets really bad as time goes on. But you come in, looking a perfect picture if I may say so, joy to the eyes and the heart."

I didn't grin because I've heard this before. Prison authorities don't like one to be "young or pretty" (not that I'm either), because that is thought to "upset the inmates". Any woman, of any age, will see to it that her hair is nice and her frock pretty. If Inmate is going to have masturbatory fantasies he'll have them anyway, tearing them if need be out of old *Playboys*. So what does it matter? Am I being sexy because my lipstick's on straight? If I sit with my knees crossed is that vulgar?

"You're a breath of fresh air, Vera, and one does miss that, rather. I've done some criminology studies, and all the authorities agree the summer months are the worst. Nothing like experiencing it for oneself though, I say."

"It's very good, Harold. I'll come back as often as you want me to. The administration's being rather flexible about days and hours. What would you like – books? Make a list and I'll scout around."

"Make a list. Yes, that's a good idea. Better plan, for the long term, wouldn't you agree?" Looking suddenly withdrawn and absent. I know these sudden depressions. I've seen them before. I'd had to learn that something one says, even something in the way one looks, can at the drop of a hat press unbearably upon a heart. However banal. It is the banalities of everyday life which get to them.

> " 'The gods have many faces
> And many fates fulfil
> To work their will.' "

Gone swimmy, eyes collecting teardrops. I may have muttered "oh balls". Softly.

" 'The end expected comes not.
God brings the unthought to be
As here we see.' Euripedes, the *Bacchae*."

My trouble is I'm never witty until afterwards. Should have said "Thought it was Hitler, *Mein Kampf*."

"Sounds like nonsense to me. We're forever doing silly things, and some catastrophic. So we have to climb out then, take a grip."

"Yes, well, that may have occurred to King Pentheus," but back in his normal voice. "By that time the maenads had made sausage of him." Still, he'd worked his own cure. "Your point is taken.

'Oh how I fear that this will be a
Sad business for my Miss Medea.'

I think perhaps some law books would do me good. Make a change from the Saint. Did I make that remark already? – one does get a bit infantile in here." It's a strength in the English and one I envy. A refusal to take themselves or their sorrows seriously. He had that face of someone trying to capture a memory.

"Got it! – it is of course Medea's Nanny.

'Oh how I wish that an embargo
Got placed upon the good ship Argo.' "

I was glad to be able to join in the laugh.

At home I found a monstrous pile of ironing. I really don't know how all these business women cope, dashing to and fro with only the barest pause to squirt themselves with deodorant, fling a few contraceptives in their handbag, and belt straight from work to swooning on a sofa, and never once does the milk boil over. More infantilisation. The idea is that the woman should watch this on television while doing the ironing, happy to be treated as an imbecile and to turn into one in consequence. I don't pretend to serious thought. But the wheels do go round.

Iris was a good few years older than me. Some fifteen,

almost a generation and stretched by the war. I mean she, born before it, seems a lot older to we born after. One is marked by that sort of thing. As witness the terrible story of the brother, twelve years older than herself but with whom she shared the knowledge she was too young to experience. She could only just remember him, the big tall handsome boy. That would make it worse, I should think. No other man could ever attain those heights. The miserable end has only made the clouds of glory the more shining. He won a Knight's Cross in the snow of Russia, and died before he could know the end, and this she has clung to. The more since her own father appears as an amiably feeble sort of type. Dépassé par les évènements.

But in between there were three sisters, surely. I can only recall one, Rosemary. Mild and rather passive, like the father, became a nun, poor girl. I remember Iris raging; that wasn't going to happen to her! What about the others? If alive they ought to be informed, surely? Won't there be an address book or something in the house? I must ask Mr Mertens, since Henri won't have time, for permission to rout about. I was only barely a friend, but I don't know of anyone else who is taking this on. And what about the funeral – and the children? I'm sure the English are arranging it all, they always show solidarity in exile.

Damn, I wish I hadn't let this pile up so. Has Henri been unusually extravagant with shirts? Or perhaps it's just the hot weather.

I can see Iris so clearly. And perhaps I'm the only one who can. What is Harold seeing? All sorts of distortions? Or is it like a crossword puzzle, full of black squares he has blanked out, so that he can now only perceive fragments?

An odd mixture of languor and vitality. She would collapse upon the sofa lamenting. She spent a lot of time on that sofa. Lying on an elbow, knees drawn up, nice draughtsman's line from hip to ankle, she kept those long rangy legs. She'd kept her figure remarkably well, despite drinking too much. Elle avait de beaux restes, the French would say, she had good bones. A few lines bitten in, but she didn't sag under the jaw. Complained that her breasts

96

had shrivelled, and she couldn't wear low frocks, but she looked very well when she took the trouble. It was going on about being a failure that did her harm.

She never did tell me how she came to meet Harold. Perhaps I'll piece it together. He's told Henri things, but are they the truth? "Grammar school" whatever that is. Seems to be better than what gets defined as "minor public school" – these nuances of English inferiority-feelings escape me. Scholarship I think to Cambridge, could it be Clare? There's a C in it and there's also a Christ I do believe, and a Corpus Christi, too, or is that what they call "the other place"? One mustn't get entangled in English theologies especially since there's a Jesus into the bargain.

And Iris' low, slightly hoarse voice, not the shrill English soprano but neither "Irish" (I suspect Eamonn Hickey of exaggerating his on purpose so that the "foreigners" don't get him muddled with Brits; how difficult it is, they can all be so touchy). "We'd been taught French and German at home by a series of incompetent governesses. We knew how to ride a horse well and play the piano badly. We knew nothing. Oh, and how to be good wives, meaning without any sexual education whatever. Oh yes, I've tried to be a good wife and learning a lot of things the hard way has left me a bit battered. There were plenty of good Protestant schools in Dublin – academically anyhow. One could have gone on to Trinity, which was a Cambridge foundation.

"Oh the hell of being Cath. The Sacred Heart, full of butchers' daughters learning how to behave in society."

"But surely," I'd objected, "there must have been other girls-of-good-houses?" Iris looked at me, ringed hand under her chin, the fine eyes drowned in tormented memories.

"I could show you a map. Dublin, with all the old houses still marked. They weren't burned down. They're suburban housing estates now. Boys were sent to England, to the Jesuits at Stonyhurst, the Benedictines at Ampleforth. Nobody bothered with girls much. Or it would be the ghastly Sacred Heart again at Roehampton.

Expensive. We were living on charity by this time. We'd fallen into the shabby genteel. We were given to understand the convent was the place for us and that's just what poor Rosemary fell into. Can you just see it? – Bride of Christ in some establishment highly recommended by Monsignor MacMahon."

"Who's he?"

"The Irish middle class," well away and paying no attention. "They all had to be doctors or lawyers. Small narrow clerical minds. Arguing about the difference between Cosgrave and De Valera. All the good ones got shot in the Civil War. That ruined Ireland, I can tell you. Why am I telling you all these awful things, am I pissed or what?" She'd been at the port a bit but wasn't drunk, just unhappy.

"It's because I'm a Czech peasant. Slovak, which is worse. Piggier. More Cath. I refused point blank to be a child-of-Mary."

"I was," anger again mastering her.

"In a white muslin frock rather too small for you and a blue ribbon? Strewing rose-petals from a basket, while walking backward simpering?"

"Exactly."

"They still do, in the backwoods parts of Poland."

"You're right, I wouldn't tell the English this. Nor the Irish."

They found means, those two, of tormenting one another. But did he kill her? Henri won't say what he thinks. Mumbles things like "If he didn't, it's hard to say who did." It has been his business, often enough, to find out. But he's inhibited, indeed actively prevented. He's no longer a working police officer, and he stands on that. It's not his business, he says, to do any investigating. Harold is his chief, and a friend, too. He says justly that even if he were still in a criminal brigade he'd disqualify himself. And there's this tricky political angle, of the Communauté, the different nationalities, the ambiguous position of it all in relation to the city of Bruce and the state of Belgium.

I keep thinking of these children, these two boys in England.

Oh dear, if Henri didn't insist that shirts should be pure cotton and nothing else, this job would be a lot easier.

A marvellous man called Mr Simpson took charge of the whole thing. How well the English arrange these matters. From a different department and Henri doesn't know him at all. "Ag and Fish," he says vaguely. They work out extremely technical things like soya-bean quotas. How many herrings you are allowed to catch in the North Sea (and who may catch them). What happened to the mad cows (burned, buried, or just eaten by the French all unbeknowing)? Wine lakes, butter mountains and Pyramids of Peaches. Worthy people and they don't get much thanks.

Mr Paul Simpson (perhaps there are others). Tall, solid, dignified and perhaps a little portentous. But a pillar, definitely. Known, we are told, as the Duke of Windsor, because of talking all the time about golf, rather than on account of the name. I have all this from the invaluable Miss Huntingdon. But a kind man, as well as insisting upon all the proprieties and the right protocol. He has the two boys in his house, to stay, although a stranger, relatively, to all concerned. The mother has died in tragic circs, the father is held by judicial decision in custody (apparently the Belgian Proc is being diplomatic and ambiguous about this, but rather firm), but we will do things properly. There is a strong turn-out from the Communauté, the Secretary-General (who's in Washington, or maybe Helsinki) is represented, the coffin is of the very best quality, there are huge piles of flowers, and there is a formal religious service. Church of England, naturally. Iris was Catholic if lapsed, Harold is nothing that anyone knows of, but we are being ecumenical and eirenical in dark suits. I can't tell anything from the looks of the two young men. Both are darkish, with Iris' looks rather than Harold's.

Miss Huntingdon has murmured a piece of gossip in my ear, that the elder, the "postgraduate one", had said "That was the marriage of Stalin and Hitler." "Of course," she said in a hurry, "all he meant was that Harold can be authoritarian and arbitrary, and that his mother he found rigid and obstinate, but people were rather shocked as you can imagine." I can well believe that two student-aged boys would be violently rebellious, but both were on their best behaviour now.

All those flowers, and underneath, poor Iris, autopsied. I wish I didn't think about it, but Henri, who has been huddled with lawyers, was muttering only this morning that the autopsy results appeared blurred and indecisive. "Bits left out." Whatever that may mean, it sounds horrible. When asked, he only grumbled that he suspected the Belgians of "being diplomatic again". I know from occasions in the past that they make one enormous cut from your thorax down to the pubis and take a saw to the rib-cage. Do they saw the top of your skull off? I forget, I'm glad to say. I prefer not to go into it, but Henri says they sew you up again, make you decent for burial. Oh my poor Iris. But bravo the English. They've formed a solid, loyal front.

We went back home and had a drink, badly needed. A "solid" whisky for each of us before I changed and put on an apron. I had lit a cigarette, and stood it on an ashtray, and the smoke went up in that thin beautiful horizon-blue thread before spiralling away into nothing, and it was goodbye, Iris. She had rather a good soprano voice. "Mezzo," she said, "meaning no good, really." It wasn't true, she sang well and had had much pleasure in earlier years, in choirs. "Oh all right, yes, it was one of the few things I did well. But I could never manage anything tricky, really, I never did manage to read music properly. I'm half-assed in everything I do." Poor Iris, convinced she was a failure. I know the feeling. I can find lots of parallels in my own existence. My mind is slow. Women aren't stupider, but their minds work in different ways to a man's. Harold, restless and brilliant and ambitious – had he been patient enough, with Iris? Henri, I, we yell often enough. Both of us have been known to throw things. We wouldn't kill each other. I've sometimes thought I'd like to.

Everyone has thought that, I'm quite sure. Those two loved each other deeply, I'm convinced of it. And as Henri says, anybody can kill anybody, any time. How are we ever to know? I wish it could all be forgotten.

"What did you mean when you said 'bits left out'?"

"The report seems oddly put together. Incomplete or superficial – I haven't seen it myself, but the lawyers are dissatisfied. She was strangled all right; that little bone or cartilage in the throat was busted. Vaginal vault clean they say, she wasn't raped at all. Doesn't match my observation. All a bit puzzling."

CHAPTER TEN

Henri Castang

stars and sun moon
and only the snow can begin to explain . . .

I'd heard rumours of legal doings at the funeral and
nobody could take exception to it, not even Mertens. It
wasn't hostile; it's an atavistic reaction and I've done it
myself. Some accident in another country obliged you to
consult a doctor and I'll bet there was a moment when you
felt mistrust of his methods. Ten to one indeed that when
you got home you ran to your own man saying, "Fellow in
Italy gave me these pills, d'you think they're any good?",
upon which he'll pull a face and say, "Well, it's not quite
what I would have . . ." Without knocking a member of the
confraternity he'll manage to convey that the chap was
probably a charlatan.

Mertens said that he was unsurprised; that there'd been
"a buttoned-up blackavised sort of personage," represen-
ting some London firm of solicitors. Grego and Laetitia
were unsurprised. There are Community rules for such
things, and local bar associations have tit-for-tat
agreements. Unperturbed, for lawyers flock like rooks and
get paid whatever happens. So I was the one surprised by
Mr Quentin Camden, who is to be sure a QC, and, of
course, Cue-Sea he became at once and was thereafter
invariably known as.

Impressive figure. Very polite. Penetrating, though. An
intense stare, saying "I'm not quite clear about your exact

status in this matter, Mr Castang", putting one in mind of death rays.

Smallish man, compact and powerful in the neck and chest, filling his clothes like a pillar. No fat there. Holds himself straight, and looks straight at one. Enormous waves will break over this without anything in the countenance budging by a millimetre. The eyes do not blink. The round sandy head is no larger than the normal proportion to the body would make it, but looks large, so that the gold-wire-framed glasses look a size too small for this annihilating blue glare: the funny thing is that the eyes when in repose are pale grey and look as if they could appreciate a joke. He didn't have any bulging briefcase. No "yellow legal pad". He had a smallish notebook in an inside pocket, and salient details went into this in slow longhand and small difficult handwriting. Black ink and a Sheaffer pen. With me he was affable, in a concentration so perfect that the workmen outside with a road-drill ceased to exist.

"Will you explain to me this open door? I haven't seen the house yet. I presume," to Gregor, "that the police plans and measurements will be made available."

"It's a villa. Solidly built, construction anywhere around 1910. Own grounds sheltered by shrubbery. Outside gate and gravelled approach. Anyone could get in, but not into the house, without leaving traces. Path around the side, to a paved area at the back. Service access, kitchen or central heating. Space to park a car."

"What in England we'd call a tradesman's entrance."

"That's right. The oil man or the wine merchant."

"And this was open. You're unshakeable on that."

"I didn't say open. I said unlocked and unbolted. My prints are on it. I tried it first thing because the idea of an intruder was the first to suggest itself."

"Have you conclusions?"

"No. I didn't know the lady. Common sense would suggest something banal like emptying a garbage bin. The housecoat might suggest that she hadn't gone to bed and was tidying before locking up."

"You don't suggest any visitor, expected or otherwise? You're a trained observer."

"But no more. It's not impossible. You'd have to take character into account."

"Quite a highish figure for blood alcohol, I see here."

"You're hypothesising drinks with somebody she knew? Washed a glass and put it away? Not very plausible. Sort of thing the police would check on carefully. No such suggestion's been made, I believe."

"Only that in the case of a breaker-in I'd expect more disturbance – flight, fluster. Coming back to this autopsy, you saw clear marks on her throat? Bruises? Everyone seems agreed on manual strangulation, but these measurements here could fit anybody. My own even."

"I'm not a pathologist. I don't know how long such marks persist in sharp outline. The photos should show things as they were what – about three hours after estimated time of death. Bit vague since nobody knows quite when she ate."

"Suppose I take somebody by the throat abruptly, to silence or restrain them? This can cause death through shock, I think, without prolonged pressure?"

"Vagal reflex yes, I've heard of it, but I've no direct experience I can bring to mind. If you've asphyxia it leaves signs, little haemorrhages in the eyes and whatever. Should be clear enough in the findings you've got."

"Very little that is clear, so far. There's this rape which turns out a non-rape."

"I've known cases of men hyper-excited who then failed to perform. That sort of functional impotence isn't even uncommon."

"Do you see that pattern fitting the police hypothesis?" dovetailed Mr Camden neatly. I gave him the blank stare.

"The police haven't told me what their working theory is. The pattern would fit anybody on occasion; you or me."

"Let me understand you. You'd postulate somebody who's had a lot to drink, who is wandering about, obeys a casual impulse?"

"I don't like the idea of the burglar," I said. "That type

104

doesn't drink for obvious reasons, and in my experience would disappear the moment he realised that there was someone in the house. They don't like complications."

"For such a person, the excitement resides in the breaking in, rather than in the stealing? This person would be in a high state of emotional tension? Let's say he finds the entry unlocked, goes further into the house looking for pickings. She's upstairs. Comes down and catches him – his retreat's cut off. He has to silence her, stop her raising an alarm. Struggling with a woman wearing only a housecoat he becomes aroused?"

"Suppose anything you like. I'm not in court."

"I beg your pardon, Mr Castang. Just taking the temperature. You're an interesting witness since you represent a police standpoint. This obstinacy in holding Mr Claverhouse – it's because they've found nobody else, and quite likely haven't bothered much to look?"

"Bird in the hand saves beating about in the bushes," I agreed. "But I've no right to say that Mertens isn't doing his job thoroughly – these things take time. Speaking as a cop, I don't much like your scenario."

Cue-Sea leaned back, tilting his chair, putting his hands in his trouser pockets.

"Mr Claverhouse remains your favourite candidate, does he?"

"Monsieur Castang," said Gregor in his air-conditioned voice, "explained his reasons to us. Perhaps he'd recap?"

"Just that I'm a cop. A house is full of traces of the habitual occupants; hair, skin and so on. A hair of his on her coat, doesn't mean a thing. They'll look for something foreign, find it or not, they're not telling me. If they do, they've got to match it; a city of a million people, out here. Eliminate any casual visitor, anyone with legitimate business, your plumber, electrician, man about the gas. Neighbourhood enquiry, for loiterer or prowler, flasher or voyeur. They're left with some fragment, thread of material or broken fingernail. Indicators are not much use. Nothing's been stolen. Failing the outside chance of some wife or girlfriend aggrieved about a chap out with

105

some woman and she'd like to know where, you've every probability of a dead end. You put what you have on the computer and hope for a recurrence in the pattern, maybe. But nine times out of ten your reasonable solution is the chap who was there all the time. Balance of probabilities."

"You've left out the psychological picture," said Laetitia.

"Cops prefer physical evidence," I said, "because your psychology – you'll have three different experts and three distinct portraits. When I saw Mr Claverhouse, half an hour, an hour after the scene met his eyes, he had no idea how long, he was in shock and disoriented. He assumed the total burden of guilt. Can be convinced that he killed her and that he has vivid memories of doing so. Association, disassociation, he doesn't know and that's the fact. He could have the carving knife in his hand and he still wouldn't know. The point is that then we would."

"You suggested he take a shower," said Camden.

"No. But I didn't stop him. He was in a sweaty lather as well as being drunk. He has a hair-trigger type of nervous organisation and my overriding idea was to cool him off. I was at fault, and Mertens put me through the mill about it."

"Not perhaps the reaction of a trained police officer?" suggested Camden gently.

"I've thought about that. In fairness, can I say that I feel myself a friend and wished to help him get composed? Could I say that I feel glad that I'm no longer a police officer, and perhaps unconsciously emphasised the fact?" Camden was smiling.

"We would, however, ask the question that I dare say Mr Mertens has also asked – what it was that put him in this unbalanced state. Finding his wife's body? – but you say you thought he imagined that." It was hard not to be annoyed by this forensic needling.

"You've got the verbal process in your papers there," I said, a little too irritably. "Harold came storming in, yelling some nonsense about killing Iris. Evidently something dramatic had happened to set him off gibbering like that. I

106

thought of a household accident; that she'd fallen downstairs, or electrocuted herself in the bathroom. Something more of a commonplace than this kill talk. I could remind you that accidents are rather more frequent than murders."

"You make your point," said Camden. "You didn't want to think like an officer of judicial police. Very well. You found yourself in turn confronted with this shocking sight. I suggest that the experience would bring you back to a professional view. You accept that? May we know now what this view was?"

I found myself huddling in the chair where I was sitting; feeling for a cigarette. "Take your time," said Cue-Sea. "We're not in court," pleasantly.

"It wouldn't be allowed as you well know. Police witness sticks to facts observed."

"You're no longer in the police, Castang; don't be an ass."

"Drawing conclusions from emotional supposition – inadmissible."

"Revealing answer. You're looking for a legal justification for your own squeamish emotions."

I looked at him with no pleasure.

"All right, let's see if I can help you. You are reconstructing from facts seen by you, and facts known to you. A further fact is your experience of such scenes. A habit of impersonal observation. Then, you say, your emotions crowded in, and this vitiates the value of your opinion.

"But I still want to hear it. Could be illuminating. It's confidential of course – privileged."

"Shut up and let me think." Suppose I do speak my mind? Candid. Does that harm Harold, now? Mertens' mind will work the same way. We are both cops.

"I formed a theory, yes, which would fit the facts. Whether it fits the personalities – that's not in my sphere. You are two men and a woman, here; you'll have to ask yourselves whether it fits your understanding of human nature.

107

"I've never liked the idea of somebody breaking in. I can't see anything to support it. The door unlocked – by itself a fact of no significance.

"A visitor then? Or an assignation? Strikes me as unlikely in the extreme, from what I know of Mrs Claverhouse. Out of character. Anyhow there'd be traces, a glass that had held a drink – something. This contrived idea of traces effaced belongs in fiction. A police team looks for it. Exactly like an insurance investigator, seeking to establish whether a fire was accidental or arson. There would be a scenario, and that leaves traces. A surface recently wiped, for example, is much more open to query than an accumulation of dust.

"My picture, thus, is of a woman alone. She'd got ready for bed, she had a bath or a shower, she simply thought of a job that needed doing. Or she heard her husband come in and there was something she wanted to say. I mean it's a domestic picture."

All three faces were still, wiped clean of expression.

"A man comes home. It isn't early, it isn't late. He'd been working or amusing himself, I neither know nor care. He may have had a few drinks, but I've no knowledge of his state of mind.

"I don't know whether relations were strained between these two. Like most marriages, went up and down I should imagine. Temperaments, and difficulties, a storm or a reconciliation, doesn't concern me. I postulate an idea, extremely simple, that a man proposed to make love to his wife. He is perhaps mildly euphoric, she's floating about in a housecoat, I won't labour the point.

"It would turn, I think, on her refusing him. I could imagine that, I emphasise the word. And conceivably, with some stinging or insulting phrase, which could arouse anger or a sense of injury, what you like but bringing about a loss of control."

I don't think that Cue-Sea was being officious. His contribution was a good one.

"Could we use the expression 'flicked on the raw'?"

"That would do well. Yes. That he felt raw, exposed. He

108

might then compensate, I won't say venge, an injured vanity, an aggrieved manhood, I'll let you choose the wording, by forcing her. You find this notion preposterous?"

"No," said both the men and the woman, all at once.

"It's within your experience? Or I'll say, your estimate of possibilities? Well, I didn't know then what I know now. I had no idea of a temporary impotence. But if we admit a fiasco, which is supported by the autopsy findings, it strengthens the theory. We'd have a feeling of humiliation there. Is it too strong to say a man, this man, no, any man, would feel emasculated? Am I overstating it?"

"No," said both men.

"I don't mind admitting," said Laetitia, "since we're making, it seems to me, an effort to be honest, that I've heard the phrase 'castrating bitch' used upon occasion."

"Bravo," said Gregor in a collegial tone of voice. It has not occurred to me to wonder whether they were married. I'd seen it only as a legal partnership. I've no evidence to the contrary now.

"She might then have said something extremely wounding to a man in that situation. You see? – I was looking for whatever could have been a fierce momentary motivation. Why else should he take her by the throat?"

"To kill her?" asked Camden, in the tenor voice, as though asking whether I'd lit my cigarette with a match, or a lighter?

"To kill her, no, surely not. If one has a sudden, a violent loss of control one might say 'I'll kill you.' It doesn't show purpose. To stop her speaking, surely, is the objective. To close her mouth which is uttering these destructive remarks. But the rest is conjectural, I'll go no further."

"Why not? It's all conjectural. Passing it through your head has brought it vividly to life in your mind. I have questions. He grips her by the throat. This continues? To stop her yelling – it would be similar to putting a pillow over her head?"

"I think not. No, no, it would be a uh, more of an . . . uh . . ."

"You're mumbling."

"More of a sharp – sudden—"

"Not necessarily prolonged?"

"Not necessarily, no."

"Could I call it an arresting grip?"

"I'd call it more of a punishing grip."

"A silencing grip if you wish?"

"More than that, I think."

"Vengeful would be altogether too strong?"

"Too deliberate, I think. He's not thinking about it. It's an instinctive, all right, frenzied effort to release the tension boiling up in him. A shot in the dark."

"You'd prefer the instinctive word, wouldn't you? A clutch, rather than a grip?"

"Yes that comes closer."

"There's no deliberation? No forming of an intent?"

"No, no. There's no premeditation."

"There'd be a wish, unconscious if you prefer, behind this overmastering need to silence her? A wish for death or destruction?"

"Hold on there. Now you're going too far. I'm not a psychiatrist."

"I wished to ascertain," said Camden coolly, "whether a sense of theatre were carrying you away."

I didn't know whether to laugh or be angry.

"If you'll just let me get my hands on your throat – I'll be nice and let you tell me when to stop." He beamed at that, or perhaps at a successful demonstration.

"Right. You're the normal man. You're placed in abnormal conditions of exasperation, mortification. The impulse towards violence, normally under adequate control, surfaces for one terrible, brief moment. Just the one more question. He has her within reach," stretching out his hands across the table. "They shoot out like that – and take her by the throat. Now one more effort, Mr Castang. Supposing she were not within reach. What do you do then with this ungovernable tension of yours?"

"Oh – I think it would be that rather heavy, sharp-cornered crystal ashtray, don't you?"

"I'm not joking," said this horrible little man. "I think you've known analogous circumstances."

Yes and no. Imagination is a powerful and a dangerous tool. It is also a powerful inhibitory block. Yes, there've been occasions when I've thrown things. Vera can be the most exasperating of women. One doesn't throw things at her. The picture of a missile catching someone on the temple is too dreadful. One throws things on the floor; at the wall. I have noticed too that one chooses cheap things; easily replaceable.

But if she were to boast of something intolerable. There we are at the heart of the matter. I'd know, you see; that she hadn't. That she wouldn't. And if I didn't have that certainty? No; do not push me too far.

Gregor and Laetitia had kept silent. A lawyer manoeuvres one, feeding, adroitly, the words, the qualifications, he wants to hear. A good one, the expert criminal pleader, seeing you stiffen at too blatantly leading an approach, tempts you out into quicksand territory, stands back inviting the jury to watch you flounder.

"Are you acquainted," asked Cue-Sea, "with a well-worn cliché in English criminal pleading – the man on the Clapham ominbus? No? *Monsieur Tout-Le-Monde*. He's on the jury, rather stuffed with prejudice and steak-and-kidney pie, but quite alive to what he'll accept as reasonable." Gregor and Laetitia were, indeed, looking a bit stuffed. "You accept this?" Throwing it at them.

"Speaking as a woman, the stinging words, yes, alas. Irrecoverable once uttered and putting a man beside himself. Momentarily out of his mind? If he were that kind of man in the first place. Then yes."

"Which no, I'm not, at least I think not," said Gregor, "but I've seen and heard and taken part in too many divorce proceedings not to agree. After a glass of whisky too many – yes, I think the paralysing grip is on the cards."

"No doubt of it," said Laetitia, thinking him too lukewarm. "I've had to plead the cause of too many battered wives. Violence can take every imaginable form. Very often these women cannot realise the role they have played in provoking or encouraging it. Men and women both have an extraordinary talent for justifying themselves." A wifely admonition, or just a professional elbow-jog, I couldn't say. Gregor was jogged, though.

"Perhaps we're too apt to consider it limited to half-educated people in positions of petty authority. The works foreman, the army sergeant. Policemen—" with a half-apologetic glance in my direction.

"The postmaster, the managing director, the ayatollah and the burgomaster," I offered him. "All authority is petty."

"The suffix 'master' occurs oddly often in nomenclature," said Camden light-heartedly. "Like 'chief' in America."

"They're being French," I told him. "A chef isn't a cook, you know. If you knew how many times I've said it," tugging my forelock. "Oui, Chef. The whole of French society is organised in a hierarchy."

"Whose isn't?" asked Laetitia, quite snappily.

"I think we've made our point," said Camden. "In England I'd expect to get the Crown to compose, beforehand. Here in Europe you've more explicit and clearly nuanced definitions, in the codes. What is it, grievous bodily harm?"

"There are several possible articles and the Proc as a prudent man will settle for a catch-all, but 'without intention of causing death'. Adequately pleaded," Gregor was saying pompously, "we should be able to work in so many extenuating circumstances as to expect a nominal sentence, most of which will have been served beforehand." Camden gave him a look of "we can do better than that", but only said jokingly he'd be placing much reliance on his expert witnesses.

"You," darting a finger at me, "and Commissaire Mertens."

I didn't want to be an expert witness. I'd rather be just a functionary, and in no position of authority.

I was feeling deathly tired.

CHAPTER ELEVEN

Henri Castang

Tired? I thought about Monsieur Adrien Richard. Long retired: my former chief in the PJ; a remarkable man. Being Tired, he said, was nothing but a state of mind. He detested states of mind.

He also took risks, sometimes monstrous; with his rank, Divisional Commissaire (like mine); with his position as a local notable, socially, and governmentally, too, as a responsible official. A great deal, he used to say, can be achieved by cheek, by brazen pretence, and by impudent bluff. When stuck, and officialdom means one is often downright bogged, seize the initiative.

I am bogged all right. I don't like this affair of Harold's at all, and there are some sharp spotlights, too, shining on me from several nasty angles. I don't feel as shrouded as I should, in a comfortable bureaucratic anonymity. Recent proceedings have exposed me. I've been given a confidential mission, and told all too clearly to be discreet about it. This means that my spying friends, from being an unpleasant tickle like a loose hair down the back of my collar, have become a thorn fixed in my foot. I didn't like that car following me to Harold's house. I pretended to disregard it, but in my gut I didn't like it at all. I've had to suffer, passively, a succession of spiteful little gags. No initiative. Time to call Adrien Richard to mind. He has been a good friend to me, on many awkward occasions.

I have a ridiculous rhyme singing itself inside my skull. From way, way back – surely it is Ella Fitz? A joke from the jazz age, origins long forgotten— "I wrote a letter to my love and on the way I dropped it."

A bluff. A piece of cheek. I wished I'd Richard at my elbow. A fine hand with "adminstrative prose". Tickle them, he'd have said. Make the chap an offer he can't refuse.

I took more trouble . . . I drafted it twenty times, that message. Now I know how the constitutional expert sweats, phrasing an enactment for proposed legislation.

Sly? A little, and it has to show. Humbled, but not grovelling; tamed without being obsequious. I had to convey that I was frightened of being unstuck; that I know how easy it is to plant a little parcel before having someone picked up, this time by a real Narcotics Detail.

Robust, though. I had to convey that I can only be bent so far. That if they were to start on Vera I'd turn, and bite. Some venality, and some remnants of integrity.

All this, in under fifty colourless words.

After leaving this piece of prose in my typewriter I was tormented by possible improvements. Esprit d'escalier, the witty rejoinder thought of while going downstairs. Too late now; a tisket, a tasket. Who is going to pick this up and put it in their pocket?

Vera complains that I never throw things away. I still have a gun, and I still have a cop-jacket, which doesn't show the gun when worn. The gun wasn't state property so I never had to turn it in. Bit of an antique. Nothing fanciful; standard .38 Smith. Nine millimetre is quite big enough for me. Four-inch barrel likewise. Revolver, of course. The cross-cut wood of the butt is chipped and greasy, and much of the bluing has worn off the metal. The belt is only a strip of stiff saddle-leather with a flat brass buckle. A blackened eyelet shows where my belly used to fit and doesn't now. There's an old half-box still of copper-jacket ammo. I've kept this gun clean and oiled. Not rusty. I am though.

If caught carrying this in Belgium, I'll be in baddish trouble with Commissaire Mertens. But nothing ventured . . . For I've had a message back. Complicated, but perhaps promising.

Right out at the end of the Avenue Louise is a roundabout, a circle where main roads branch out between woodlands: Bois de Cambre, and here there are well-worn paths and clearings; the "Louise" bourgeoisie walks its dogs here. Nasty big ones and yappy little ones. A place chosen by my unknown friends to appear and disappear as it may suit them, but I had hopes there wouldn't be more than one. To make acquaintance; a cosy-up, quoi? I parked the car on the ragged fringe of the wood. Look like a chap taking a quick pee. A man was walking a dog, but it was raining enough for him not to stay long.

Bench. Paths were difficult to follow in the dark and a drizzle. There are more benches, but this one was marked with an old Marlboro packet, silver paper neatly folded; signal, so I sat. Trees about and scrubby shrubbery. Plenty of dog-shit, too.

Signal; a torch winked. Then it shone on me, long enough to dazzle, so that I couldn't make out much, but the spy costume, hat pulled down and trench coat collar up, and about the right height for George Raft. So I stood up, and held out a hand to shake howdy. My stomach is flabbier, but I'm still fairish on my feet, for a chap pushing fifty, and deskbound. I used to be handy in a gymnasium.

Mistake. I got a grip, but the friend slid in to me, got under my chest and slammed me straight over his head. Hip throw, neat as one will find. I was on my back, and no doubt in the dog-shit, too. Hip; the back of his, the front of mine. One has sometimes stuck the gun in front if it's wanted in a hurry, but mostly it's around at the back. So I waited for breath, and then sat up, looking to get my eyeballs back in place. My night vision's only so-so. I had landed heavily, and the damned gun had bruised my kidney, which hurt. He was standing there, shaking his head at the foolishness of me. So well, chum, nothing else for it. I fished out the piece and let him see it.

I hoped it would startle him; it did.

115

"Oh fucking hell – put it away you silly ass." I got startled. It was a woman's voice. Goddam judo experts.

Drop-it-good-dog? Not startled enough for that though. Time to apply the Richard formula; some preposterous cheek. So I laughed like a maniac and put one into the ground right between her feet.

"Fucking Hell," voice jumping half an octave, "there are cops around here, you clown." Very probably: the bourgeoisie expect plenty of protection. I laughed some more and put another two into a harmless little chestnut tree behind her. Makes a hell of a noise close up and we were only a hundred metres into the wood: I had to say prayers. She turned to run, and judging by the previous athletics she could run faster than me, so I bellowed.

"Next one's in your leg," and she stopped as though run into the wall. This time I got the wrist, but I stuck the gun roughly where her arse would be. Roughly.

"Your car, or mine?" I hoped I'd Find mine. The Polizei might find it first. But by then I knew who she was.

"We need a talk. Don't you think?"

Hers was in the other street. It, too, I recognised: the little Alfa Spyder and in a trice I knew what had been following the Lancia a few days ago.

"My flat, then." On home ground she'd regain initiative, hm? So in another trice – whatever a trice may be – my dirty Volkswagen was following her. Dainty little thing. Word is, among the fans, that Alfa will put it back into production. The Respectable streets of Ixelles. Five minutes and a little top-floor flat, dainty, like the car. The drive would cool her, and she'd be confident she was cleverer than me.

She took off the hat. Black velours, broad brim: the things these girls wear . . . Tidied the trench coat neatly on a hanger. My jacket smelt of wet dog so I put it on a chair. But I still had the gun.

"You'd like a drink," in command now, shaking out her hair. Miss Huntingdon is a highly skilled personal secretary and a natural blonde into the bargain. She's very well paid. The girl-bachelor residence was full of tasteful

116

objects. I pointed the gun at her and said, "Take off all the rest, too," just like George Raft spinning the silver dollar in the air.

"Jesus a rapist yet. Castang the married man, ringing her up every five minutes. Should he wear the red tie or the green one this morning?" A nasty laugh. It stung. I sighted on the nice crystal flower-vase, popped it, and there were all the gladioli in a pool of water. Goody, I hate gladioli, nasty things. The bullet, deflected, went on into the wainscot.

"And one mousehole, one."

"God, the neighbours. That was Saint-Louis, cost ten thousand francs. God, you'll pay me that, you swine."

"Strip," I said aiming at an Empire mirror.

It could have turned into a nasty scene; violence and cheap drama. We had been exciting each other, judo throws, guns, and does it end with a good-hard-fuck on the carpet? It doesn't, but the idea cleared the air.

Harold's secretary and good at it. His tough rampaging act is not all self-indulgence. He hasn't made a success of his wife; he must have had relationships with other women, but none ever came right or satisfied him – until Marieke.

I don't even know Huntingdon's first name – Harold was forever inventing new ones. "Pearl"; "Diana". Her job was to see that he functioned, in jargon "to keep him structured". His self-indulgence was to lean on that; his vanity was to slide over boring detail, fudge his homework. When concentrated he was brilliant, but he used her, abused her. I don't mean sexually; she said he'd never slept with her or suggested it, and I'm sure that's the truth. The moment when I wanted her to take her clothes off, and she was ready to, set off an understanding between us.

She was in the same boat as me; she'd been told to use her position to gather any information the British might think useful.

She had a cry and I don't blame her. Emotional strain; prancings in the woods, having cannons shot off at her. But a stable, sensible woman. No wonder the Assistant Naval

117

Attaché, or whoever, thought her good material. Just as in my own case; the Brits are terrified of malign influences (French, mostly) upon any aspect of policy in Bruce. Harold was English but regarded as 'not very sound' – true, he's not that sort of patriot. Huntingdon's first job was to keep Mr Claverhouse in the paths of political virtue.

"But you know, things in Bruce aren't what they may look like in Watford." Yes, I said; I do know.

She'd been told to keep a sharp eye upon the French bastard – me. She had not thought up the little tricks; there were other people for that. Yes and they've all been reading these little spy books. The death of Iris gave them a drama: what does the imbecile she reports to get into his head? This is the French "destabilising Claverhouse".

She gave me a single malt.

"I don't have to sleep with you, do I?" We both broke out into slightly nervous laughter.

She could always tell them she'd been to bed with me. It would give them the same idea. But they'd already had it.

It gave me a fine notion. I could write a flaming report to my General, in Paris. These Brits had been tedious: well, I'd have them pestered by the French. The Stapo and the Sipo could sneak about destabilising each other to their hearts' content. It would get him off my back.

No it wouldn't. I'd get an instruction to start infiltrating Nato.

We parted friends, and as friends of Harold's. She promised that there'd be no more outrages upon my peace of mind. I did not mention Vera. For all I know, Huntingdon could be a Stasi agent.

I'd be less irritated by all that expert-witness talk if it weren't cropping up in another context.

Police work is like that, sure. Things crop up; they seem entirely irrelevant; one day they fit together.

Vera's neuroses – for lack of a better word – about Europe: they start tying in with the work I've been set to do. This story of Harold's is mine because I am part of it.

On paper we are talking about the procedures of

criminal law in European countries. We'd like to try to co-ordinate them, a bit. Based upon our recommendations, eminent jurists will draft a proposal for a European code.

But our nice clean paper gets crumpled, gets blood on it, looks dirty.

Vera's petty doings, her family affairs, these are relevant. "Child," said her mother, "whatever happens it will all, always, be the same." That's exactly what we're afraid of.

"For you and me," answered Vera. "But not for the children."

And so, too, with the Accès thing: so, too, with Marieke. It's time I tried to pull all these threads together. It was at this moment that they all started to fit. Marieke – she's quite a famous girl in fiction, but she was about to become a reality to me. Jacques Brel wrote a song about her. In French; the language of bourgeois Bruxelles.

He was always voluble in contempt for "Les Flamands": that's endemic here, seethes and smoulders, will take generations still, before it dies out. But Marieke is a Vlaamsch girl and he compares her to the Flanders sky: there is a sudden rare intensity of warmth and love. The immense sky, of piled cloudscapes never the same. In silhouette upon it the towers and spires of the cloud-capped cities. "Bruges et Gand" – Brugge, we should say in Vlaamsch, and Ghent. Marieke herself – suddenly he apostrophises her, and in her own language. It's unexpected, and since the man is seen now as the fine artist he was, there's a metro station in Bruce named after him, and up in Brugge in a public garden there's a statue of Marieke. Quite probably bad, I haven't seen it, but I can be sure of one thing; it doesn't look like her. Because I know her.

Accès the same. Unimportant – it's a do-gooding sort of social work to which I give a few hours a week. Vera talked me into it; I was lukewarm. To me it's business for professionals, and whole-time at that. Because one gets involved, beyond wish and beyond capacity. I would never have known about Marieke if it hadn't been for the "girls". They were exactly the type that come into Accès and cause anguish; because plainly something urgent should be done about them, and it isn't easy to decide what.

Even with a decision made, there's no guarantee it'll be carried out, or handled with the skill and patience needed.

Isabelle, the elder, was fifteen; Natasha twelve. Close to the age of my two. There was, yes, a grain of emotion in my attitude.

Fact and fantasy become so entwined in their tales as to be interchangeable. One had better disbelieve everything until it's checked. Isabelle had a lurid story, but I couldn't be sure even of her name nor how old she was, nor where she came from.

So this was a village well up to the north of here, in Flanders. How had they come? By train. How long had it taken? Nearly an hour. Ghent is the provincial capital, the "town".

I don't know it well. Full of mediaeval and renaissance glories, but the modern town to my mind is not very inspiring. Pretty prosperous; that area is a Silicone Valley. And there's a big industrial fair for flower-growers. The soil is good; there are whole villages given over to nurserymen. And this, she said, was one of them. Her father worked for such a concern. New plant varieties was the best she could do. Entreprises de Wilde. So that this was the moment to leave them with a cup of coffee, to go and ring up. What sort of man was this? A monster perhaps in a young girl's eyes – the little sister didn't utter much – but what did his employers have to say?

"Yes, quite true. Good solid chap. No, not highly qualified. Not very bright, you know. Pushes the wheelbarrow. But people like that who can do what they're told and do it reliably are themselves valuable. Been with us a few years now, and no cause for complaint. Character? Oh, quiet chap. Highly conscientious. Not highly paid, but doesn't, you know, do badly for himself. Doesn't drink. Lives here in the village. Not much more we can say; try the Mairie."

I glanced over to see that the girls were still parked. When they see that their stories are not taken at face value they'll often run out on us. They had their heads together, chattering vigorously, looking at ease. How had they got here? Pinched the train money out of the housekeeping. How had they heard of us? Well, a boy in the railway station . . . Had they any more money? No! What had they expected then to do in Brussel? Don't know, find a pad somewhere.

A Town Hall in Flanders keeps pretty good tabs on the people registered, and this was a "foreigner". Which saves a lot of trouble. "To be sure we know him. Italian immigrant. But been in Belgium, let's see, twenty years. Married to a Belgian. Nothing in the least irregular about his situation. On the contrary, nothing but good references in the neighbourhood. Steady chap. The wife? – seem to have heard she works at the hospital in the town. No problem with rent or debts that we've ever heard of. What's that? Girls run away? Not our concern. Quite right, two little girls, I've looked it up for you, registered at the local school. All above board, as far as we're concerned. Claim that the father's brutal? Nothing that we've ever heard about."

I went back to Isabelle. She's quite a pretty girl, mousy of hair and feature. Healthy-looking, apparently well-nourished. A bit tatty in appearance, but that's nothing: T-shirt, short denim skirt, bare legs, down-trodden loafer shoes. What is one to make of this tale? The younger girl has nothing to contribute but a few tears and snuffles. To add pathos to the tale?

"So you've run away, you tell me, because your father beats you. For misconduct, or is it just how he feels? And you've marks? Now suppose I call one of the women who works here. You think you could show her some sign of this?"

"Sure," agreed Isabelle readily. "I can show you, any time. I'm telling the truth, you know."

Quite likely, but there are more precautions one has to take with girls of this age. Vera wasn't here and the only

121

woman who was said, impatiently, she was busy. Very well; commissaires of police, inspectors, and agents, too, however lowly of police, witness a pack of stuff that one should call a doctor for. We have one on call, naturally. But I can't rout him out for something as trivial as this.

"You stay there," she told her sister, who sat and sucked her thumb. "I'm just going with this guy a moment." We have a back room for this sort of thing; needle-marks, cuts and bruises. She was perfectly matter of fact; they often are about maltreatment. Made no bones – I hardly had the door shut of that ignominious cubby-hole when she turned and hitched her skirt up, pulled down some rather grubby knickers and presented her behind.

Sure enough the child was striped right across with nasty marks. She had insisted, seeing me dubious, and she had not lied.

I didn't like it much; it looked like a dog leash, the diamond pattern of plaited leather visible on her skin.

"I've more on my front."

"You have?" I was a little shocked at that. I had two witnesses to this being a quiet and kind man. She thought it a tone of disbelief.

"He makes us take our clothes off. I can show you if you like."

"No, that's enough." More than enough. "Your little – Natasha has these, too?"

"I'll call her and you can look."

"No, that'll do. But your mother – what does she say to this?"

"Say?" puzzled. "Doesn't say anything."

I lit a cigarette, age-old police reaction when one wants a moment to think. Seeing which, Isabelle produced a crumpled packet and lit one, too, jauntily. I should take them away telling that they're bad for her? There is more that's bad for her.

It's a familiar problem. How much bad treatment should one close the eye to before taking a child away from the parents? For if I signed a complaint, the Juvenile

122

Court might well decide to have them put in care. Which is bad. He might even decide to prosecute the father, which is worse: the man might lose his job, and at best be blackened by village talebearing. He might, as easily, throw out the complaint. The children have been beaten. But we have all seen so much worse; far smaller children flogged with cable, burned with cigarettes, with electric irons; with broken bones.

Why had they been beaten? Where had the money come from, for the train, for cigarettes? Pilfering, and then lying about it? One can get several of these instances in a week, and none of the standard procedures are of any real use. Asking the local gendarmerie to look into it . . . most of the time, more harm done than good.

The obvious thing to do is to have a word with the father. He would be surprised and quite likely indignant. He had only corrected the girls for bad behaviour, he'd say, as was his perfect legal right and moral duty. Yes mate, I dare say, but a slipper on the bottom is one thing: stripping them naked and taking a dogwhip to them is another. Well, what was stopping me? Laziness, mostly. I had small relish for a drive out to a village in the backwoods. I didn't even have the car.

"Stay here a sec," I told the girls. I went over for a word with Ivan, one of our few professionals, who as I suspected made a face.

"We're rather short-handed, Henri, right this minute." Apologetically, because we always are.

"I'll see if I can get Vera to fill in for me. Need the car, anyhow."

Phoned, Vera was lacking in enthusiasm, which was no surprise. She did agree, dragging her feet.

"Oh well, I can leave things ready, and it won't do Lydia any harm to get supper I suppose. You're not sentimentalising the situation a bit?" Perhaps I am. Two girls of this age remind me too sharply of my own. A woman in general handles these things better.

"I don't think I can send them home alone."

"All right, I'll come on down. A pest, rather. Oh and

123

there's been a journalist lurking about. I sent him packing, but he wants to see you, and he's the adhesive type. So watch out, when you get home." I wasn't surprised. The Press comments on Iris' death had been moderate enough, but the English papers had started smelling a story. I'd been expecting something of this sort.

The girls' eyes lit up with fear.

"But if you bring us back, he'll know where we've been, and that we told you. He'll whack us again and it hurts, it hurts terribly."

"No, he won't. Not after I've had a quiet word with him." And indeed I had every hope that it would work. He sounded a decent enough man, narrow- and righteous-minded but able probably to see that he'd exaggerated. One wouldn't throw a scare into him unless it proved needful. It was more the wife that sounded a worry. But there was a strong argument for going to see for myself. Still, to pump some courage into them took most of the half-hour before Vera appeared. She tossed me the car keys and went over to talk to Ivan. I put the girls in the car and—

"Mr Castang?" said a voice at my elbow.

It's that sugary voice they have. Insinuating, ready to be ingratiating, equally ready to be bumptious as the situation may allow. "Press. Daily—"

"I'm busy, I'm afraid." It was obvious enough. Hanging about in the street waiting for me to come home, and deciding to follow Vera and see where that led: their instinct is unpleasantly smart.

"Yes, that's what they all say. But we'd like an interview, you know. You seem to be some sort of vital witness in this Claverhouse affair, and we'd rather like to know about that." I'm used to them of course – or was, formerly. It is always best to be polite.

"Look. I understand what you're after. Come tomorrow morning to the office, and I'll give you some time, can't say fairer than that."

"Yes. Rather like it tonight, so's we can catch the morning edition. They're rather keen in London. There'll be half a dozen by tomorrow. Like to get an exclusive."

124

"See for yourselves – I've work to do. Sorry but—"

"These your girls?" eyes taking a good poke at the two ragamuffins in the back.

"No, but this minute they have to be taken home."

"Only half an hour. That won't make any odds. Here," flashing money at them, which they gripped. "You'd like to buy yourselves some chips. We won't keep Mr Castang long." This was getting out of hand. I was embarrassed, too. I didn't want the bloody Press getting interested in — shit, these are my private concerns. There's a photographer, too, Goddammit. These English ones are more pushing than — oh, hell.

"No photos. I want to be polite and you're making me angry. This behaviour is intolerable."

"But Mr Castang," greasy now. "Why make it all so hard? We come to your house, perfectly correct, and sorry but your wife is not very helpful, even rather rude I'd call it. So we come on down here, farting about in the street, and now it's you making things tough for us. Only doing our job. Now you want to drive off under our nose and all we can do is stick to your tail. You wouldn't like that either. Give us half an hour while the young ladies have a hamburger over there in the McDonalds, we pay them a nice milk shake, we buy you a drink and where's the big problem?"

Ground – it always happens – between these two millstones . . .

"This part of the social work you do? Interesting!" They know damn well; they have me – what's the English phrase? – by the short hairs.

"I'll do a deal with you. This has nothing to do with you at all." The girls were getting excited and interested by a fellow being generous with McDonaldtalk. And that I had to cut off. "I'll give you half an hour, in the pub across there. Look, girls, I've some urgent business here. You'd better take the train or you'll be in trouble for being out late. I've got the address, I'll be up tomorrow, I'll have a talk with your father, it'll all smooth itself out."

The girls set up a wail. Tears trickled from the big one;

125

the little one started bawling. Not only was I diminishing their importance by failing to take them as seriously as they liked, but I was even diddling them out of a drive home in the car, which they were looking forward to.

It turned out a bad mistake. I plead guilty to it. With extenuating circumstances, and try to understand them. These bastards were twisting my arm.

I even gave the children more money.

"Here. This is for your fare. Don't stop at McDonalds. Take the first train, eat when you get home. Say what you like, but don't say you've been to see me. Cool things off. It'll be better anyhow when I come tomorrow, there's less of a link with you being missing tonight." And they bawled: a second occasion for arm-twisting. The journalists, I could see, were loving it. What will I do about it – sue the Daily Whatever?

One speaks of making the best of a bad job. And I succeeded in making the worst of it. Of course, the children with pockets now full would stop and revel in the fleshpots of Bruce. While I with even less enthusiasm than Vera's, coming down here from Schaerbeek, was getting steered to the pub to be interviewed.

But what would you have done in my place?

CHAPTER TWELVE

Vera Castang

I suppose Doctor Jung would be calling it synchronicity. I've experienced it once or twice. Henri says it is always a factor in police investigations. He doesn't, he says, have much confidence in fancy academic jargon from Zürich, but there IS something which disturbs the comfortable glib patterns of "detective" fiction.

I cannot in all honesty find any blame for poor Henri. He was irritable and upset because he could see nothing – nor can I really – for those two tiresome girls short of a "talk" (tiring, a bit nerve-racking, one has no guarantee that it's going to work) with an ignorant peasant of a father. I do it better, because I'm a narrow-minded peasant myself, and my father was another. Do you know that up to the age of twelve, if I misbehaved – and I, too, have lifted cents, and up to a half-dollar, from the housekeeping money in my mother's purse (a thing every child I've ever heard of does occasionally) – I got my bottom slippered. Way of speaking. My mother put a stop to it. "That child has begun menstruating: you can't beat her: I won't have it any longer." My father was a disciplinarian. A railwayman, and the railways work on discipline. Slip up, and you'll face punishment. It was all quite normal to him. Corporal punishment to me was part of life. I knew, without being told, that he loved me dearly, and that it cost him more than he would admit to whack me: he felt the pain, more than I ever did. And he respected a child who was a girl. I got his belt, yes, for crimes like pilfering or lying. Pretty half-hearted and it didn't even hurt much, but the humiliation was still considerable. Never, never, never were my knickers taken down. I got hauled into the bedroom and given a few licks on my skirt. They hurt and I bawled. And then I begged his pardon, and he asked for mine. It was a very old-fashioned procedure, and it had some formality and dignity. And then it stopped dead.

Henri, rightly, instinctively, didn't like the situation he saw. Two girls, teenage or verging on it, forced to strip naked and getting a dogwhip all over the body – no, no, no; he had to show stiffness over that one. It's hard to know what he could have done better. And those journalists. I'd been brusque, told them smartish I wouldn't have pestering on the doorstep. So they took it out on him, poor Henri. He's too much of a professional to feel guilt-stricken, but I know . . . he worries about "inadequacies" where our own girls are concerned. Once – just once – and it's some years ago, she might have been ten; Lydia had been poisonous all day. I was tired and my nerves were ragged; I did something unforgivable and shoved it off on to him. "Your father will have a word to say to you, young lady, when he gets home." And poor Henri, exasperated after a lousy office day. "All right, you, come with me." Took her into our bedroom and put her over his knee, turned the wretch's nightie up and I (agonising, outside the door) counted eleven ringing slaps. She howled the house down, had a lovely self-pitying cry and went to sleep happier than she'd been for weeks. It did her no harm, quite the contrary, but Henri was thoroughly upset all evening for beating a child, and I'm sorry to say I crept away quietly and was sick in the lavy, because it was my fault.

It isn't like beating a naked child with a dogwhip though, is it? I have nothing but sympathy with Henri, and the more because I felt guilty: I sulked and flounced when he asked me to come down and fill in.

So it was I who first met Marieke.

More synchronicity. She had come to the house, miserably unhappy. I had just gone. Lydia aswered the door: or didn't, rather, we give them instructions not to, because who knows who may be outside, with what plausible tale (like journalists)? So that Lydia opened the first-floor window and looked out. She saw a girl, a stranger, and bawled (rudely, probably), "What d'you want?"

"I'm looking for Mr Castang."

And the innocent – for all she's fifteen now and thinks herself terribly sophisticated, 'He's down in the town, you better look there.' Lydia had "told me off" an hour earlier for being "rude" to those fucking English journalists, who caused the whole thing. But what could they possibly know about responsibilities?

"You were rude, Ma, telling them to fuck off, like that."

When Marieke appeared I made two mistakes: being unreasonably abrasive, and telling her (guiltily) where she was likely to find Henri. That much, one can get buggered about by one's own teenage daughter.

Henri had just left on his fruitless errand with the girls, and as I later learned, a fruitful (he says fruitless and harmful but he's wrong!) session with the Daily Whatnot in the pub.

I saw her, I heard her, sailing in with her inborn bourgeois poise, saying to Ivan, "I'm looking for Mr Castang. I was told he was here."

"He was here – I think he still is," said Ivan who didn't know one way or the other: the whole thing turned on a minute. Synchronicity how are you.

"I'm sorry. He just left, he had an emergency. I'm Mrs Castang." God, she's pretty. I honestly didn't know whether I was on my head or heels. I was devoured by curiosity. And was I jealous, too, of such a pretty girl? I mean, one did wonder, what her business could possibly be with Henri.

Because this isn't the type to wander into the Accès office. Most of them are scruffy, more than a little dirty. I'm being unfair.

But she was so over-perfect. Tall and blonde and beautiful. Eamonn has a comic song: it dates from prehistory, the 1940s.

And I'll wear my hair—
Like Veronica Lake.
But things like that – never happen, to me.

Hm, the men won't need much help from me, in being lyrical about this. Fields of waving corn. But what earthly reason have I to be snide? She looked to be a nice girl as well as a pretty one. Certainly her shy manner was attractive. One does rather acquire a distrust of these ones who are demure. The English have an odd phrase: "Butter wouldn't melt in their mouth." I don't understand it, but I know what it means.

"But since you're here, why not sit down?"

"You see it was really Mr Castang I wanted."

"He said he wouldn't be back for a few hours. He'll want to go home then, to be honest. Does it have to be him?"

"Well really it was about the thing in the paper. About Mr Claverhouse."

"My husband is a friend of his, yes. So am I, come to that."

"I don't know." Tears began to well in those lovely eyes.

"What's your name? You can tell me that much. All right, I don't want to meddle in private business."

"No I don't have – I mean I don't know him." Crying now. "I know Mr Claverhouse."

"Oh." Trying not to make it sound like Oho. "If there was a message I could give it him. Where to get in touch with you. A *boodschap*." I don't know why I used the Vlaams word. True, she had a Flamande look, but her French was better than mine is. No country accent.

"Oh, *spreekt U Vlaamsch?*"

"I'm afraid not, but for the odd word." Still, the odd word seemed to have broken the ice. I floundered.

"My husband—" (oh dear – "My Husband and I"), "he could meet you somewhere."

She was struggling with caginess and distrust.

"Perhaps the Danish pub? In the centre, on the boulevard?"

Yes indeed, the best Treffpunkt in the city, and why on

130

earth feel indignation that she should know it, too?'

"Tomorrow morning?"

"I can't promise that, I'm afraid: he's pretty busy." The door opened – and Henri blew in.

I was furious. It made me look a liar, and as though I were trying to keep her away from him. My hope was that she didn't know him, but of course he caught my eye and came straight over. I couldn't wink or anything.

"Sorry, things went wrong," he said. "Bloody journalist caught me, twisted my arm. I had to send those girls home and I hope nothing comes of it. Wait till you're clear, shall I?"

"Oh, are you Mr Castang?"

"I am."

I got up. I couldn't help feeling nettled. "This young lady wants to talk to you."

Eyebrows arched. He was rinsing his eye, as the French say. I couldn't blame him – pretty girl.

"I'm going home. Car keys, please. Try not to be too late." I can't pretend I was being only tactful, and I could only hope my bottom did not flounce when I went out of the door after signing off in the day-book. I was in no frame of mind for any more juvenile delinquents.

"Who's the blonde?" asked Ivan looking up.

"Made a fuss about wanting Henri."

"Lucky Henri. Doesn't look our usual type." She was only wearing jeans, but even across the room she had an expensive bourgeois elegance.

"I know nothing about it, she wouldn't tell me. See you tomorrow."

He would not be interested in Harold's affairs. I was. The girl looked like trouble to me. If he had been giving way to any little unprofessional frailties, it might complicate matters. That would have got under Iris' skin, all right, if she had got to know about it. It would have got under mine, I can promise.

It's the men, who airily refer to inconsequential frailties. Adultery is what I call it. As long as one doesn't know . . . I can remember twisty feelings in my own inside about

131

Carlotta Salès in Paris. Not that I had any evidence. Told myself it would be out of character for them both. Jealousy – one suffers so, and tells oneself one would suffer less, if one actually knew. Which is nonsense of course. The only person who could have told me was Madame Morandière, the archivist, and she never would. Too nice a person. I took off my clothes and went to bed, in rather a pet, I'm afraid.

Henri at breakfast was sombre and uncommunicative; tramped off to the office. Harold or no Harold, the work of the Communauté continues. As we're forever told, nobody is indispensable. I had plenty to do, getting the girls organised. They are cross, because all this nonsense means the summer holiday is going to be upset. They want to go to Prague. Sudden new interest in discovering themselves half-Czech. I have to fix this, because I don't know when Henri is going to be able to get away. Damn Harold Claverhouse. No, undamn. He's in a worse fix than I am.

I was dressed, mercifully – I hate loitering about in dressing-gowns. Iris a great one for dressing-gowns, never in her clothes before lunchtime, drinking cups of tea. Is it very Irish?

As well for me because the bell went. Another journalist, but this time I was better prepared. This was the wheedling kind rather than the bullying, and chatted me up (perfectly politely) until I agreed to take the door off the chain and let him in, but only after I'd looked at his press card pretty carefully. At least the girls were out and Henri gone. This one, too, rinsed his eye, on my untidy living-room, pricing all the furniture.

I am well drilled because I have been briefed, by Henri of course, and by Eamonn Hickey, a lawyer himself, and the Irishman's view of England is fascinating. They understand "the psychology". And on the legal aspects, by Laetitia, Jewish woman, warm and spontaneous, I like her a lot. I don't know whether she can understand Iris, and don't know if I do, either. She tries.

132

The English interest goes back, of course, to the episode at the football ground. Hideous affair but "legally interesting" (I'm quoting Eamonn). Even more interesting, for the victims, I should have thought. So much of the English attitude was that it was anyone's fault but their own.

Well, now that they've a criminal case with no possible get-out, for if they decide to try Harold try him they will, there are editors in London and elsewhere who are trying again to beat the tom-tom about Sovereignty, the rights-of-the-accused, I don't know what-all, all the old bogyman stuff about us being in the pocket of the Germans, so terribly old-fashioned, but what they'd like is that we take the place of India and they would come and Administer our provinces. That in their view being their God-given Mission.

Well, anyhow, hence journalists. Be polite, tell the truth, say you don't know. But he was polite, too, a nice young man and I made him some coffee.

No Henri at lunch either — in the Danish pub, I wondered, with la belle Flamande? And I've rounded up a few of the books Harold wanted, so this afternoon I'll pop in to see him.

At the prison they know me by now. Beaming smiles, and nicely slack about rules. I have a lawyer's privileges, and their two nightmares, escape and suicide, do not occur to Harold. They don't even pat me down, content with a casual glance at my shopping bag. Harold comes, gives me a kiss, an affectionate hug. He's glad to see me, and I think, too, I'm "real" to him. Nothing much else is, even now. Laetitia tells me that with them he shows a bland indifference: is it an act? – a mask? – a psychological fact? That "all this" is academically quite interesting, illustrative of a number of nice points — thesis material? It's all happening to someone else.

I looked up "real" in the dictionary (like Harold). I had it muddled with the Spanish – Latin "regalis", royal: no, Latin "res", the Thing.

He's privileged too. Even for "detainee awaiting trial"

133

(are they going to make up their minds to bring him to trial?) the rules are stretched. They bolt the door at night, yes. He has a biggish cell to himself, I gather, smokes cigars in it, leaves the bed down, and lies on it if so inclined, has a big table with writing materials and books a-plenty, now, has a shower or takes exercise as he pleases, almost. If he were to say (with of course a little contribution to the widows-and-orphans) that he'd like an hour alone with a woman, I almost wonder whether they wouldn't turn a blind eye.

When I used to do this visiting job, years ago, besides my knitting and a bag of sweets, I used to bring a few topics, to interest the people inside, and get them to focus on something actual. They all have this "reality" problem, more or less. I would bone up beforehand, too, on football or the Tour de France. They didn't have television, then.

For Harold I try simply to be alert, or informed. For example, he is much involved in the work of a syndicate of Communauté people who labour to protect the city and environment from bureaucratic excesses of planning and building. Not just architectural and aesthetic monstrosities but the consequences to parking, traffic, pollution – the fabric. Or the coming opera season. Or some happening, absurdly small but with unforeseen comic consequences. Or "a good scandal". At the lowest level a "Belgian joke". I had one today.

"The Belgians decided to go in for space travel. So the Russians have Mars and the Americans have Venus, and so they thought they'd go to the Sun. Somebody complained that this would be too hot. That's all right, they said, we'll go at night." It got a guffaw, which is what it was for.

"An English Minister said the BundesChancellor was Hitler and the French were poodles on a lead."

"What did the French say?"

"Oh, what you'd expect, tnat Brits thought themselves bulldogs and looked more like wet hens." Another guffaw, but he was dull today and withdrawn.

I was dull myself. I hadn't done my homework and my

134

mind was full of that Accès incident (Harold has some interest in the criminology of this, but only moderate. To him it's a "social sideshow"). I made a bad mistake.

"There was a girl among the delinquent children, asking to see Henri. Says she knows you. Flamande crumpet — very pretty, I must say."

Harold went "quite white". I mean it. He's not florid but has normally a healthy, quite high colour. It left him. Eyes glared at me.

"Oh God. Marieke."

"Is that her name?" I'm so slow on the uptake.

"Her name is Marie de Wilde." Tight, hard voice, quite unreal.

I had made a fearful gaffe. "I'm sorry. I didn't know."

We sat there, "looking at each other".

"Vera! Do me a kindness? A great, a personal kindness."

"Of course." I thought it would be "Don't mention this again."

"Take your clothes off."

I'm afraid I "just stared".

"Nobody is going to come in. Nobody will ever know."

It knocked me completely crooked. I turned into an old, wooden clothes-horse. "Harold, have you gone quite crackers?" Soprano, very.

"For the love of God stop talking. Do as I ask."

"You must know it's out of the question." I was standing up; frightened, and clutching my shopping bag.

"Vera, if that means a great deal to you, to me still more."

I suppose that I was remotely beginning to understand, but what use is that? "I won't. Or I can't. Does it matter which?"

He had got himself back in hand. "Go away then, you silly bitch," in a conversational voice.

"By all means." On my dignity. I looked for the shopping bag, which was in my hand.

"Don't go away."

"No."

"Sit."

135

I sat. Why am I holding on to this infernal bag?

"Try and listen then."

Harold's face was burned up with torment, anger, bewilderment. What was happening to him? Well might I ask, and well might he. I hoped he wouldn't drag me round the parlour by the hair. He stared out at the view, which was an exercise yard where a dozen detainees were throwing a basketball. I scuffled with my skirt which seemed tight. I didn't want to be caught with prim knees glued together. Crossed them. Didn't that look still more self-conscious?

"I apologise. You are a trusted and beloved friend."

"So was Iris," rose to my lips and got swallowed.

"That girl sent me out of my mind."

"Not really out of your mind. Off your balance I'll accept."

"Jesus she's turning into a lawyer yet."

"Please don't roar like a bull, the gatekeeper will hear and I mustn't upset his notion of a virtuous and trustworthy *bonne-femme*."

He stopped roaming about, to stretch. "Perhaps it's like this being taken off a heroin habit. You crawl about the floor begging abjectly. They feed you bars of chocolate."

"I've one in my bag if you want it."

"Be thou chaste as ice thou shalt not escape hanging."

"Maybe not, but you'd better settle for the bar of chocolate. I'm not, anyhow, at least I hope not, but whatever I am it's me, I'm sorry."

"Thank you for the law books."

"Tell me what else I can bring, next time. I can't bring you her, you see."

"No. Nor any substitutes. You know – this isn't in the least funny." I stood up. He took two steps, caught hold of my shoulders and enveloped me. He is big, and strong. I didn't fight. I knew he wouldn't try to abuse me. I got a very big kiss in the hollow of the throat, but there was more affection in it than passion. He let go of me gently.

"Dear Vera. You're a great comfort to me."

Before facing the guard I whizzed in to the lav. An

American once said, "A woman who's been laid Looks laid." Well, I hadn't, but I combed my hair a bit, and I had a chiffon scarf in my bag. I hoped that mark on my neck would wear off.

I don't know much. My experience has not been wide. I mean if they just ask, like do you want a second cup of coffee, or still more so if they don't need to ask because the body-talk has made it pretty plain, what becomes of passion? The day after tomorrow you'd want a new one, I'd imagine.

I mean, I can see she's a pretty girl, but what's special about her?

CHAPTER THIRTEEN

Henri Castang

> one day anyone died i guess
> busy folk buried them side by side
> little by little and was by was

Three in the bloody morning, when the phone rang. It always is, or always used to be, and I felt aggrieved that it still was. The extension in the bedroom has the buzzer turned down low, but it went on going brr brr until it poked me awake and by that time even if it is a bloody wrong number one may as well get out of the by-our-lady bed because anything else is nastier still.

"Yes, Castang. Yes, Patricia. Yes you did, but come to the point. Oh dear. Oh hell's delight. Well, isn't that just lovely. No, I don't suppose there IS any alternative. Thanks a lot. I'll have to, I suppose. Keep them quiet until I get there. No, better not call any more police. I'll have to do, at least until it's sifted a bit more. You think it stands up or you wouldn't have called me. No, no, Patricia, you were quite right to ring. But you know the Irishman's curse? May you marry a ghost, and bear him a kitten. Put that in your pipe and smoke it. Yes, about half an hour." I was rewarded by her giggle down the phone. But she's a sensible and experienced woman, and she wouldn't be giving way to hysteria. It was Eamonn Hickey, taught me that one.

Vera had rolled over and was peering with big alarmed eyes from under the sheet.

"Don't worry. But I'd better go down to the Accès house

because it's too much for Patricia to handle and sounds like a nasty mess. It's those two infernal girls. Go back to sleep, and I'll try to be back for breakfast." And there was me. When I got unstuck from my criminal brigade – and how long ago that is, now – I pitied myself no end. And by the sound of it now, it's going to be like I was never away.

As you can imagine, with only two or three full-time people, which is all they can afford to pay, at present, the night-duty thing is a problem, and that's just the time when emergencies blow up. One shuts the door because of drunks, but there has to be a night bell or what's the point of "access"? And with anything up to six or eight brats kipping in the sleeping-quarters, they often get restless or have nightmares. Patricia is a Godsend, one of those valuable women who actually like being up at night, and she's competent. Thirties, post-graduate psycho-socio something, doing a Ph.D. Dryish, thin, flat-breasted female, gipsyish looks, nice eyes – no, no, she's a nice woman and good at this job, and thank heaven for her, say we all. No she would not have got flustered, or called me without good need. She knows very well when to call SOS Médecins. And when to call the cops. Or the fire brigade, and not just because Johnny's got his head stuck in the railings.

I rang the bell with the code to say it's one-of-us; she can press the release from upstairs.

"Yes, Patricia?"

"The little one's asleep, I gave her a pill. She'll do, till morning. The big one's rampaging about, wouldn't calm until I called you. They hitch-hiked in, they said, on a vegetable lorry going to the market, from some village up near Ghent, I gather, but you know more, she says."

"But the father's dead, she claims?"

"Well," said Patricia, cold and dry, "the little one's clothes are covered with blood."

"Ah."

"The big one says she'll tell her story, but only to you. I'll send her down, okay? I have to keep an eye open, up there." She works on her texts, at night.

139

"Hallo Isabelle." She caught me having a shot, out of the staff whisky bottle.

"I want a drink, too." I had better not start with an argument.

"Let me smell your breath."

"I had a schnaps. The driver bought me one, at the market. He said I needed it. Only one, I promise. Cross my heart." Mm, she seemed fairly coherent. I gave her a small one and she threw it down like a truck-driver. She shuddered hard, but she quietened down. I gave her a cigarette which she drew at gratefully. What use to argue?

This girl is sounding, behaving as though delinquent. Or maybe how she thinks delinquents would behave. She looks like a demure missy, nicely-brought-up. In fact, of course children in need, as the euphemism has it, of care and protection can appear sullen and ruffianly, or look perfectly angelic. What they do generally look is dirty. Tattoos or spiky hairstyles, being greased or varnished, when female gaudy cosmetics may or may not accompany this, but the first sign of neglect is dirt. Perhaps, too, I am less immune than is a practising police officer to bad smells: he, or she, gets insensitive to stinks. They'd better.

Surely I remembered this one as windblown, dishevelled? Was the memory accurate? Had I even paid close attention? I had been distracted, unconcentrated, throughout. Her hair was shining clean and in a neat plait tied with a ribbon; her ears and neck – look, I'd be a bit dusty after a couple of hours in a vegetable truck. Her clothes were modest, clean, and unextravagant.

I kept quiet. The bright and breezy "Well Now" is to be avoided. They hate being hustled. I stubbed out the cigarette.

"Got me out of bed then. To listen, was it, or what?"

"I knew how it would be. I Told you how it would be. You didn't Listen. You didn't want to know. You promised to drive us home and it was too much trouble. You wanted to go off drinking in that pub with that man and we could just be paid off with a dollar for ice-cream, wasn't it."

140

Sounding like Lydia with a grievance. If anything, a politer choice of wording.

I can't reproduce all the monologue. That would be graphic, but would take too long. She rambled, and sometimes she froze up, and then again floodgates would open, and by now I was making notes, and spoiled the natural flow because one has to stop them, asking them to go back over a vague or inconsistent point, or looking for some corroborative detail. One will have to "prompt", but one mustn't "suggest". Quite a lot of skill and experience goes into taking a statement. Letting the cheesecloth drip, one of my early teachers put it. "Straining the jam through muslin" Adrien Richard used to say. Two homely, housewives' metaphors. You musn't push, or squeeze. Inevitably, because you're always in a hurry, you do stir a bit.

With money in their pocket they'd hung about, of course, and got home late. Wished it on themselves, you'd almost say: they'd been bellowed at and had their hides tanned.

I was getting a clearer picture of the mother now: this had puzzled me, on the earlier occasion. Belgian, and this marriage with a very traditional-minded man from southern Italy did not work too well. A nice enough woman, too damned concerned about her own freedom. Lazy perhaps, sloppy, self-indulgent? Fille de salle in a hospital a few miles off. These women supposedly do only the domestic chores; cleaning, tidying, serving and clearing meals. Hard work, and they have to be disciplined and conscientious. Inevitably, because of the shortage of trained nursing staff, they are drawn into doing a lot of other work; nursing work. They aren't paid much, the hours are long and there's a lot of unofficial extra responsibility.

She'd do this well, from what I could make out. It became too much of her life, to the detriment of her home and her children. Too much away, keeping her own money, ("I've earned it, haven't I"), hanging about after hours with cronies, "relaxing" in local cafés.

Drinking, gossiping, gambling, maybe too easygoing

141

with the male staff – nothing really wrong and everything wrong.

The man didn't understand it. He got still more rigid and discontented and anxious: this to him was "a bad wife". Two nice people, but neither very bright and too far apart in mentality and upbringing and general attitude. Since his wife was often away he got into the habit of household chores when he got home, cooking meals and looking after the children. Too strictly, too exact and conscientious according to his lights, too wrapped up in them.

You get a vicious cicle then. The wife comes in at all hours, slovenly and smelling of drink, no time for anything but getting herself and her clothes ready for the morrow, often tired and irritable, and impatient with fusspot Italian ways (and there's no Calabrian granny to take the burden off them both). Before you know where you are they aren't sleeping together either, and it's all breaking down. He's increasingly over-strict and exacting with the children. Self-respect becomes fanaticism. The children are disobedient and unreliable, and the real trouble begins. He loves these girls and he loves them overmuch. There's a horrid inevitability. They get whacked – and they're made to strip naked. He's bothering about things which are the mother's job, their clean underclothes and washing their hair properly, and the mother's not bothering enough. Sooner or later the nubile girl will be taking the mother's place in bed.

How recent all this was I could not easily tell. At times in her tale it was yesterday, at times seeming to date further back. You see, these girls are full of modest withdrawals and circumlocutions, and also they come out with farmyard terms picked up from the village boys.

Talking like a cop (but will I ever be anything else?) the caressing is ambiguous and bewildering; being cuddled goes with being beaten.

It is quite possible that he doesn't really know himself where he's headed.

The little sister knew without realising: it's a secret. And the mother? Possibly she had been drunk, to have spoken this brutally. Tired and harassed as well, to do her justice. The child had said something, timidly, and she "hadn't wanted to know". A terrible phrase slips out and cannot be recalled. What can Iris have said, to drive Harold over the edge?

"Fais pas d'histoires, pour ton petit cul sans importance. Make less fuss. Your little behind interests nobody." Working in a hospital, where one gets insensitive to a lot of physiological detail – yes, like a cop. Smell? What smell?

She may have regretted it as soon as said, and been ashamed to admit her wrong. Thus slapped in the face, the child would keep silent, thereafter. The wife sees, and decides not to notice; stays out the more, and longer? These things are cumulative, and one reaction provokes another.

What the little one made of this we'll never know. When too many neutrons are squeezed into too small a compass, you get a chain reaction. Too much happened in forty-eight hours, and the alternance of punishment and what was passing for love was too rapid.

From what I could understand, the children had been under the shower, and washed their hair. The little one had wandered out into the kitchen. The big one had still been in the bathroom, not yet dressed. The bathroom door had been left unlocked.

Lying on the kitchen table was a largish sharp knife. It had been used to trim bacon rind.

I don't know and I'm not about to ask. I should guess that the little one walked in on this. Does she recognise it for what it was, or imagine some new and fearful punishment? But she thinks only of deliverance from torment. The knife was on the table. A wooden handle with a grip cut in, that even a small child can hold firmly. A stiffish triangular blade, and a sharp point.

What have I here? Four pages of notes. But it took me till seven in the morning. Patricia came down and made some coffee, and I went out for fresh bread. I got a moment to telephone to Vera. The child could not unwind, refused to rest. When one of the day people comes on (mornings are the slack time here when one tries to get tidy) somebody will get the girl a medical and put her to bed. And I must hie me to Ghent because – has the mother come home? The police may be looking for these children already. Yes, technically I could have laid it on the cops here. But I couldn't get it out of my mind that last time I hadn't gone back with them.

This man's employer is Marie de Wilde's father.

Raw, all this? Yes; I find it so myself.

When we got into the house, the gendarmerie, a doctor, me, we found that the man had not died at once. He had got as far as the kitchen. The wife had not come home. When found, I dare say, there would be long, angry, incoherent explanations. She wouldn't have wanted to find her own daughter promoted to wife-status. All right. I have also indulged in a lot of self-justification. The girls panicked at the sight of blood and ran. Where to? There wasn't anywhere to run to but me.

So many of them are like this. It wasn't anyone's business. It isn't anybody's fault. So now it's just another stupid muddle. Typical of the poor, the uneducated, the ignorant? No. Incest, if that's the example which comes to mind, that's a crime, is it? A "blood" crime? Thinking is fairly muddled on the subject. Maybe it's a felony, maybe it's merely a misdemeanour. I had better say only that it happens just as often among the educated and the privileged layers of society. Anywhere.

These distinctions are misleading. Like saying that a kitchen knife is not a bourgeois weapon. Well of course Iris (speaking of examples which come to mind) was not a Calabrian peasant. She wouldn't have left knives about because she wouldn't have thought of boning or trimming a piece of bacon. She wouldn't have known how.

I went to see Mr de Wilde.

It's a neat village, in the trim, clean Flanders countryside. Two or three minutes off the Brussel-Ostend autoroute, or five from the train line to Ghent and Brugge. The district is given over to nurseries, so that all

144

the houses have smooth clumps of rose and hortensia, well-behaved examples of suburban conifer. Nothing to shed dead leaves in autumn for the traffic to skid on in wet weather, no awkward branches to come elbowing in at the primly-curtained bedroom window. Even the plants, you feel, multiply by artificial insemination rather than through earthy fornication.

Mr de Wilde has a prosperous business. He has built himself a pleasant villa on the outskirts, with gravel, and lanterns, and illustrations from his catalogue; deutzia and spiraea and a fine weeping laburnum. A notice round the side says "Bureau": push the door and it rings a bell, and the linoleum is highly polished. Beyond was an office and two men with some pale-grey IBM machinery. Mr de Wilde is grey-haired, grey-suited, soft-spoken. A slightly harassed or absent-minded expression as though wondering where the plants have got to, but he has gardener's hands. He is a Flamand, and in a highly competitive business, and it is run by the computer on thoroughly modern lines. He is proud of it, and gives it his entire attention, and sees to it that it runs well. Anything you buy from him will be healthy, hardy, well-shaped, full of happy buds, guaranteed free of any disease or infection, carefully packed, strictly according to the genus, species and hybrid variation described in the catalogue, and at a most competitive price. Flanders is not like Wallon Belgium, which always looks as though left over from the last century.

After meeting him, I did feel I understood Marie just a scrap better.

I did not mention Marie. Perish the thought. He was a nice man, a kindly man, and had quite enough to worry him as it was. He was much disturbed at the appalling news, and asked at once what he could do for the family. He did not – as the gendarmerie most decidedly did – enquire what on earth all this had to do with a French commissaire of police – and ex at that. Flanders, and Wallonie, too, have an immense mistrust of anything coming from Bruxelles, instantly suspected of meddling

145

incompetently in their affairs while simultaneously managing to neglect them. He spoke French quite as good as mine, said "Poor people" a number of times, and was plainly in his mind already choosing and assembling the flowers for the funeral, while composing the death notice to insert in the local paper. "We will guard and respect the memory of a devoted collaborator who served faithfully." He confirmed what I had learned already; the man was a field hand, not very bright, with no real technical qualification. Just a planting, weeding, hoeing and manuring peasant, trundling about with his wheelbarrow. But it's very Difficult to get good, reliable, trustworthy field hands. Especially to work without constant supervision. I sympathised. It's exactly the same in the police.

The gendarmerie said, gruffly, they'd see to the girls. Work, no doubt of it at all, for the Accès office. We'll have cops pouncing in, armed with legal orders, dragging these children off to some orphanage where the holy nuns will see to it they're properly looked after and virtue instilled. Or is there any chance that the mother won't be punished? I feel sure that the hospital authority will stick up for her, and say that whatever calamities she made of her private life, she's a good woman, kind, clean, cheerful and good-hearted. It is also very Difficult to get good staff in any hospital – anywhere. I rather suspect that if the Proc comes down on her and takes the children away with lectures about her unfitness, she'll go to pieces and start smelling of gin on the premises.

I drove home thinking about all this. Thinking about Marie, too.

Mr de Wilde does not rattle round in overalls and a rusty Renault pick-up with tools in the back and old sacks. He has a smartly polished new six-cylinder BMW outside his door, and a smart suit and he shaved this morning. Only his hands still give him away.

La Mère de Wilde is likewise a lady now. I'm sure that she still works hard in the business, knows her customers by name, has that computer well drilled and obedient, misses nothing. She has her house, too, to run. After plenty of hard work all day she'll look forward to the holidays, Austria for the snow in winter, Dalmatia for the sun in summer, and something nice to bring home each time, to adorn her house and keep abreast of the fashions. Smart modern clothes, Ghent once a week to have her hair done, and not too proud to put her apron on if the cleaning-woman's child has the measles.

They've brought Marie up well. Her brother has gone into the business, after a diploma in business administration, and practical stages a year at a time with one of the big growers' firms in Holland and England. Knows German, speaks correct English, has been to the USA and Japan, too, most likely; conjugating the verb I–you–we enlarge our mind. There's nothing of the peasant about the younger generation. Except perhaps an attachment to traditional values and beliefs that may be deeper, grittier, more tenacious than they realise or count upon. I know little about Noel. Marie, who is very fond of her brother, has described him. He appears as a personable, bright, modern young man, secretly hoping that Pa will make his mind up to retire quite soon, since the only thing wrong with this biz is a bit of a generation gap.

Marie went, as a weekly boarder, to the College for Young Ladies, where the holy nuns have high academic standards and are still more exigent about behaviour. Good matric-marks, rewarded by lavish presents from justly proud parents. A year in London for "polish", au pair with a very nice family in Richmond.

But how to get some flesh onto these dry bones? I must try to see her the way I tasted. Awkward word, and I haven't found a better. As she came across? The word "impression" is too tame, too blurry; like a worn-down rubber stamp. Carlotta used to complain about applying this word to painters. "Not what Claude Monet understood by it." The problem of getting light into opaque pigment is indeed alike to my difficulty in getting something as alive as Marie into my tired, stale, bureau-musty words. When she appeared at the Accès house, horribly embarrassed, there was no glow to her at all. The Danish pub, as Vera calls it, suited her better. She'd taken her resolution.

Yes, this is where I have to start, with physical description, painting the background first and then trying to work her into that. Laborious. But I can do no better. And she's worth the trouble. Vera may well sniff at that phrase, but won't jeer.

The pub is dark inside, and chintzy, but well lit by lots of bright brass lamps and brackets. The big vase of flowers on the bar counter is bright, and so are the scarlet uniforms and white shirts of the waitresses. The wooden panelling is dark, but there's a sparkle of good beer and smart service and colourful Danish food. There are two balconies as well as the floor, and little alcoves where you can be in the light of the front windows, or the dimness of the back, as you please, but always comfortable and even as private as you can get in a public place, because the neighbours don't encroach upon one. It was designed by someone with a thoroughly good understanding of café architecture, and that is a great rarity.

Nor is it a place only for the old. Sure, there are plenty of desiccated old ladies and superannuated but natty gents, absorbing cake and coffee, but there are just as many pretty young Bruxelles girls who come to meet exotic and often Arab boyfriends, glamorously overdressed. Marie did not look in the least out of place, and I melted into the background, at least I hope so. To be unnoticed like the salt-and-pepper shakers is the result aimed at.

Marie – I am not going to call her Marieke, that was his name for her and perhaps her village-name as a child – is tallish, slim (the proportions are textbook for a twentieth-century beauty) and ravishing. Sniff, as you please. A great beauty, haute-époque, a Danae or a Europa for Titian. Hair, corn; eyes, sapphire; skin, I haven't seen her undressed; the arms are modern and thus tanned. Bare feet in sandals, no paint on the toenails, I didn't ask her to put her foot on the table. Possibly not very good since few women have good feet. The hands are not painted either, and a bit too thin. But the ears good. No jewellery at all, or not for me. Cotton frock well cut, no emphasis either upon

148

absence of bra or that horrible indecent line when their knickers show through.

So what am I to say, if I am not to run away with myself? That I'm a sober fellow? (I had one of their dark beers; marvellous on a hot day and even in Munich it isn't better.) That I'm not all that susceptible to young girls, even if I am getting close to fifty years of age? That it isn't an erotic stimulus: there's nothing like this in Harold's picture collection. I can't judge of her intelligence, which seems normal, nor of her character, because I don't know her. So that I gave her a standard, even a conventional answer.

"Can I come back to you? I'd like to think about all this, for a couple of days. Have I got your address?"

I was in search of a lawyer because those girls would need one: a Juvenile Court is all very well, but they vary in quality. We know a few who do "access" work, but the one I thought of was on holiday. Looking for another, said to be "in court", I was getting sore feet in that impossible warren of the Palais de Justice when I ran across Laetitia. Now there's an idea. Most of Gregor's work is in civil cases, but she is a criminal pleader. How Mr Quentin Camden (whom God Preserve) will fit in, if and when they bring Harold up to trial, is for her to worry about.

"Buy you a cup of coffee, in the canteen?"

"Can do. I'm finished; it's not a jury case."

"Ever take on any *pro Deo* work?" "For God" is a technical term for legal-assistance cases.

"Upon occasion," warily. I told her about "the girls". She listened, the head cocked, that hard Jewish intelligence following closely.

"Yes, that's quite a headline number. Where is all this? – up in Ghent? Mm, very Flamand. Well, I can do the necessary, whatever's urgent. I can get somebody good to watch it. See how it goes, then. This one of your Accès things, is it? Mm, Castang, you're quite a sentimentalist, aren't you?"

"Indeed I am; it's hard not to let that side of one get atrophied. I quite agree, open and shut, no interesting legal facet, no nice feminist angle, two tiresome little girls who've given me a lot of trouble. If they hadn't been the same age as my own two – purely an emotional involvement. Perhaps it struck me; emotion, instinct, no question of state of mind at all . . . Mr Camden, I take it, has gone back to England?"

"Yes, of course. Nothing's going to happen here till after the holidays. Tough on Claverhouse, but that's his bad luck. They say they're waiting still, for a few expert reports, but they're preparing a case against him, there's no longer any doubt."

"I just may have found you the missing witness."

"Show, show."

"Defend these girls for me, Laetitia. I'm working hard for you and I'm not getting paid. I'm not a cop any more. I'm not bound by any oath to state or institution. What I'm bound by is confidence and I have to think it all over." She nodded; looked at her watch.

"I must fly."

"So must I. See you . . ."

CHAPTER FOURTEEN

Vera Castang

I was none too pleased. Henri pulled out of bed at ungodly hours, running round the countryside after two delinquent girls. This Accès work is valuable and vital, but one mustn't get over-involved. Henri's cop-experience is worthwhile, but he sometimes forgets that he's no longer that sort of state servant, that he isn't paid for it, and that he can't afford to invest so much time and effort in this sort of affair. Do I seem hard? Young girls do get sexually abused. That is appalling, but it's also a historical constant. The Regency in London, the Régence in Paris, oh, any moment you care to look at that's at all documented – full of thirteen-year-old prostitutes.

Heavens, didn't we have enough trouble when he found out about the goings-on in the lycée classes, last year in Paris? Lydia wasn't even involved, save through a couple of her little school friends. But Henri got himself tangled up with the scruples of a doctor and a magistrate, nearly got Lydia into bad trouble, and all for what? Losing his own job, and as I keep telling him, the fact that it was a rotten job and not one he wanted is irrelevant. He counters this by telling me to have-a-look, we got This job as a result, and now we're sitting pretty. Pure accident. Would I have let professional life make an impact on my personal affairs, if I hadn't been emotionally upset by a nasty experience of my own? Where does one draw the line?

Hard question. He gets involved, and I get cross, but if

one doesn't get involved – then one turns into yet another parasite. Prudent cowardly egoists are not in short supply. The lily-livered, as Henri calls them. No stomach for getting their feet wet.

He's quite right. I know it, but I keep arguing, because it frightens me.

And who or what is this ravishing blonde that he's running after? Nasty-minded, petty, jealous woman. I know perfectly well that the man I love and trust is not snuffling behind my back at luscious young girls. But I know, too, what suckers men are at this age.

Henri has just come home. He has been to a village in Flanders, where those two children come from. Bad news; the younger has killed her father. Incest with the sis, a horrid tale.

He was right to take trouble. Children's courts can be good, and can be – he's got Laetitia to look after it; good.

I'm going to twist his arm about the blonde.

The blonde, I must say this great beauty, is or has been Harold Claverhouse's mistress. Yes, I had pieced that much together. And she's extremely worried about this; I am not surprised. A Flamande and a Jansenist; rather like me. A very Catholic upbringing and I can sympathise. There are plenty of parallels between Slovak peasant girls and this Marieke; another peasant even if in Flanders – they're all bourgeoisie now, and rich.

So that now I feel personally involved. But I am blocked, too. Henri has told me.

This is not easy: one is told things in confidence.

Marieke met him in the Danish pub. Irony; the place I had suggested. She told him her story in confidence. Am I now going to break this? For Harold confided in me, and am I going to break that? Even to Henri. That he asked to make love to me? I had determined to say nothing.

Marie is in a hideously tormented state, because since learning of Iris' death she blames herself for it. Yes, I see her point.

But what am I to do? I can tell Henri. But can I tell Laetitia?

I wonder whether I am being over-simplistic.

Is it so grotesque to think that Harold cannot bring himself to speak about this girl Marie? Literally to utter, form words? Was that offer, to make love to me, a way of telling me so? It is so, so preposterous, in any other light.

Harold is not going to speak of this to Henri. Or the lawyers. But might he overcome the barrier and talk to me? I am the only other person with access to him.

Accès – isn't it the same trouble that we always have? To persuade them to talk. Their problems seem to them so tangled, so impenetrable.

This amalgam is not very clever. The constant factor is immaturity. They are by no means all unintelligent, if the general level is pretty low. A miserable emotional state – there's always a family problem. How can there be any parallel with a man in his fifties, highly sophisticated, very brilliant, a senior international bureaucrat, a distinguished jurist – dear God how inadequate I feel.

I can but try. He listens to music, can I bring him some tapes? For somebody as operatic as Harold – yes, but what hits the right chord? Not Mozart surely – too urbane, too tempered and balanced, and equally surely not Berg or Janáček, and Perish The Thought of Wagner. But a nice piece of Verdi – Falstaff, say? And then standing in the shop like a fool, an idea struck. Marie de Wilde, and Princess Eboli, have both made the discovery that being very pretty is the quick road to misery. They share the fatal gift.

Have I perhaps got that much right?

These scribblings have been gushing and incoherent. Now, I am breathing a little easier. Writing it down is supposed to clarify. These are not supposed to be passages from a schoolgirl's diary, whatever they sound like.

Verdi was a success. Harold much more himself, buoyant and talkative.

"Don Carlos, splendid stuff. Philip the Second among one's favourite historical characters. To think of him all by himself in the Escorial, worried out of his mind, the whole

153

of Europe on his back, reading and annotating every single diplomatic report. You know legend has it that Philip himself had Eboli walled up in the convent for playing him false. One needs perhaps to have been in prison oneself to understand all this."

"You aren't walled in, Harold. Philip walled himself in. It isn't necessary." I was determined to take this bull by the horns. "If you want to talk about it you can." He was looking at me oddly. Relieved, if anything. I don't like dramas, even grand ones by Verdi. I am not about to launch into an aria about any fatal gift of love. "I'm sorry to have behaved so badly, last time. I apologise. Can you talk about it, at all? I'd be happy, if you did." English has good curt phrases. For example, looking like you'd "lost a quid and found a tanner". Then why not sometimes the contrary? Scrabbling in the gravel for a dropped sou, and come up with a gold napoleon. One can wake from a nightmare that had seemed interminable, and find that the real world is not that bad after all.

Harold lit a cigar. He drew at it awhile, turning it and watching it until it was going nicely, even all round. "Shut your eyes," he said suddenly.

"I was giving one of those talks; och. 'Aspects of Sovereignty' you know, British Council stuff for university students. I really don't recall what: can it have been German Unity? She'd remember, no doubt; if asked.

"These are fairly well-worn numbers, there's not a great deal of juice in them. Officially approved, the public relations service of the Community likes it, professors like it, there's often a *vin d'honneur*, drinks and you mingle, after the show.

"So that there's nothing unusual about a girl looking you in the eye and saying something intelligent about Flanders. Speaking quite good English, and then getting out of her depth and reverting to French. You ask a few things yourself out of polite interest, it's a pharmacy student being open-minded, deciding she ought to know something about political economy, why not go and listen to the Efficient Baxter lecturing? Maybe he'll be funny.

154

"But you're not interested in the how, are you? Just the why."

I was listening to it from a long way away, a slow, light voice pausing to make room for the cigar and for being dispassionate.

"There's not, in fact, a shortage, ever, of young girls doing tricks to draw attention to themselves. You play a little game? Flirt with them a little, friendly, unserious, you aren't ever going to see them again; of course now and then one sets her cap. And what do you do then, you make your choice, you don't have any emotional involvement, and then as long as you stay away from the ones who do . . . hm? But that's more fiction than fact. If you have a relationship already, something profound, given and received . . . Suchlike have a way of being tougher in life than in fiction.

"Some women, they say, are elegant and detached and intelligent and funny about it all. Not the ones I know, they aren't.

"You knew Iris, didn't you. You'll have known that she was a woman of unusual qualities, and of remarkable character.

"Not going to say any more. Not going to say that Iris did this or Iris did that, nor more to the point what she didn't. Not here to defend herself. In parenthesis, that was a thing she was extraordinarily skilled in. Not perhaps in a lawyerly or forensic sense of the term."

I did want to open my mouth there, to say something like We have need to be. But I didn't.

"Not going to talk about myself either. To say I'm good at this or I'm bad at that. Supposed to be an adult, when all is said. Confine myself to one remark since that you know already. Having made a monstrous ass of myself, last time you were here. Felt admiration then, you handled it well. That I have physically a powerful appetite. Like to eat and drink. Like to make love. Possible to say, then, in passing, Iris was a woman quite normally constituted. Man comes to you snivelling about his wife being frigid, tells you more about the man than about the woman.

155

"However, no news to you, very likely, woman at menopause age, number of upheavals, psycho as much as physiological. All quite commonplace, all discussed openly and sensibly, any woman's magazine knows how to handle that.

"Talk about Marie, instead? Shy away from a difficult subject, hm? Find yourself there, out of the frying-pan maybe, and your ass on the fire. The thing about Marie, she set a very high value on herself.

"I don't know how well you know her."

"I don't know her at all," I managed to say. "She came to my house. She wouldn't talk to me. She may talk to Henri. I don't know, he hasn't told me."

"Henri is no sort of fool." Harold's voice and manner changed completely. This was the businesslike Harold.

"The one essential thing is that this mustn't get out. Seal her off, Vera. No lawyers, no journalists. I must not allow a second innocent woman to suffer.

"Marie thinks she's coming to my aid. It must be stopped. There's no real damage been done to her. Young, intelligent, heart as well as head. Nobody need know.

"I don't have to tell you: my thought is not to protect myself. That is clear enough: foolish, irresponsible, in the end criminally so, I must answer for this.

"It's right that you should know. You know so much already, and I can trust you."

"As far as I know from the lawyers," it was the truth as I knew it then, "there isn't any real case against you. The Procureur is lukewarm. Because of, oh, politics; scandal and bad publicity. Not the moment to be seeking a conflict between the government and the Communauté. You'll know all that better than me. But if you'll just stay quiet and keep patient.

"You know – working out a face-saving formula."

Harold was smiling, I suppose at my innocence.

"That's as may be, my dear. On my own account, I should try to do a little better than that, shouldn't I?" He examined his cigar which was showing signs of neglect.

156

Giving it a skilful poke, so that it would burn up afresh. The traditional male, 'smoking-room' world of the Victorian era, where women had no place but the men understood each other. The English going Erm, while administering their Empire. I've read about it. As long as India was six months away, sailing ship round the Cape, everything was fine. But as soon as the Suez Canal was pierced, and the Memsahib arrived – ruin.

"No, have to look it in the eye, I corrupted that girl." Was Harold sillier than he looked? One of those men balanced in all their other views who become uncontrollably silly at whatever point of contact with young girls? My face was looking acid? Perhaps, because a glance at it drew a glimmer of a smile.

"Oh technically . . ." with a look at the cigar and reassured to find there was plenty left, "fifty-fifty you could call it, as to Seduction. She's the type to find older men attractive. But there's no watering it down. A basic answerability."

"As long as you don't grovel, breast-beating." One of his likeable traits is catching on fast.

"Mm yes, Italian pictures in great number if dubious authenticity, Saint Jerome waggling a big stone and a pious beard in reproof of the Fiend. Hardly, hardly.

"Know the Danish pub, do you? Met her there a couple of times. Not at all lascivious. Can you think why I should give rope to it, to so absurd a — well, Iris, you know, Iris . . ." Pain alters a voice, one doesn't need to see the face. "Iris never stopped arguing. Challenged every damn thing." It had changed again into a voice slightly querulous, saying the ashtray hasn't been emptied. He did not wish to complain – to a woman – of his wife. "Every conversation a confrontation, it becomes so damned tiring."

"Yes. Female trait." Henri also gives way to exasperation.

"Marie's a level-headed girl. That's very Vlaamsch, all that hard common sense. When she doesn't know, she shuts up. There isn't all that backchat, because they have to show themselves certain.

157

"Oh well, yes, she also seduced me. Food, you know. We won't say dainty little dinners.

"Poor Iris. She was a rotten cook.

"Being Irish, probably."

"Peasant food?" I asked. I had to laugh at this, because Henri is the same. Men who eat out a lot in restaurants get the hankering for stew like granny used to make. There are pubs in Bruce where one can get Flamand food, but they're apt to be crowded, noisy and smelly. After a bad day in the criminal brigade, Henri used to crash in screaming for my own distinctly rustic efforts. And I do see Marie (with a mother proud of her own clean kitchen) shyly offering one of her unexpected talents.

"She has a little flat back of the Sainte-Cathérine. Those old well-built houses which have gone slummy, cheap because they're full of Turks. I don't mean a studio. One big room with a bath behind a curtain and a kitchen corner anywhere. Dad paid the rent because it's too far to get home except at weekends." Yes, I know, I've been a student too. "Can be very attractive a room like that," tailing off lamely.

But I know. Not for oneself they aren't; it's such a struggle to keep them clean. But given some oddments from junk shops, plenty of posters and a few pots of geraniums (there are often lovely big windows once one gets the dirt of centuries scrubbed off) and plenty of handy bits of curtain, these squalid quarters can look wonderful to an eye accustomed to bourgeois comforts. Yes, I remember Prague. To the romantic eye, but Harold's is an English and a very romantic eye.

"So I brought some bottles of wine. And determination hardened to get her into bed."

"Mm. Make a fuss about that, did she?" Spitting it out was plainly going to include details of female anatomy which leave my own temperature fairly hivernal. But there was no stopping him now.

"Vera, I beg of you, don't be cynical." Said with dignity. I felt ashamed, because from what I've seen of Marie she does have dignity.

158

"Never have I known Anything as difficult as getting that damned girl's clothes off." Highly querulous and then at once seeing the unconscious humour of his own situation.

A man — of, I suppose, any age — is earnestly single-minded in pursuit of this particular object. Not really able to laugh about it at the time. Henri keeps telling me how humourless I am. So look at it, Vera, with a painter's eye. Cheap — but nice — rug on a bare, stained wooden floor (Bulgarian, wool and cotton). Curtain of faded but pretty old brocade, concealing primitive washing appliances. Bed formerly a sofa, narrow and uncomfortable; one had got accustomed to odd lumps and hollows. Prague wouldn't be that much different to Bruce. The difference was that I'd had sense enough never to get caught alone there by a boy. There weren't these tremendous wrestling matches with my countrified and shabby underthings. But lamps, one went in rather for lamps. Wine of much better quality than the Hungarian plonk featured at our parties. A good many girls did get their clothes pulled off. Not mine, but at gym school as much emphasis got put on the values of Stalinist virginity as at home in Slovakia. I do remember what a delight it was losing mine to Henri. Yes, I can sympathise with Marie.

At art school, naturally, it was fashionable to take one's clothes off and not wait to be asked. And lovely, by lamplight, as well as paint-light, they did look. Lots of Bonnard, not to speak of Modigliani. So yes, I can sympathise with Harold, too. You can see through Marie's clothes, a lovely plastic body. But I won't write down the heated lyricisms Harold had to wrench out of himself. Tearing himself up in the parlour of the House of Detention. I would have to be very insensitive not to see the charcoal sketches of Marie's breasts, her bottom, the articulation of the magical curve in that muscled, tendoned space between her thighs. The shrine, or just a rhythmically complex area, for dancers say, or for anybody drawing the female body. It is not just the Hole in

159

the Wall. I myself am about as lesbian as the Brandenburger Tor, but my mind does not turn simply to childbearing.

Art is about this – this obsession? The word is all wrong; Harold is trying to find words and my hand is fidgeting for a pencil. This word "plastic"; to a Czech it does not just mean Semtex explosive.

Harold is trying to get rid of all the literature, the rhetoric, the dishonesty; the shields and pretences it is so difficult to abandon. But all he's really telling me is that Marie's triangle was something of intense beauty.

Which it often isn't and my pencil has faced the innocent problem of putting it in, leaving it out, or drawing a shadow. Flamande girls (I found an excellent model when we were living in northern France) have fine, sparse hair which does not obliterate the line. Harold is telling me about this in detail: yes, I know.

And yes, when one is a man, and that tiresome penis, difficult to draw because easy to idealise, becomes the petrified giant, the difference between life and art, worrying at the best of times (making Flaubert's parrot feel awfully sick) . . . oh dear, Henri reading this will be in stitches of laughter. "Oh my poor dear Vera."

Harold is the same. He doesn't know whether to laugh or be sick. Whatever the lurid adjectives left in or kept out (like the triangle), whether we conjugate that simple verb to fuck in the indicative, subjunctive, or imperative modes; life and art both become abstract. It's difficult to talk about "crime" in this metaphysical context. The Japanese drawings of joined couples – better, the linear scratches on Greek vases of a man with a stand and a girl with her thighs apart – are they bad art? Wagner's music to *Tristan* – is that bad art?

I must have been making faces; at least what Henri calls "wearing an expression", because Harold said abruptly, "Tell you a story. A very old German story. Highly moral. The teacher said to the class of small children, 'Name a flower.' A little girl held up her hand and said, 'Primrose.' 'Good,' said the teacher, 'and *schön, schön.*' Another little girl said 'Poppy.' 'Very good. And *schön, schön.*' And a little boy at the back put his hand up and said, 'Sexual Intercourse.' 'But that isn't a flower.' 'Maybe not,' says the little boy. '*Aber schön, schön.*' "

Oh dear, invariably I get caught; I am the perfect pigeon.

A pity one cannot tell this story to the Judge of Instruction. This unmitigated pest has sent for me, and my heart is in my mouth rather. I have seen him before, of course, because I am "a witness". It was to my house that Harold came, after going home and finding Iris there on the floor, and it was in my house that he stayed, more or less gibbering, while Henri went to see what reality there could be in this frightful tale, before ringing up the police. So that the Judge examined me pretty closely on facts; timings; states-of-mind: what did he say and how did he look when he said it.

A youngish, thorough, earnest man. Polite, nowise hostile, but it's a session with the dentist's drill. I could tell the truth then? First because I do. Second because Henri has taught me that there are two sorts of liars. The ones who lie all the time, systematically, who know that you know, and who just don't care. And the ones who tell a teeny, little cover-up lie. Who get caught, because an instructing judge is exhaustive, has dozens of cross-bearings, and gets a fix on you.

And then I knew nothing. Now I know a lot, which Harold has told me, and he has told in confidence, and I have given my promise, not to tell, ever.

So that this time I was frightened. The Judge was sitting in shirt sleeves. The sun was on that side of the Palais and it was hot in there. He stood up and shook hands, smiled, pointed to the chair, pulled the "dossier" about, extracting bits and mulling, with some sotto voce mumble and pencilling annotations and sometimes pushing his pencil into his neat curly hair. While I sat stewing. It's one of their techniques.

"I beg your pardon. It's that I'm going on holiday

161

shortly, and I'm anxious to get this wound up before I go. So were there any gaps or holes?" tapping the pile with the pencil, while his clerk sat at her typewriter, staring out of the window and probably thinking of her shopping list, waiting to be switched on. "I have one or two points of enquiry about Mrs Claverhouse, aspects of her character and personality, you knew her quite well."

"But very briefly."

"Quite. We'll be quite brief."

I felt a bit damp round the armpits, but it was with relief. The rhyme is unintentional, but fits. A sort of couplet, huh? Iris, yes. That proud, secret, awkward, tied-up woman. Whom I suddenly felt I could know, and like, and understand, that afternoon when she let her hair down and talked about Ireland. But I must be careful, and very much on my guard. Judges of Instruction are a Pouncing sort of race.

CHAPTER FIFTEEN

Henri Castang

all by all and deep by deep
and more by more they dream their sleep

One or two things stand out in that month of July; month
of bright sun, sky as blue and blank as the eyes of the little
German girls in Vera's "schön" story. Petra, Clarissa,
Gundula. Vera . . .

Because yes, I've heard the story now. She had to tell it
me, and it didn't break any confidences, because I'd heard
all the other side, you see, from Marie, yes. We've had
sessions in the pub, over a beer, and very politely and
nicely she has asked me to come and see her "flat". Only
the one room but a big one. Big windows and a rickety
little balcony, nice solid old house behind the fishmarket.
Bang in the centre of town, would cost a fortune but for
the street being full of Arabs. So, oh yes, I've seen this
"Tatort", too. Do not imagine that I have seen Marie with
no clothes on: I have not. But I have imagination, too. Not
perhaps the same sort as Vera's. Mine is slightly more
carnal. But Marie is a very ladylike and well-brought-up
girl, out of the most self-respecting sort of Flamand
family.

Other episodes stand out. Meeting Laetitia, to set up
some strategy for those two village-girls, because though
this is technically a murder trial, and thus Cour d'Assize,
even a court realises that this is a show trial; juveniles. And
there is urgency; one can't leave children like that hanging

163

about. So they'll come up immediately after the holidays, and Laetitia is organising. But she makes me pay the price, dammit. I wish I hadn't told her about the "missing witness". That was before I knew about Marie – or Harold's tale to Vera. Laetitia is unduly keen about all this. We had glasses of tea, Jewish for the hot weather, in her cool expensive office building. Orange-blossom weather here, too, in Bruce, but in a fuggy, humid way that even a tough Jewish lawyer complains about. Lot of bargaining going on. Laetitia wants me as an "expert witness" for the girls. I'm not any expert witness, and don't want to be, haven't any intention of being, told her so, ex-cop and staying that way. Tricky, lawyerly, tea-drinking cow. She has all sorts of ways of twisting one's arm.

They, she tells me, will be "bringing up Claverhouse". When? Soon. The instruction is "just about finished" and the Proc is talking about a certain celerity; i.e. slap the trial through, to avoid any journalists, especially English ones, being snide about leisurely Belgian justice. Another grievance for Laetitia; everybody having holidays and here's me run off my feet. "These little girls are troublemakers," (don't I know it), "and will you just look at the calendar, I'm supposed to be pleading in Bruce and running to Ghent practically the same minute, I should never have agreed to represent these infernal children."

The process, making every bone in my body ache, is known as bending me to her will.

Standing out are visits to Harold. For these are not so frequent now. It's Vera who's kept up the steady rhythm. And Suarez is a much harder taskmaster than Harold, largely because he knows so much less about the subject. She reports that Harold's calmer these days – hard to imagine him placid. But hot weather notoriously hits hardest those in prison: it's always the time of year when they get up on the roof and throw broken tiles at the police.

He won't say anything about Marie. I understand; his confiding in Vera (who won't discuss the subject either, beyond telling me to lay off) must have been a huge effort.

So much was at stake; his own self-esteem; his position as a senior Community official; his standing as my superior in our own pyramid. So that talking with him, I stick to technical matters. Work; the tactful handling of Mr Suarez. The lawyers will have told him that we're confident of getting him a non-lieu, technical jargon for discharge. Nothing can be proved. None of the medical (nor, I'm told, the psychological) expertise is conclusive. Mr Camden will let off some fireworks in court, the President will go through face-saving manoeuvres, justice will appear to be seen to have been done. And then the Communauté will clasp Harold to its bosom and it will all have been forgotten in another month. The gossip will be that there must undoubtedly have been an intruder who used unconscionable violence in keeping poor Iris quiet. Experience has taught me that the police are cast as scapegoat in such circumstances: they must have been lazy, incompetent, bribed, or all three. Mertens must be as used to that as I was. But it's all forgotten inside a week.

A lethargy, probably heat-induced, had overcome him when I did come bustling in full of glad cries; he didn't want to talk about anything much, save perhaps the Tour de France. That's all right, I'm a great expert on the Tour, as pretty near as anyone French or Belgian is, at least while in the Café de Commerce (and all of Italy, Spain, and Holland, too.) It's the great spectacle of the year, since going up and down mountains makes hair-raising television. A downhill run, on the bicycle, filmed standing on the back of a motorbike with the speedometer on a hundred-an-hour, puts any gangster car chase to shame. But it's the climbing, naturally, which captivates the imagination of the onlooker. Harold had never seen a Tour before and was transported.

"The appalling heat. The thirst. The terrible dramatic failures. '*Il faut savoir souffrir.*' To know how to suffer," he repeated thoughtfully. "This can be horrible to watch, one's cast as a sado-maso voyeur."

"We're broken to it as children. Much like bullfighting, but there's no blood, thank heaven."

165

"Heroic struggles, *mano a mano*, like Hector and Ajax. And moments of pure farce. A Spaniard made a fantastic sprint climb on the Causse Noire, and all he could say at the top was 'My mother told me I was a lazy bugger.' One is stupefied."

I had to laugh.

"Yes, the chief problem is that it spoils one for every other spectacle. The utter bogosity of football, the triviality of tennis – ashes in the mouth; the one thing left possible to watch is pure skill, like snooker."

"They Maintain," said Harold with huge glaring eyes. "Even when it's excruciating. It can burn like a hot iron, inside the mouth, the soles of the feet – asphyxia, the lungs give way."

"Yes and the arse, too," I said, being cheerful. "All those hours on a saddle like half of a broken razor-blade – frightful anal fistula."

Harold recovered his sense of humour. "I found – the most extraordinary sight – Pedro Delgado. Wanting to win and – apparently quite deliberately – preventing himself from winning."

"He's an extremely odd character. Threw it away last year for five minutes lost on the startline. Said he'd gone for a cup of coffee and forgotten it was so late. Psychological complications, very Spanish."

"I must think about this," said Harold with great seriousness.

Vera got a note from the Judge of Instruction, bidding her attend, because obviously he's winding his alarm clock prior to going on holiday. So that I wasn't surprised to get one too. I found him calm, as though fairly content with the job done, while feeling pretty sure that it's been a waste of time. Courteous, and formal.

"Have you anything to add, Monsieur Castang, to your depositions as previously made? Or anything you'd like to alter?"

"Not that I can think of. Or recall. Don't believe so, no."

We're all agreed; the entire question of Marie de Wilde

is better kept from the children, to use a Camden phrase. Suppressed for her sake quite as much as for Harold's. Nobody would ever persuade the public that it was something more than just Sex. It didn't figure in the police reports. Harold – whatever else – had been discreet.

"Well," I said blowing in brightly like the nurse of a morning with her trolley full of Instruments, "Only a couple more weeks and we'll have you out of this."

"So they tell me," said Harold. "I don't know that I regard it as time misspent. To a certain extent wasted, that's inevitable. Quite an invigorating experience, if it didn't go on too long. Rather to be recommended, I'd say, for all those people terrified their accents will give away their social origins. Infinitely preferable of course to an English boarding-school. Even indispensable for people like you and me, interested in the processes of penal law. If you aren't a cop, be a prisoner. I have betimes felt envy of your professional background. Ever been to jail?"

"Been close a couple of times. Plenty of cops get thrown in and a great many more deserve to – nearly all, come to think, at one time or another."

"To perceive the nature of the punishment," said Harold slowly. "This of course has been a piece of cake. I have been vastly, immoderately privileged. Not like Captain Dreyfus, or maybe Oscar Slater. Some social stigma will always attach. One will always be seen, by a lot of worthy people, as the man who killed his wife and got away with it because the Belgians didn't want to embarrass the Community. But one goes on being privileged. Like Nato, everybody talks about reducing the troop strengths, but nobody suggests sacking a hundred or so superfluous admirals."

"Come, come; this is cynicism."

"I'll be dining out on it, no? Man who killed his wife in order to gain practical experience of various penal processes like the Assize Court which he thinks stand in need of reform."

"Now you're acting."

167

"Of course I am," wearily. "We all are. All that bothers me really is how my children view the matter . . . Ever tell you about my father, did I? I was ashamed of him for many years. An old Radical — had no more use for socialists than he had for the Tory Party. Hopelessly individualist, he despised and loathed unions. The sort of artisan who worked ninety hours a week and still called himself a free man. Got most of his education in the public library, but one mustn't sentimentalise it: he never did. Refused to be sorry for anybody because he was never sorry for himself. Valuable old boy. My children are avoiding me and I wonder how long they'll keep it up. I can understand, because I did the same to him. Rather trying, the old boy, to talk to. But I like thinking about him, now."

One doesn't know people, ever.

Interpellation: Eamonn Hickey

That's right: if I were seeking a literary parallel it would be from *Treasure Island. Narrative continued by the Doctor: the Jollyboat's last trip.* Not that it will be as exciting (my sister, in moments of stress, used to say, "You take the gun Trelawney, you're the best shot.")

But he's an honest chap, Castang, and like a nineteenth-century novelist he wants a Narrator, and he can't narrate what he doesn't know (unlike Conrad in *Chance* who cheated abominably over episodes that Marlow couldn't possibly have witnessed).

He hasn't told me but I think he's preparing a sort of paper about this whole business. It would be a kind of professional viewpoint to illustrate his ideas (Harold's ideas?!) about reforming the criminal law.

He is a witness in this trial, so two aspects appear here. One is technical: a witness can't sit about in the courtroom before he's called. Evidently, for he might pick up notions there which would colour his statements or even prompt him to change them. After his release from the witness box

168

he can take a place if he pleases among the public. The same applies to Vera. Who as I gather is contributing to this "paper". An old hand at this game, he has worked out that he won't be called before mid-morning, and there may be interesting things to observe before then. So he has asked me to sit in, to cover a small gap in his narrative. I would have been coming anyhow. I'm a Celt, I like trials.

Castang, as I gather, has a sort of watching-brief for the Community (which naturally, having a big bum and a tender one, doesn't want to find itself suddenly sitting on a pin). On a number of social occasions, and even in the office once or twice, we have discussed this second aspect of things. Me, I'd work it up, if I had that sort of talent, into a crime novel. We both hold the conventional notion of "crime novel" in some derision. But as I said – I'm a Celt, a romantic. I suppose that this romanticism played a rôle in urging me to take up the law as a profession. It's a dusty subject, but the other side of a Celt's nature gets a sort of satisfaction out of it. Back in *Treasure Island* days I loved all the picturesque ceremonial and nomenclature, I rolled words like "Procurator-Fiscal" and "Lord Justice-Clerk" around upon the tongue of my imagination. Very like dear old Stevenson. And today as an adult, asked to put my finger on the finest piece of crime fiction I can think of, I'd not hesitate. *Weir of Hermiston* – it has absolutely everything. Or am I being "Celt"?

This daydreaming passed the time. Lawyers began to appear, opened briefcases, took out pieces of paper and frowned at them, exactly like businessmen on planes, puzzled: "Simply can't think how this got into my bag." They yawn, make faces, scratch, whisper; now like badly-behaved schoolchildren in church. I do not know why my Celtic imagination presents all the women lawyers as preparing to sit upon the lavatory: the combination of black robe and white bottom is somehow irresistible. There seem a lot of them and I suspect they've come to see the Englishman's wig. There he is, head together with that tall, statuesquely handsome Jewess.

Now the Press, bustling in with its knowing look of never

budging from the bar before the last possible second. And here sure enough is the Huissier, that mediaeval beadle, a wide-armed ecclesiastical movement to lift our asses off the bench and the lips framing "Stand" before intoning "La Cour". The "rather dirty Wykehamist" as Betjeman put it, "broad of mind and broad behind". And here come the judges befurred and splendid like the Lord Mayor, as usual clutching great dossiers looking too heavy for them to carry.

Surprise number one and quite a big one, a court dominated by females. The assessors are men, but the President is a woman, a big square dominant Flanders face, florid with good living but agleam with intelligence, authority and Hanoverian majesty. An Archpriestly "Sit" before taking her hat off and running a big competent paw flashing with rings through short grey hair. And languidly smoothing her skirt into the throne of the Prosecutor is not Coninck's long nose, distinguished and slightly impotent greyhound looks, but a tall beanpole wearing the red robe and ermine with ease and elegance. Curly neck-length hair between fair and grey, long clever eyes, biscuit-coloured face with a slash of lipstick to match her robe across a wide mobile mouth. A handsome woman and a dangerous-looking one, which makes two of them. One's brow knits a scrap; does this portend any trouble for Harold? Simply that the Court is going to take it all more seriously than we have been led to believe? Or what? Harold has been produced, as prescribed by regulation, between gendarmes all shiny boots and funny hats, but not handcuffed (I should hope not, indeed). Looks well; not in a suit or tie, in which he would have looked deplorably like a peculating financier extradited from the Bahamas, but an open-necked shirt nicely ironed by good careful Vera and a stomach rather slimmed in plain brown trousers. A little bow to the Court, quiet and modest; excellent impression.

As is their disconcerting way, instead of getting on with it the Court starts muttering about legal quillets. I have difficulty in catching the meaning at first until the

President's voice, quiet but resonant and beautifully audible baritone, settles the matter: Mr Camden QC is being presented and accepted. He speaks French, well and with a good accent (Westminster School, no doubt). The usual little English error; he says "Madame la Présidente": saying "Madame le Juge" sounds illogical to an English ear.

"There is no difficulty. The Court takes note of the presence of a distinguished member of the English Bar. It is common form that witnesses who do not speak our language are provided with an interpreter. Following practice established at international congresses, to enable counsel to address the Court freely, it has been agreed that simultaneous translation facilities be made available to the jury and the officers of the Court. These facilities have been extended to the press benches. It is regretted that these for technical reasons are not available to the public. This will not be seen as an infraction of the rule that justice be open and comprehensible. That lies within my discretion. The Parquet assents? The defence assents? Very well."

Public mutters a bit, but for heaven's sake, they're all well used to it by now; happens every day, television doing a voice-over for Russians or whoever, let's move along, yes, Harold's curriculum vitae, in detail. Madam Chairman friendly, courteous, informal.

"The word is given to the Ministry-Public." And up gets Mrs Beanpole, hiplessly slim, long lovely legs and high-heeled shoes as well. Pleasantly feminine, but not a whisper of bulge in that lean abdomen. Her voice is tenor, unimpassioned; there are no emotional-contralto effects: well-trained it floats effortlessly around the courtroom, whose wooden panelling and coffered ceiling make for fairly unencumbered acoustics.

There's been, of course, no How-Say-You, Accused, Guilty or Not. In European courts the preliminary instruction and the filtering through the Chamber of Accusation give everyone to understand that the matter has been gone into at exhaustive length, and that there is

171

definitely a case to answer, or we wouldn't be wasting the Assize Court's time. This leads uninstructed observers used to Anglo-Saxon procedure to conclude that the accused is thought guilty and must prove himself innocent. This is prejudice, though a bad tribunal can show itself biased. A prosecutor still has to prove his case, to the satisfaction of a jury and professional judges, in open court and in fair manner. And her manner was eminently fair, conspicuously moderate. The wide mouth seemed sometimes to sketch a faint smile, but that may have been its unusual flexibility. Her fingernails are not painted. She's a good forty-five. I don't know why, but I have the impression she'd warm up a good deal in bed; am I being Celt?

"I will not have it thought that I should seek to damage a distinguished Community servant. A jurist, to officers of this court an illustrious confrère. This does not absolve me from the duty towards clear sight and objective word. Does that create a pressure? You will hear more of this word, and it will be well to ask yourselves what true weight or value you should attach to it. You may ask whether political or diplomatic bargainings can influence judicial process, and to what degree these so-called pressures are media-inspired, designed to feed an avidity for the sensational.

"In front of us is a death, a death induced by violence; a fact in itself sensational. To hear of it creates a sense of shock. To meet with it, to be an ocular witness of the result, increases this shock. Such a sight, the fact is undisputed, can bring about a sense of outrage, to an extent a doctor will term traumatic, which is to say that the normal senses of eye or ear become perturbed and even to a degree where a witness is no longer reliable in his description of what he has experienced, nor what he has done. You will look at Mr Claverhouse here and you will see him as an able and intelligent man, trained in wise judgement and prudent forethought and you will be quite right. You will hear witnesses to his achievements and abilities, and also to a delicately-balanced nervous system, to hair-trigger sensibilities and, it may be, susceptibilities.

"You will hear the experienced officers of the criminal

172

brigade testify that the sight of this dead woman was indeed exceedingly shocking and might well bring about a momentary but grave imbalance in his state of mind, which could lead them to throw doubt upon his account, and that, in fact, they did not place great reliance upon his words. You will hear that questions formed themselves in the minds of the judicial authority. Some of these questions remain unanswered. We are here to try to arrive at the answers, and you to judge whether they are true answers."

As you notice, Henri, I took her down in shorthand, but it would be pointless to quote her at length, and indeed if you wanted that you could always get access to the verbatim transcript made by the court stenographer. You asked me rather for impressions made or given; imprinted on the mind of the listener which weren't to be found in transcripts. She was effective, moderate which made her presentation the more telling; built her arguments in logical sequence: impressive. She reviewed the medical and psychiatric reports, to wit that the marks on the throat were inconsistent with a claim of accident, and that HC was/is perfectly in his right mind; gave good, lucid legal definitions of traumatic amnesia and the doctrines of temporary insanity; reviewed the statements by Mertens and yourself (one could see that she was going to give you a roughish passage . . .)

But then she got on to Iris, and her state of mind – that this was in the highest degree relevant. I knew that she'd be questioning Vera about this.

We anticipated that Harold would get closely examined by the judge, over the whole area of inconsistency.

"That this woman was in a state of violent excitement will perhaps be demonstrable. That Mr Claverhouse returned to his house in the same state is admitted. You may perhaps think him less than altogether frank about the quality of his recollections, but he says that he was tired and overworked and had been drinking a good deal, which we have no reason to suppose is an inaccurate picture. He has a vague memory, according to his statement, that earlier in the day there had been a quarrel, or some hasty words, about some photographs of an erotic nature in his possession. I should say in passing that I have seen these. They are of some historic and aesthetic worth and of monetary value, and there is nothing in them to arouse rage or jealousy, but we will hear that this woman held rigid and puritanical opinions on the subject.

"We may believe it possible that a further altercation took place, perhaps on this subject, and that it took a tragic turning.

"Now as you will hear from Mr Castang, his friend and colleague to whom he turned for help and advice, his original contention was that he found her dead. This was initially accepted, and a tentative conclusion formed that some robber had gained entry, been interrupted by Mrs Claverhouse, and that she had been killed in an ensuing struggle. Commissaire Mertens will tell you that doubt was thrown upon this theory when he could find no trace or indeed any scrap of evidence to support it. None has since been brought forward.

"We must bear in mind that Mr Claverhouse, while shocked and in great agitation of mind, claimed responsibility if not actual authorship for his wife's death; a claim treated rightly with scepticism, for as I can myself tell you it is a commonplace psychological pattern. When a violent death is reported in the newspaper the police will see or hear of a number of people, thought normally to be of soundish mind, accusing themselves upon no good grounds of the crime.

"We must now look closely at this woman's state of mind. Modern criminology agrees that a victim may bear a share in responsibility for his or her death. That the author's share may thus be only partial. Such a question would be for the Court to determine. The question exists, and will be a factor in deliberations. Much turns thus upon her character, and we will hear that she was proud, virtuous, and puritanical, to a degree perhaps obsessive."

This brought her naturally to the sex angle which has been such a worry, and she handled it cleanly. We haven't

174

spoken about it much – I am Irish enough to think myself as puritanical as Iris, if it comes to discussion of my friends' private manners. She didn't overdo the feminist angle, but laid down a pretty good doctrine about marital rape. I was a bit scared that she might try that out on Vera. Camden would have put a stop to that, I should think, but one can't tell, with a judge. The President heard her out with a bleak expression. Her conclusion, incidentally, was much the same as your supposition, that "a man" (we won't talk about HC) could well be under the circumstances, in such a violent uproar as to rape (physical overmastery) his wife, but that the circumstances (and plenty of alcohol) would inhibit his actually having-it-off (her forensic language was politer than mine, but she let us have it between the eyes). She's nobody's fool, and she stared down the journalists; as tough a Belgian cookie as is to be found in Bruce, hm?

A word about the President. Vlaamsch, to be sure, and (this is written that evening, before we got any verdict) tough as they come, too. And four women on the jury! One can't compare a modern magistrate with a hanging judge of the nineteenth century (even if these still exist and indeed proliferate in dear old England). But I must admit I was often reminded of the Lord-Justice-Clerk. "I have been the means under God of hanging a great number, but never just such a disjaskit rascal as yourself." I am a bit alarmed by the idea of a guilty verdict, of a severe condemnation. Not much point in now saying "*T'as voulu, Georges Dandin, tu l'as voulu.*"

What is to become of Harold?

175

CHAPTER SIXTEEN

Vera Castang

Well, I suppose I'd had some warning. I mean the Judge of Instruction had been pretty exhaustive, abounding in shots at hemming me in about Iris. I wasn't prepared to be dislocated, put on a rack and stretched, by Madame Proc (who came herself as a nasty surprise). Fair, though. She was taking pains to bring out that Harold lived sitting in a thornbush, with Iris. Everything I knew was wrung out of me: her pathetic, awkward little ways, the moods of black sullenness. I did try to say that her life with a character so demanding and violent couldn't have been any bed of roses either. I would have been inhibited, spouting all this out in public. I was concentrating so hard on the woman in front of me that I forgot I was in court. This often happens, Henri has told me since, to comfort me perhaps? The President asked Camden whether he had questions for me; he smiled and shook his head. So I can't have been that bad, I thought (comforted). Realising later that it was deliberate. If he'd tried to make me change or even rephrase some of my answers, it would have been an admission that I'd said damaging things.

Naturally, I can see that now. Painting this picture of Iris as life-companion, desperately loyal and, of course, physically faithful, but at what a cost (it sounds like me, doesn't it), the Procureur was nailing down the certitude that Harold killed her. Poor Harold, having to sit through all this. Henri has told me the sad anecdote about Harold's identification with a Tour rider. You have to know how

176

to suffer, to get up that hill. Quite literally: to know how to resist the pain, the torment.

I mean, it's obvious enough, surely, and to all, that he killed her, and as evident that she brought about her own death.

Writing this — but there's nothing to say! It's all in one of "my pieces of poetry" which everyone laughs at me about – I don't care! And not even good poetry; a piece of nineteenth-century doggerel, famous only because it "needed saying".

> And what good came of it at last, asked little Peterkin.
> Why, that I cannot tell, said he, but twas a famous
>   victory.

All trials are like that, says Henri, sententiously.

I was pretty stunned, by my passage. I went and sat, next to Henri, limp and sweaty. He took my hand, which I thought nice of him. He had come just before me, so I missed his part in the proceedings. I gather he had quite a hammering, too. But he's a professional, he's used to that.

So that the next hour, too, I'm afraid, flowed by me rather (or over me). There were the medical and psychological experts.

This, apparently, was heaven-sent for Camden, who demolished them utterly and gave a dazzling performance, even impressing Henri, who always says that the only thing one can be quite certain of with experts is that ninety per cent of the time they're wrong.

The next thing which hit me, really, was the President saying, "A good moment, I think, to break for lunch." We went across the road, to the pub on the boulevard opposite the Avenue Louise. Eamonn Hickey had reserved places for the three of us. I had rather a lot to drink, I'm afraid, and only remember that whatever we ate it was too fancy, Avenue-Louise prices, not very good, and a rude waiter. The two of them discussed progress in mutters, very much in the style of professional keen-types, connoisseurs of the Assize Court. Like the Press, who were stuffing away all around us, with undiminished appetites. All that talk about how it always looks worst at this moment, when the defence hasn't even begun yet. I was trying to remember the name of the battle (yes, then already). Hohenlinden. I've no idea where it is (the river Isar flows, I recollect, through the city of München). Who fought? Why? Keine Ahnung! It was a famous victory.

"Do you want pudding?"

"Black as winter was the flow of Isar rolling rapidly."

"I said d'you want pudding?"

"No."

"Come on then, children, back to the bordel."

The President fidgeted a second to make herself comfortable, allowed a moment for the fuffle to die away into silence, and, *La Parole est à la Défense*. The Word: in the beginning was – and the Word was . . . I must not allow myself to wander. I'm still dozy as though from too much pudding, and I'd had no pudding.

Laetitia is on her feet; not going to let anyone doze. Straight of back and with a cool carrying voice, lower-pitched and more resonant than the Proc's conversational tone. She is not quite so tall. She could not be described as horse-faced.

"May it please the Court." Presence she has, and everyone's attention. "We have heard a lot of stories, haven't we?" The Prosecutor looks up, smiles a little; gives a faint nod. No love lost, perhaps, between these two women. "Each little tale, told by witnesses adroitly steered, flattered or comforted, seemed quite consequent, consolatory to the theory adduced, which is that Mr Claverhouse killed his wife, and being of perfectly sound mind is – so runs the deduction – a murderer.

"And then all this fine argument trickles away, like a glass of water spilt on a polished surface, leaving nothing but a few little globules of wetness. I use the metaphor since it happened to me at lunch.

"In plain terms it doesn't cohere. All the skill of the prosecutor cannot make it cohere. Why? Because the synthesis doesn't add up, makes no sense. It is quite likely that the jury realised this, too, over lunch. They may have felt surprised, having been impressed, or should I say deluded, by forensic talents attempting to glue it all together. I wasn't surprised, because I knew.

"You heard the technical evidence and you heard it demolished by my colleague. They don't know what they saw, or thought they saw, and they don't know what conclusion to draw. There was some kind of violent scene, and the woman died, according to their interpretation – which varies – of the signs and marks upon her body. But behind the smokescreen of technical jargon they don't really know, because they weren't there.

"You've heard the police evidence. Commissaire Mertens wasn't there either. His subordinates formed a number of impressions, and there was a bit of misplaced zeal, but we aren't complaining about that. Afterwards he attended the scene, and with the aid of a number of technical tests, some peering through microscopes, the most he feels able to say, because he's a scrupulous and a fair-minded man, is that he found no sign of an intruder nor indeed of any third person, beyond Mr Castang who had himself come at the request of my client to try and understand what had happened.

"They were none of them there! Nobody was there except Mrs Claverhouse, who is dead and cannot tell us what happened, and, at some time in the evening, Mr Claverhouse who was so greatly disturbed and shocked by the happenings that his memories and reconstructions were and are quite unreliable. He doesn't understand and he doesn't really know. Now you might feel that this cannot be so, and that perhaps he is telling lies, distorting or suppressing details. But the President will tell you that it is so, because it is a well-known and well-described mental condition consequent upon violent shock, in which whole areas of recollection are telescoped and displaced, until one can no longer be certain whether some memories, even vivid and detailed, belong to another occasion altogether, widely separated in place and time, and can even be totally imaginary, although the witness is perfectly honest and quite convinced of their purity and verity. If the President feels you need further satisfaction on the point we can call an eminent authority to describe the condition for you. It has nothing to do with insanity."

But it has to do with tricky ground. Having denounced one lot of experts as numskulls she must be aware that the Proc can do the same. But the Prez has let it pass.

"So that what we want is a straightforward, simple and sober account of what actually happened. Not the Prosecutor's complicated and difficult patchwork, full as it is of gaps and holes, but a coherent construction. And this, as so far you may have come to believe, is an impossibility?

"I don't think so. I think it can be put to you quite simply and briefly. But I have to apologise because the last piece in this pattern only became clear to me yesterday, when as it happens I was pleading another case, in a courtroom some distance from this."

Henri, sitting next me, patient, suddenly uncrossed his legs and began to fidget. The President, who had been rolling her pen to and fro on the desk with the flat of her hand, looked up.

"You can't influence proceedings in this court by telling us what happened in another court, Maître."

"With your permission, Madame le Président, I have a witness. Present in this court." Henri glared and shuffled visibly. "Nothing can be easier than to recall him so that he can tell us directly."

"Counsel can proceed but must be prepared for me to stop her."

"I will give a very brief account," said Laetitia enjoying the beginnings of a slight sensation, "and the President will rule whether the witness should be heard.

"In the course of social work among disturbed adolescents, Mr Castang, whom you heard this morning and is sitting here, came to know of a tragic happening – the death by violence of a simple working man, brought about by a child who did not know what she was doing.

"Mr Castang who was called as an expert witness feared the possibility of justice miscarrying and called on me to

180

watch the proceedings. Because this was a sensational affair, involving a father-daughter incest."

"Has this case been judged?" asked the President abruptly.

"Yes Madame."

"In open court?"

"No, under the generalised rule in cases of children and morals the court was closed."

"So that there was no press coverage. Well, insofar as this is admissible at all, a point about which I am not yet convinced, there'll be no mention of the matter here, either. You're close to the edge, Maître."

"Yes, Madame. The tragic occurrence was that this child loved her father, was driven out of her mind at the sight and knowledge of her sister, a year or so older than herself, obliged to submit to sexual abuse, and stabbed him fatally with a kitchen knife. That is as far as I can go or need go, without the Court hearing the witness."

"What is the relevance?" in a freezing voice. And with a damned hanging face.

"With respect," staring it out and voice unperturbed, "the child was not insane. I used the phrase 'driven out of her mind' which is imprecise. I should have said 'driven beyond endurance' by an overmastering passion. I submit that we are here looking at an act of overmastering passion and a man driven beyond endurance."

Madame Beanpole put her tall body together, and said, "I must protest," in a carefully colourless tone.

"I will order a short suspension," said the President. "I will hear this argument in private from counsel, and from the Ministry-Public. I will then decide whether it can be countenanced."

A ripple, and a rustle, as of a lot of people unwrapping chocolates. Harold, looking unhappy, was ushered off by attendant spirits in need of a smoke. Henri, plainly furious, sat and glowered, like "Up the street came the rebel tread, Stonewall Jackson riding ahead." Camden who had been sitting Englishly slumped on his spine with his legs stretched out and his hands in his pockets, came to

181

life, and muttered at us. "I know nothing of this, we're being upstaged. Damn the woman, she'll fuck us up unless she's lucky. That's a poker bet and could weaken us considerably, perhaps gravely. If she'd consulted me I'd have said no." I wished he'd go away. I was also wriggling for a pee. "You've plenty of time," said Camden kindly. Eamonn Hickey, that prudent man, eyes cast piously towards the ceiling, had found a silver hipflask in his pocket. Journalists, on the same errand as me, were treading out cigarette-ends on the marble pavement outside.

"Bring in the accused." Her special way of sitting down, probably to do with not getting her robe creased. The President of an Assize Court is a magistrate of the Court of Appeal; the assessors are *Grande Instance* judges. "The Court will hear the witness," gathering to put the questions herself, and like a large bird putting its feathers in order, appearing to gain in size and stature. Henri marched forward heavy-footed but with aplomb; Marshal Ney before the firing squad. "You don't imagine I'm afraid? Faced more loaded guns than you've had hot cups of tea."

"You heard the preliminaries," in her polite, conversational voice. "You were called in this affair as an expert witness."

"I disclaim 'expert'."

"Put it in your own words."

"These girls ran away from home. I heard their story in my capacity as a social worker, down there by the station." We distinguish, in Bruce, between Ville Haute and Basse. Grand buildings like the Palais de Justice are at the top of a steep slope. Low things like railway stations are at the bottom. "I formed the opinion that it could be a serious matter," leadenly.

"Based, you would say, on your experience as a former police officer?"

"Quite so. I thought I'd better talk to this man. I was unhappily prevented, by other circumstances. When I saw these children again the damage had been done. They fled here, to Bruxelles, early in the morning, hitch-hiking. They'd nowhere else to go. I called the police. I mentioned

182

the matter to counsel, fearing that their – that they would need better than perfunctory representation in a court."

"Very well. We've heard this expression used, act of passion, ungovernable, urged in mitigation of this man's death. Speaking as an impartial witness, and against your background of police experience – did you agree with that definition?"

"If forced to express an opinion, yes I did."

"And did the Court agree? This was the Children's Judge, I take it – this child would have been too young for the Assizes."

"He held that the child was not responsible and must be placed in care."

"Evidently, from the sound of it. And in the very different circumstances which we here are asked to examine, you heard counsel claim a possible parallel?"

"Yes Madame."

"Had you discussed this previously, with counsel? Or with anybody else?"

"No. It happened only yesterday. I have not seen counsel, since."

"So that this possible parallel has never struck you?"

"No."

"Now I will recall, for the jury, that you are a former commissaire of criminal police in the French Republic, at present employed in the legal-advisory services of the Community. The accused is, in fact, your hierarchical superior in this service, and you are on terms of friendship with him. As is shown, I think, by his turning to you when in trouble as we have heard described. That is fairly put?"

"Yes."

"He sought, we can say, your help. Now give me a careful answer. He sought, also, your impartial opinion on a legal point, that of his responsibility, and eventual answerability?"

"I think it's fair to say that he relied upon my experience of a startling and shocking sight, such as a violent death. I have no means of knowing whether any such legal doctrine crossed his mind. I should not think so. As I hope

183

I made clear before, he was very upset and confused. His claim to have somehow brought about this death was not one I could take seriously, in the event. It was in any case ambiguous. I could not even be sure that there was any dead body. A directly concerned witness in such circumstances is not to be relied upon."

"So that you'd agree that you were, and are considered a professional observer."

"One could conclude that."

"Counsel has laid claim to your value as an impartial witness. Now without throwing strain upon friendship, can you say whether you will agree with counsel's estimate of this possible parallel?" The pause was long and the judge unmoving. Henri stared at her heavy, level face.

"I'd have to reply honestly that I think I do." I don't know if anyone else breathed out heavily; I know I did.

Proc was there like lightning, leaning forward pointing her pencil like a gun.

"One moment, Monsieur Castang. On the one hand, we're talking about a small child."

"Eleven, I believe."

"For whom you felt sorry."

"Sorry? A delinquent child of that age will say anything. One has to get at the facts."

"Eleven. All that could be gathered together of the impressionable, the inexperienced, the vulnerable. You agree?" Shouting.

"Yes."

"And you are seeking parallels with a highly intelligent, worldwise and extremely sophisticated man in his fifties? A trained jurist, a senior civil servant with weighty public responsibilities?"

Poor Harold, that Goddam mountain still stretches up and away interminably in front of him. Keep pedalling. One thing about Henri, he stands up to browbeating. He's had lots of that; lawyers, judges, senior police officers . . .

"Oddly enough, yes I am."

Fair dripping with acid, "Would you care to attempt to make that clear to the Court? Because I have to admit that

184

it is not very clear to me."

"A man such as you describe can still be a child of the age mentioned in his personal emotional relationships." A sudden brilliant smile travelled across Camden's face.

"That, Monsieur Castang," leaning back but still aiming the pencil, "will be as the Court may see, and decide."

As smoothly as though there had been no interruption the President said, "You may stand down now, Monsieur Castang." Turning her majesty upon Laetitia, who was standing head bowed like a nun in church. "Onus now lies upon you, Maître, to find support for this view, which the Procureur understandably sees as extravagant. You cannot rely upon Monsieur Castang. His opinions may have carried weight and been upheld, in another court and in this other instance, where judgement has been given and it would not be proper for me to comment upon that. Here he disclaims expertise, to my mind rightly, and he distinguishes between the impartiality to which a serving criminal investigation officer may lay claim and his present position as friend and colleague. If you are going to lend substance to your conjecture you will need testimony. Or I would find myself leaning to the opinion of the Ministry-Public, which saw your argument as a rhetorical device. Latitude goes no further. In the popular phrase he who says a must also say b."

Laetitia had endured this with the fixed sunny smile of any advocate getting a telling-off. She looked up and said, "I believe I can satisfy you, Madame le Président." I was scared she was going to ask for me again; she took an ostentatious drink of water. "I should like to ask the Doorwarden to summon Mademoiselle Marie de Wilde."

"No!" Harold shot to his feet, amid scandalised gendarmerie going shush. "I forbid it." Red in the face, eyes out of their orbits.

"Sit down, Mr Claverhouse," ice now. He had himself in hand at once.

"I beg your pardon, Madame. May I not—?"

"No. You have no authority to forbid here. I direct these

185

proceedings and if you make a disturbance I shall have you put out."

"With respect, Madame, I should like a moment in which to instruct the advocate."

"I have given a ruling." Kindly. "You will have the opportunity to speak on your own behalf, and you may also ask me to raise new questions and to put them if need be to the witness. For the moment you must keep quiet." He struggled with himself, obeyed, and leaned over the barrier to whisper to Camden sitting below him, who stretched up backwards, blank-faced, and shook his head. I felt a clutch of sympathy. Harold is used to giving orders.

Young and plainly vulnerable, Marie made a brave entrance. She also looked very pretty. That would not impress the formidable woman on the bench, even if one of the assessors was appraising a melting eyeful with an indulgent expression. The Procureur, too, was examining her with a faint smile, exactly the look with which an older woman's eye travels up and down the figure of a bride in white, who happens to be carrying a rather large bouquet of flowers.

She's a legal adult, an intelligent girl from what is termed a good family, carefully brought up and expensively educated; at present a student in the faculty of the University of Bruxelles; living independently, it is presumed capable of independent thought and action. Laetitia is bringing this out quietly in the brief conventional questions, getting answers in a clear soft soprano. Marie looks composed and keeps her eyes on the interlocutor. Harold who has his head in his hands hasn't been able yet to bring himself to look at her at all. Which is childish?

Meetings now. Tea drinking; the "flat" at the back of the Place Saint Cath. "Simple tale."

"So you became his mistress," said the President, uninflected, matter-of-fact.

Eamonn Hickey was having another surreptitious go at the hipflask. "Does the jade tell us she was the panel's mistress?" he muttered, being Lord Hermiston. "Faith ye make a bonny couple."

Marie took her time deciding whether the intention were hostile. "We made love. I saw a difference."

'The difference," dryly but not unkindly, "you are here to make plain to us, if you can." I liked Marie then because she flung it back, one Flamande peasant woman to another.

"I have to say it in court and it's not easy to say even in private – I saw nothing dirty in it because it didn't come at all easily to either of us and we were always trying to respect each other."

"Let me understand this. If I press you, for precise answers, I wish you to follow my meaning. You are upon examination, as might happen before a professor in biology or chemistry. Much may depend upon the exactitude of your replies. You follow me?"

"Yes. Do you think though it is just a biological or a chemical process? I don't." There was a laugh. The President smiled, too, before folding her arms, leaning her elbows on the desk, keeping her conversational tone.

"You have a man here. He comes to your apartment, talks kindly to you, treats you as an equal, you make him a cup of tea. You're a student, he is a distinguished professor. The situation flatters you because he is important, amusing, experienced. It flatters him because you are a pretty young girl. That covers the situation?"

"Not altogether I think. I was frightened and I felt insecure."

"Come. You aren't a child. You knew very well that he would be wanting to get you into bed."

"Yes, I was frightened of that."

"Prior to this idyll,' remarked the Proc, "were you physically experienced?" Marie looked at her slowly.

"One at a time I think is fair."

"I was about to suggest the same," Camden's lightest tenor.

"Touché," drily. "Now answer the question."

Marie blushed all over her face and neck. "No, I was a virgin."

"Answered," snapped Camden.

187

"Counsel will intervene when the time comes," said the President. "And so will the Ministry-Public."

"I apologise," said that lady, with grace.

"May I speak?" asked Marie timidly. "Of course I knew about this, I'm not a fool, I thought it certain he'd ask or . . . or do something and I'd made up my mind to say no, and I didn't have to because he never made that sort of suggestion and some weeks later I said he shouldn't come any more because I was frightened of saying yes, and afterwards again – I'm sorry, this is a very stupid story – I made up my mind to say yes and then I don't want to talk about it because I said yes without being asked and it became rather a Thing."

"Rather as one would expect. Very well, Mademoiselle, we won't need to go into it." Laetitia sat looking at the girl as though wishing she herself were twenty years younger, and I thought the Proc had a bit of rueful look, too; as indeed I was sure I had. Camden looked relaxed, making the odd note on what Americans call a yellow legal pad (why yellow?). A lot of English people don't understand that European judges aren't as distant as at the Old Bailey, but it's not a bad method, they modulate and dedramatise, they aren't promoted advocates but professional magistrates, and quite often they are good ones.

"Now you were of course aware that this was a man long married and with children of your own age."

"Yes." (And why aren't any of them here?)

"I ask you, what did you know about this woman?"

"You mean was I told that his wife didn't understand him? No I wasn't." How I envy this self-possession. I would have been quaking and stammering. These modern girls aren't intimidated by authority, where we were brought up to grovel. The judge didn't react to the sarcasm. She may even have liked the girl standing up to her.

"I was aware," said Marie slowly, "that she was always true and loyal and devoted. And that I didn't have anything as good. I tried to measure my responsibility. You'll say badly. But I tried. I felt much respect for her. And I felt sorry because it didn't sound as if she'd had a happy life. I didn't think it was in her to be mean or petty unless she'd had a rotten time. I was stuck." With her candid blue look meeting the old, experienced eyes.

I missed the following exchanges. I don't know how much I missed, because my mind skidded off the road, and tumbled into a ravine.

I felt sorry for Iris, and I was only feeling sorry for myself. We had a lot in common, and it went beyond feeling inadequate. I have never been able to forget those words spoken by an Englishman in 1938. Czechoslovakia was a small and unimportant country of whom few people had heard. And, of course, it still is, in English eyes. Never mind that this is a characteristic expression of smugness. As Iris remarked, they think of Ireland in exactly the same terms.

And if, ten years from now, it should be Henri who finds this girl . . . just look at her, nineteen years old and a Rodin come to life. She thinks, and she feels. She would look at me, at the little Czech peasant. Might she then remember that Flanders, too, is a very small, unimportant, far-off piece of the world? Or would she only look at herself and think that she was nineteen, and beautiful? Harold is as sensitive as they come, but he is English, with the "fatal gift" of imagining himself superior. Iris had not been able to cope with it.

She had lived as a child in a grand and a beautiful house called Spanish Point, already by then irrelevant, shabby, the rain coming through the roof; but hers, her home, immeasurably marvellous. As indeed is a village house in Slovakia; peasant, a hovel. Iris had been forced to let go, and never really succeeded in coming to terms with a world outside: everything went on being measured by truths learned as a little girl. Lonely woman, Iris had felt instinctively that I would understand, that she could confide.

Thirty years from now, Marie. You are still only nineteen. If you were to look at me you would only see a "good woman" trying hard to be a good wife. All right, to a difficult and temperamental man. She has borne his children and cooked his dinners and turned the collars of his shirts and kept the house – well, vaguely clean, relatively comfortable, sometimes tidy. They've shared a lot, hardish times and poverty and yes, fear. She's always been "faithful": well, it's something, I suppose. Not exactly a banner to display with pride, any more than it was a sheet to hang out of the window after the first night.

Marie has so much more, in thinking and in feeling. It isn't just that glorious body and those striking looks. Tja, marriage. Long row to hoe, and hard stony ground, and under the blazing sun. A woman loses her looks.

They've let her go, the Marieke. I haven't been paying close attention. The President told her to open her mouth wide and looked at her teeth one by one. The Proc, a hard-headed woman – well that's her job – hit her with some fairly brutal questions. Laetitia is being gentle, being skilful, but Lordy that's a lot of women there, isn't it. Coincidence, this "feminine" Court? Hard on Harold.

It's going to be his turn now. Nearly at the top, mate. But is it a steep climb the whole yardage to the finish line? Or will there be a faux plat; that last kilometre looking easy and even level after the hairpin bends and the fearful gradient, and which a rider can get caught on, and passed. He can leave his heart there on the roadway.

190

CHAPTER SEVENTEEN

Henri Castang

summer autumn winter spring
reaped their sowing and went their came
sun moon stars rain

Vera, next to me, has fallen into a trance. I don't blame
her; a trial in the Assize Court is a jogtrot, wearisome
business and I've known "accused" lose all interest and go
to sleep: the professionals grind on, up, down, to, fro, in
these airless courtrooms, terrible lot of talk there is and
most of it meaningless, but that's the law. Mechanical,
heartless, men and women (both dong and ding) taken to
pieces and dissected. We've a chance still of finishing the
same day. If Camden isn't too long, if the examination of
Harold is not too exhaustive, if the Proc is not too crass, if,
if, if. This President has staying power, but the jury is
getting glassy-eyed, I fear. "Nearly" at the end though.

Camden made a brief address, to pull the strings of the
thesis together. Had he really not known of Laetitia's
surprise? – no, no, that was a ploy, definitely, adopted
because he saw that I was furious as well as "surprised",
and pretending to know nothing about it was meant to
soften my anger. They had discussed the possibility of
using Marie as a way to cut the ground from under the
Proc's feet. Quite certainly, ever since I had myself given
the game away by mentioning her existence, fool that I
was. "We won't tell Castang." And we won't tell Harold
either. Spring it on him in court. Sorry chum, we didn't

know we'd have to amputate your leg until we had you under the anaesthetic. Beuh, lawyers are like that. They'd have debated it – would Marie stand up, under some nasty questioning? Had they known it would be a "feminist" Court? – ach, I feel too tired now to be angry, really. But poor old Harold, they're ready to castrate him in order to win their technical acquittal.

Camden does it well. Smooth, professional, not in the least handicapped by the language difficulty. I am not here for a load of chicanery, he is saying, in efforts to exonerate football hooligans, to extirpate a man from a charge of – no, not murder. That cannot be. You have heard the medical evidence and you've heard that not one of the experts is willing or able to go into the witness box and claim this was not an accident. For murder there has to be malicious intent formed. None is suggested. At the very most, homicide through imprudence, through loss of self-control, through passion. Here, yes, we do have some small passing resemblance to the hooligan situation. Passion. Those boys were blinded by passion, too, for their loyalty to their team, for the ignorant, yes, and loutish nationalist passions culpably cultivated and whipped up by the Gutter Press. That was the process of "the media". Which had now the authority of chose jugée: it was recognised that these oafs were unable to withstand the passions whipped up – passion, yes, there is indeed a connecting link. No comparison with this educated and sophisticated man? Sexual passion has nothing in common with the chauvinist, xenophobic fears and hatreds of a football crowd? Yet overmastering passion is the link. We have heard Miss de Wilde, and with much respect, wouldn't you agree? She has shown you her efforts to withstand passion, her fairness and honesty, her sympathy and love.

All right, Joe, but don't go on too long.

No he didn't, he's too adroit. The one missing piece is for Mr Claverhouse to tell us how he got trapped – as Miss de Wilde has described it – how he has tried to be honest with himself and with her, how he struggled in the trap.

192

Mrs Claverhouse? – he has neither the need nor the wish to show her in an unsympathetic light. She was a proud, a virtuous, a puritanical, yes, an obsessive woman and these fine, indeed noble qualities combined to catch her, too, in the trap. She could not cope with the rigidities of her own strong character. But let Mr Claverhouse speak for himself.

One tries to avoid clichés like "shaky on the pins" or "walking like an old man", but Harold had taken a bad knock. His face looked patchy, as though these summer months in detention had – physically – been a lot more damaging than he pretended. They are, too. And the marvellous voice was no better; unsure in pitch. He answered a few easy questions from Camden rather badly, at too great length. The President's voice struck a brisker note.

"Mr Claverhouse – we've heard your counsel explain matters. We've listened also to Miss de Wilde. She has spoken, one may say with courage and determination, to conflicts and distress. To divided loyalties, which she thinks led to a situation – it is suggested – from which you found it difficult to withdraw. You have now the occasion, which before I refused you, to speak of these matters in your own words."

So come on Harold. It's that moment the rider dreams of, to take off and leave the others standing. The classic Spanish climber has the choice of two tactics. To take the initiative no other can follow or to let another tire himself out before placing the counter-punch. Both are devastating, but what he must never do is hesitate. As, this year, Pedro Delgado hung back, to his undoing. As Harold did now. He made two or three false starts, and they sounded pitiful.

"You'd like a moment, to collect yourself?" she offered politely.

"No – no. I have not understood all of these arguments. Much that has been said seems to me quite irrelevant. I loved my wife. That she was a difficult or a troublesome woman strikes me as beside the point. I loved Marie. This word love is ridiculous. We no longer use it or admit to it. We'd prefer to banish it. We no longer have faith in it. It frightens us. We can't cope with it. One would prefer not to try. To love two women is an odious as well as an absurd spectacle. I am doubly ridiculous, doubly impotent.

"I am, however, a jurist. The fact has been mentioned and remarked upon. Since you invite me, I will make a technical point." The voice had grown firmer and more flexible.

"An English judge gave an interview to the Press. An old man, and in retirement. Now in a notorious criminal case there had been an equally notorious miscarriage of justice, which could only partially be righted by the freeing from prison of those originally accused and wrongly condemned, upon evidence later shown to have been corrupt.

"This old man aroused much scandalised protest by suggesting that the miscarriage, if indeed there had been any, lay in their not having been hanged. For then, he maintained, the matter would long have been forgotten. The public would be quietened, he said, by an assurance that even if mistaken, justice had been dealt firmly and impartially. And that this was needed.

"As you can imagine the uproar was considerable, and senility perhaps the kindest charge laid to the account of this very old man. D'you know, I'm not altogether sure he was wrong."

This is – in a sense – amusing. Harold's conversational tone sounds as though he has completely forgotten where he is.

"He's been misunderstood, I believe. He remarked that he was the only judge still alive who had in fact been called upon to pass a death penalty, and that he had done so when required without any particular emotion, without what we should call *états d'âme*. Simply because such was the law." The Court was absolutely quiet.

"This judge has in the past been well known for applying common sense to technically complex or difficult deliberations. He never had a remarkable legal mind; he was no outstanding jurist. He's on record as having

194

frequently maintained that if one followed a moral principle in passing judgement, this would invariably turn out to be good law.

"I think that somewhere in his mind was the venerable principle that it is expedient that a man suffer for the good of the people. He was saying, I believe, that it might be a very dreadful thing that people should be hanged and afterwards shown to have been innocent, but what above all else should be upheld is that an English judge is impartial upon the evidence set before him and that English police have integrity in presenting such evidence. Both principles being at present badly shaken.

"It is possible, anywhere, to claim, and often rightly, that the police have been bribed or that judges have bowed to political pressures. What matters is the principle. If crime, then punishment – you have to maintain that. Pay no attention to lawyers. I killed my wife. That's a fact. I don't have any more to say about this."

He turned around, walked back, and sat down, exactly as though he'd been giving a little talk to the second-year pharmacy students – including Marie – about the problems of deontology.

The President never turned a hair.

"Exactly as with anyone else before this Court," in her usual voice, "you have also the right to the last word, after the final arguments have been heard and before the Court comes to deliberate." Clearing her throat, "The Ministry-Public will now present the requisition."

Lady Beanpole did just that, short and to the point, no fioriture of rhetoric and in a quiet, reasonable voice.

Mr Claverhouse had made a good point there, hadn't he? Disregard whatever is irrelevant. Nothing in the evidence shows a deliberately formed intent to terminate life, and she doesn't think so either. That could be suspected, since the man has acquired a young and pretty mistress, and kept quiet about it. There is a quixotic argument that he did so to shield her, but this won't impress you much.

Non, mais! I'm sorry but they're going on! I mean, I'm

an old hand at courtrooms but . . . What phrase to use –
that my attention wanders? Or "farcical" – is that the
word? I thought a farce was supposed to be funny; that
you roll about, slap your thighs, wipe your streaming eyes;
purged by laughter. The word in English has become
misshapen, I think. Harold uses it often – "this is
becoming farcical" – without laughing at all.

Neither am I.

Vera, bless her, is listening attentively, brow knitted,
mouth slightly open. I caught Eamonn's eye, beyond; he
has been showing restlessness ever since the Proc started,
knows as well as I do that there's no point in going on. He
made the sort of grimace English actors use when
pretending to be French: huge shruggings and rollings of
the eye. I jogged Vera's elbow.

"Let's get out of here."

"Oh, but we can't. We owe it to Harold." Her loyalty
outraged.

Stuck with it, are we? Yes, I suppose we are. I'd caught
the President glancing at her watch. She's going to try to
finish, all on the same day. Respect the unities, quoi, of
classical drama. These long summer evenings . . . but in
winter under the electric light turning everything yellow,
from the panelling to the lawyers' faces, one would have
this same feeling of time-suspended.

"Liable to go on till late. Sneaking out for a smoke is one
thing, but we'll need to eat and drink, or we'll fade away."

"But the pleadings . . ." worried Vera.

"Fook the pleadings," said Eamonn, almost loud enough
to be heard. It was like the classic Dai-and-Shoni story –
"Fook the women." "Yes, but have we the time?" Vera
looked frightened, but yielded to Irish firmness of mind.
We went to look for beer.

"Look, Vera, it's 'Our revels now are ended.' "

"Rather like German Unity," suggested Eamonn.
"Exciting at the start, but all it boils down to at the end is
whether a Social Democrat or a Christian Democrat
becomes the first Chancellor."

"I couldn't understand," said Vera, "why she didn't just

stop the proceedings. She went on as though nothing had happened. Don't they take him seriously then?"

"Law says, man has to have a fair trial. Can't just say Sorry, but we've all got bored."

"Typical male invention. And when I think that they're all women, too . . ."

"That may still play a rôle. Laetitia suddenly producing the Marieke like that, look, hat, look, rabbit. Effective, but he – poor Harold – couldn't cope, choked on it. She had a chance of getting him off, I thought – it's a non-proven anyhow."

"But we can't miss the verdict." Vera was still worrying.

"The journalists will tip us off. Plenty of time. Camden will make a long technical speech."

"I don't see what he's got to plead with now."

"Football hooligans. We never meant to kill anyone, and even if we did, all the fault of the police."

"You're cynical," said Vera sadly.

We got it timed quite well: the President was "summing up". A Belgian court isn't like a French one. For the initial deliberation, about guilt, the jury's on its own, as in England. If they bring in a guilty vote by a seven-to-five or better, then the judges join them for a further deliberation about length and mode of punishment. We tiptoed in: the courtroom public had thinned by now, but there were still a few earnest students eating things out of paper bags. One girl was knitting.

"The first question . . . The second question . . ." All according to Cocker – who was Cocker? A Law Lord, perhaps.

Did he kill her? If so, was there intent? For that would be homicide. Merely taking her by the throat would be blows-and-injuries resulting in death. Malice? – the doctrine can have complex features in such a situation. Could it be thought that this woman had been provoked into showing malice? That might be felt as an attenuating circumstance, but it should be borne in mind that this woman set a high value upon trust, and that an infidelity

197

such as has been heard described could constitute a grave breach in – oh, and so on . . .

Eamonn had been scuttling about to gather news; we got our heads down to whisper. There'd been rather a severe requisition – five years; the Proc hadn't liked the behaviour of a man in a position of trust – but that was where we had broken off, and this is where we came in.

While a jury is in conclave one has to bet on how long they'll take. We hung about in the passages, in the well-named Hall of Lost Footsteps. Instinct was rewarded because quite soon there was the Doorwarden flapping his sleeves at us.

To the first question – yes. To the second – no. To the subsequent, there would be recommendations . ∴. they at least had listened to Harold.

And the Court would now withdraw to consider these. The snack-bar is long closed, but the Press has been smuggling beer bottles in, so that we settled down for a picnic. And a foretaste of the journalists' opinions. Not what they'll be phoning in to the copytakers.

"Camden would have done all right if that Jewish woman had kept her mouth shut."

"Oh, I thought she was good."

"So she was. But one should have kept to the purely technical aspect."

"See a court full of women like that, you know they're not going to listen."

"Moment the judge threw out the sex stuff, that incest thing the woman was pleading, in Ghent was it, nothing really to do with us."

"She could have had the court cleared."

"No. Only when there are children involved."

"Senior civil servants aren't supposed to have any sex life. Like politicians, their interest is only in power."

"Can't manage to have it off, because your wife's castrated you, pretty rough to hear it all coming out in court. Mean to say, could happen to any of us."

"Wouldn't care to find myself in bed with that Procureur woman. You'd be expecting her to have the razor-blade in her other hand. Getting it up is difficult enough at best."

"But I could, for that young girl – couldn't you?"

"Yes, well, that's just the point, isn't it?"

That horrible electric bell was thrilling in the passages.

"Get fell in – the whistle's went."

The motivations get read. These are in legal shape, and prickly with jargon, and take some time. "Passion" isn't an easy concept for the legal mind. There's a lot of "Seen that" and "In the light of this". Harold stands as though on parade, thumbs down the seam of his trousers, absolutely blank-faced. Very quietly, she has asked him what he wants to say. As quiet, as polite, he has replied with thanks for courtesy and consideration shown, and that he has no further comment at all.

"In view of the aforegoing the sentence of the Court is two years deprivation of liberty." Everybody bows to everyone like royalty; levée; we all should be wearing knee-breeches. Belgians have a liking for formal manners. The big Flamande woman who has herself an eighteenth-century face, rather that of a field marshal, nods, surveys the battlefield impassively, picks up some papers and puts them under her arm, her robe billows, she sweeps. Oh well, could be a lot worse.

Eamonn took Vera off in his car. I have a little job to do. It isn't really late. There are those who complain, saying that Bruce is a provincial town and there isn't any Night Life. Nonsense rather; the Bruxellois have quite a taste for belle-époque bordellos, but they're fairly discreet about it.

I didn't see the lawyers go, or the public (why have they come, and what do they think?). My mind was elsewhere, as it's called. The tribunal of Aix-en-Provence, where I'd once been called as witness in a Fine Arts case: it is lodged in the former convent of a mediaeval hospital. The judges, the lawyers, are cynical about it.

"You expect justice – here? The courtroom is the nuns' chapel, Instruction's the former childbed ward, and the archives used to be the morgue."

199

A voice called my name: I looked up, and it was Miss Huntingdon. Why hadn't I seen her before? Perhaps she had popped in just to hear the end? Or, more likely, I hadn't been looking, hadn't been seeing.

"Welcome to the garbage bin," in the words of that embittered magistrate. "Climb in – there's plenty of room." Tribunals! What does it matter whether it's a tumbledown Middle Ages slum, or a Palace on top of a hill?

"I don't think I agree," she said calmly. "I thought it a good Court, and I think they got it right, and I believe, too, that it's what he wanted." She had her self-contained look, but the handsome face was drawn, as though she'd been overworking.

"Probably you know him better than any of us," I said in a tone of apology.

"No – I wanted to apologise. For having been such a fool, in my attitude to you. I've told all those – those secret service people, that I won't have anything further to do with their capers. They are grotesque. There is injustice enough, without our making the world more chaotic still. You know, I had truly thought, that you were trying to work up the scandal, to destroy Harold. You have been his friend. And I feel ashamed."

The court had emptied. We were alone.

"Policemen never do agree with verdicts," I said. "They get it wrong and does that mean we've got it right? We have it wrong all the time, but we have to think it right. We must believe in it. Do our work, with the conviction that it's worth doing." She gave a slight nod; slipped past me.

"Goodnight," she said and was gone.

I sat on for a moment alone in the empty courtroom. Thinking about a famous spy. They had him on television, not long ago. Polite, quite throwaway, "This gentleman sitting on my left is Gunther Guillaume."

I dare say you remember him: he brought down a West German government, and Brandt was forced to resign as Chancellor. That's right! – the famous Stasi "mole". Everyone asks now how many more Stasi agents there are, close to the seats of power in the West. Nobody knows.

An oldish man now, thickened, with a grey beard. How long was he in prison – eight years?

The interviewer was gentle, and only once showed a sharpened tooth. They flashed a still on the screen, showing Guillaume sitting on his heels reaching to pat Brandt's dog, which shrank away while his master observed the scene, paternal and benignant.

"In those days, only the dog showed mistrust." And perhaps once at the end— "Tell me, Herr Guillaume, what do you live on, these days?"

"Yes, that is rather a sharp one. I have an unemployment benefit. Luckily for myself, my wife still works."

Notoriously, the Stasi is ungenerous. Ideals are supposed to be enough to live upon. All secret services are like this – forgetful. Always, after the "usefulness" is finished, there are unaccountable hitches over the payment of the pension. It is important to have a wife, who earns.

And more important still – have a wife who is faithful.

I remembered, too, the RG General, back in Paris. He'd had a phrase; somewhat enigmatic, as no doubt it was designed to be.

"Recall, Castang. We can recruit you. We can also disrecruit you."

What was that supposed to mean? Giving me up as a bad job? Or the trapdoor to the cellars; of the Gestapo Headquarters in the Prinz Albrecht Strasse?

I have still got my magic key. Harold has been whisked off to the incredible maze of catacombs such as exist below every Palace of Justice, but my authorisations and permissions, and perhaps the stamped-in cop look, hold good here, too. The boys in leather gaiters have all hustled off home in a hurry, complaining of the Leisurely Ways of justice, and with the familiar grievance that they never do get paid their fucking overtime. But there are a number of quietish grey characters whose job is to look after the central heating and see that the cleaning women are there in the morning. They look after Harold, too, bring him in some supper and ask how many blankets he wants. He was sitting on a wooden chair, hands in his pockets, looking quite content with the world.

"Henri – how nice of you to pop in."

"Thought it possible you might like a cigar."

"Bless you, I was out. Supplies might get interrupted, now. Ah – just what was needed."

"Momentary interruption. We'll organise all that's wanted. Don't know where they'll send you – a Fortress, in the Ardennes? Think of poor Toussaint l'Ouverture, killed of cold in the Château de Joux. This is a doddle. Subtract your detention time and the Good Behaviour of Soldier Schweik, won't even be a year. Six months, we'll have you out as good as new. Christ mate, think of England. 'While the gang will still be in Pentonville, in cells for all their days-O.' Screws, cocoa, slopping-out and constipation. No more law books. You don't have to be Fabrice Valserra, terrified of the Spielberg. We won't need to bring you the *Complete Works of Sir Walter Scott*."

Harold had his cigar going nicely now.

"One moment, Henri. Let's get this clear. Wherever it is, whatever time it takes, no, warmest thanks but I don't want any more popping in. Not even Vera with the library books. Nor even Marie – especially not Marie. Take her away. Impress upon her that her life is not going to be ruined by this contretemps. Be as brutal as you need, I think I can ask that much of you. As for me, just don't bother. Forget, like Marie. 'My revels now are ended.' Prospero departs from the magic island of Bruxelles." Odd, that he had picked up the same reference as Eamonn.

"There won't be any more cigars though, will there?" Harold was enjoying this one.

"Avoid any sentimental attitudes – making an event out of it. We'll have none of that. Goodbyes are tiresome occasions. Worse though, for those left behind.

"I'm both glad, and sorry, that you came. I'd just as soon it were you, to make my goodbyes to."

"It's because I'm a cop, still. In the days when I used to have enquiries, and they ended with a prison sentence, I used to find myself popping in. One saw quite a lot of a chap, when one felt pretty sure, and was searching for legal ground, to knock him over. While he of course was working tooth-and-nail to get off the hook. A sort of understanding grew up. Almost a comradeship. No sentiment about it, but a certain emotional bond, no doubt of that."

Harold drew on his cigar, thought about it, admitted the justice of this, nodded.

"I have sentimentalised. Now I pay the penalty. That's as it should be. My life is at an end – both ways." He meant, I suppose, his professional life – the Secretary-General would expect a little resignation note – as well as Iris.

"A death penalty," thinking about that. "A bad moment to pass, but the worst about it would be the fuss made. The paraphenalia. The pretence made at dignity and solemnity. But then it would be finished with.

"It's bad principally because it corrupts those who order it, as well as those who carry it out. It's another sentimentalism.

"All the authorities agree that the victim comes out of it best. Nearly always, they show courage – the sort which comes with a prospect of relief from pain. A prospect – who knows? – of happiness.

"Just as every authority agrees that a prison sentence is bad – fundamentally.

"Worse. The prison is in ourselves, as all thought, all art, makes clear. There's no escaping that.

"So that this, too, becomes romanticised. Is there indeed anything – crime or punishment, entering this life or leaving it – which people will not turn into sugar-pink greetings cards?

"One will hear people say that they welcome going to prison. Aha, one will be free of a lot of tiresome little worries. You won't have to bother about anything. Quite; I've seen enough of it to know this to be the worst of temptations; the headlong rush into irresponsibility.

"Some golden syrup, too, appeal to the bogus intellectual: in the hermit's cell suffering and solitude will purge one of vanities and follies.

"Make the cat laugh, if it weren't busy throwing up. The best political writing is done in jail – that's another one.

"I've been caught already by a few of these traps. I've carried irresponsibility as far as asking – no, begging – your wife to take her clothes off for me. She hardly bothered to tell me off.

"Don't mention that I told you that: it would only cause her pain. In fact, self-indulgent of me to mention it. But all this speech is self-indulgent, isn't it?

"The goodbye is difficult, Henri: forgive my dragging it out. I've learned something about being sorry for oneself.

"All the cigars you want – books, anything. So that you'll scarcely notice the imprisonment. Candyfloss humanitarianism at every turn. You want a sleeping-pill? A television set? A psychiatrist? At least in the Spielberg there was no pretence about rehabilitation. You were there to be punished, at the whim of the tyrant.

"Today's humane prisons – make a note about this, Henri – our usual complaints are only incidental. The forcing-ground for petty crime, the promiscuity, the homosexuality: trivial. You can find all that outside. The diminishment and the degradation are real.

"So don't give me this stuff about it's only six months or whatever; that's quite enough to destroy a man. They didn't sentimentalise that, in the Spielberg. The six summer months were tuberculosis and the winter was pneumonia.

"What happens when I get out, eh? Rehabilitated.

"I'm going on too long, Henri. You'd better bugger off. My goodbyes to Vera, and my thanks, and my love. Marie the less said the better: say nothing at all."

An ashtray was provided: Harold put the cigar out neatly without squashing it.

"So why did I volunteer, Castang, tell me? I could have kept quiet and let Camden squirm me out of it. That woman with her talk about passion – they'd have disregarded it.

"But now, you see, I realise.

"This way, Iris forgives me.

204

"She has told me so."

I made some sort of signal with my hand and walked out. The old boy with the keys looked up from his book and nodded: to him, as well, I sketched a kind of hand salute.

There was a man in England – many years ago – who looked up when the executioner came into his cell; a little nervously.

"Hallo, tosh," he said, timid, as though frightened that the greeting might not be returned.

POSTFACE

It's not among Brel's better poems; the matter – a mere nostalgic reminiscence – is trivial and the music is unremarkable, a pretty little melody with a catchy lilt. Still, like a late Latin lyric, or a border ballad, it has his talent for brief, bare words.

> Ay Marieke, Marieke,
> Le ciel flamand—
> Entre les tours
> De Bruges à Gand.

It is also memorable as the only occasion on which he dropped into Vlaams in the alternate verses, in Singspiel and a powerful Bruxellois accent:

> And scours the sand over my land—
> My flatness-land, my Flanders-land.

One is struck by his use of the possessive adjective.

There is a statue of Marieke in the city of Brugge which I have not looked at; a fear perhaps unreasonable that it would be Peter-Pannish. However – I was shaving, on a bright sunny morning, in a hotel overlooking the mediaeval gate: alerted by a noise like ten thousand seagulls I went out on the balcony. An immense horde of schoolchildren and students from the surrounding countryside, out of train and bus, afoot or by bicycle, was pouring through the gate. Among them, quite certainly, was Marieke, and at that moment the book began.

Equally plainly, her lover was no adolescent but a much older man, to be found among "the Europeans" in

"Bruce". I must apologise, too, for Harold; not to Jacques this time but to a senior governmental servant whose Cuban cigar and extravagant conversation propelled— writers really should carry bells, like lepers, so that one would know how to avoid them.

The Palais de Justice is real, defies the imagination as both monstrous and hideous, and needs no apology from me. So is the Danish pub real, and very pleasant it is.

Grandfontaine 1990

THOSE IN PERIL
Nicolas Freeling

The little girls who go to Monsieur Dampierre's special
Literature class know they are lucky: not many eleven-
year-olds have an Academician and – more important still
– a TV personality paying them this kind of attention.
How different these meetings in a riverside inn are from
ordinary lessons ... Just how different soon becomes
grimly apparent to Castang when first one and then
another of his daughters schoolfriends shows signs of
sexual interference.

And what an irony that Castang, now living in a Paris
suburb and commuting to the sleepy offices of the Art
Fraud Squad – for he has been removed from straight
criminal work – should find himself and his family deeply
and dangerously involved in a world of criminal vice ...

'The most searching of all his recent books.'
The Observer

'Disturbing and morally probing.'
Sunday Times

'Full of stylish ambiguities.'
The Listener

COLD IRON

Nicolas Freeling

Henri Castang, lately moved from the city to a provincial northern town and unsure whether it is promotion or punishment, is still finding his feet in the unfamiliar surroundings when he is plunged into the very centre of Flanders society to investigate a death.

For Madame Lecat, found asphixiated in her luxurious and fortress-like villa, is no mere tycoon's wife, she is part of the ruling class. And her equestrian sister, her military brother-in-law and her alarmingly nubile niece are as much suspected of her killing as the servants and business associates.

With passionate irony, wit and irreverence Castang discovers the psyche of the land which still bears the scars of the Great War and which is a compelling background to this intricate story of corruption and death.

'It is time to pay tribute to the most eccentric, the most idiosyncratic, and the most European of crime writers.'
Anita Brookner, *The Spectator*

'I, for one, would be lost without my regular fix of Freeling.'
Ted Willis, *Sunday Telegraph*

LADY MACBETH

Nicolas Freeling

A dazzling variation on the traditional crime story in
which the question, for Castang, is not who did it – but
whether it happened at all ...

Successful landscape gardener Guy Lefebvre is driving
through the Vosges mountains with his wife Sybille when,
tired and irritable at the end of a long day, the couple
have a flaming row. She slams out of the car and is never
seen again.

Many people smell a rat, convinced that Guy has done
away with his over-ambitious and exacting wife, and
Castang is a prime mover in following this hypothesis.

Touching, harsh, funny, suspenseful – this is Nicholas
Freeling at this most original best.

'Flinty, sardonic and quite inimitable.'
Philip Oakes, *Literary Review*

'This is crime-writing at its best. Don't miss it.'
Sheila Upjohn, *Eastern Daily Press*

☐ Those in Peril	Nicolas Freeling	£4.50
☐ Cold Iron	Nicolas Freeling	£4.99
☐ Lady Macbeth	Nicolas Freeling	£4.99

Warner Futura now offers an exciting range of quality titles by both established and new authors. All of the books in this series are available from:

Little, Brown and Company (UK) Limited,
P.O. Box 11,
Falmouth,
Cornwall TR10 9EN.

Alternatively you may fax your order to the above address. Fax No. 0326 376423.

Payments can be made as follows: cheque, postal order (payable to Little, Brown and Company) or by credit cards, Visa/Access. Do not send cash or currency. UK customers and B.F.P.O. please allow £1.00 for postage and packing for the first book, plus 50p for the second book, plus 30p for each additional book up to a maximum charge of £3.00 (7 books plus).

Overseas customers including Ireland, please allow £2.00 for the first book plus £1.00 for the second book, plus 50p for each additional book.

NAME (Block Letters) ....

....

ADDRESS ....

....

....

☐ I enclose my remittance for _____

☐ I wish to pay by Access/Visa Card

Number ⬚⬚⬚⬚⬚⬚⬚⬚⬚⬚⬚⬚⬚⬚⬚⬚

Card Expiry Date ⬚⬚⬚⬚